INK EXCHANGE

INK EXCHANGE

melissa marr

HARPER TEEN

An Imprint of HarperCollins*Publishers*

Ink Exchange
Copyright © 2008 by Melissa Marr
Tattoo image copyright © 2007 by Paul Roe and Melissa Marr

www.harperteen.com

Library of Congress Cataloging-in-Publication Data
Marr, Melissa.
    Ink exchange / Melissa Marr. — 1st ed.
        p.   cm.
    Summary: Seventeen-year-old Leslie wants a tattoo as a way of
reclaiming control of herself and her body, but the eerie image she
selects draws her into the dangerous Dark Court of the faeries,
where she draws on inner strength to make a horrible choice.
    ISBN 978-0-06-121468-4 (trade bdg.)
    ISBN 978-0-06-121469-1 (lib. bdg.)
    [1. Fairies—Fiction. 2. Tattooing—Fiction. 3. Kings, queens,
rulers, etc.—Fiction. 4. Self-realization—Fiction. 5. Fantasy.]
I. Title.
PZ7.M34788Ink 2008   2007040106
[Fic]—dc22   CIP
                                                         AC

1 2 3 4 5 6 7 8 9 10
❖
First Edition

*To all the people who've been in the abyss and found
(or are finding) a way to reach solid ground—
you're proof that the seemingly impossible can happen.*

*And to A.S., who shared his shadows with me—
I hope you found what you needed.*

ACKNOWLEDGMENTS

The past year plus has seen *Wicked Lovely* (my first book) go from revision to being on shelves—and *Ink Exchange* go from concept to completion. This was daunting, but the warm encouragement I've received has made it possible. To everyone at HarperCollins US and HarperCollins UK; to my publishers abroad (especially Franziska at Carlsen in Germany); to librarians, booksellers, readers, parents, journalists, teachers, and the folks at the fansite (especially Maria); to my amazing financial manager, Peggy Hileman; and to the innumerable others I've met online and in person: I've been humbled by your kindness and support. Thank you, all.

Special thanks go to Clare Dunkle, who has touched my heart first with her novels and then in the past year with her wisdom. It's been a privilege.

My agent, Rachel Vater, makes chaos look like order. Whether you're talking me down, keeping me company as I wander, or flashing those pretty fangs, I am ever grateful.

My two passionate editors, Anne Hoppe and Nick Lake, continue to exceed expectations. Your insights, notes, and hours of chatting have made the text clearer and closer to the ideals I strive to reach.

Kelsey Defatte read the very earliest versions of this manuscript. Craig Thrush read through my conflict scenes. I am indebted to you both. And I am extremely indebted to Jeaniene Frost for hours of talking, revision letters to rival editors' letters, and so many epiphany-stirring observations. Thanks, J.

My tattoo artist, Paul Roe, read the tattoo sequences and answered innumerable questions on the minutiae of the art and its history. For this, for decorating my skin, and for all the rest, you have been essential to me.

Some rare people have given me their affection through years of chaos and calm—Dawn Kobel, Carly Chandler, Kelly Kincy, Rachael Morgan, Craig Thrush, and most of all, Cheryl and Dave Lafferty. Thank you for keeping me steady. Words can't cover what you mean to me.

None of the rest of this would've meant a thing if it weren't for the people who enrich every aspect of my life—my parents, children, and spouse. I'm fairly certain I exist only because you are beside me.

—June 2007

PROLOGUE

FALL

Irial watched the girl stroll up the street: she was a bundle of terror and fury. He stayed in the shadows of the alley outside the tattoo parlor, but his gaze didn't waver from her as he finished his cigarette.

He stepped out just as she passed.

Her pulse beat too fast under her skin when she saw him. She straightened her shoulders—not fleeing or backing away, bold despite the shadows that clung to her—and motioned to his arm where his name and lineage were spelled out in an ogham inscription surrounded by spirals and knots that morphed into stylized hounds. "That's gorgeous. Rabbit's work?"

He nodded and walked the remaining few steps to the tattoo parlor. The girl kept pace with him.

"I'm thinking of getting something soon. I just don't know what yet." She looked defiant as she said this. When he didn't reply, she added, "I'm Leslie."

"Irial." He watched her struggle and fail to find more words, to make him want to notice her. She was starving for something. If he took mortals for playthings, she'd be good fun, but he was here for business, not collecting trinkets, so he kept silent as he opened the door of Pins and Needles for her.

Inside the tattoo shop, Leslie wandered away to talk to a dark-haired girl who was watching them warily. There were others in the shop, but only the dark-haired girl mattered. Because he'd made the curse that had bound summer so many centuries ago, Irial knew exactly who she was: the missing Summer Queen, the problem. She would change everything.

And soon.

Irial had felt it the moment Keenan had chosen her, had stolen her mortality. It was why Irial had come to Rabbit: change was coming. Now that the Summer King would be unbound—and able to strike out at those who'd trapped him—true war was a possibility for the first time in centuries. Unfortunately, so was too much order.

"Spare a moment, Rabbit?" Irial asked, but it was a formality more than a question. Rabbit might not be wholly fey, but he wouldn't turn down the king of the Dark Court, not now, not ever.

"Come on back," Rabbit said.

Irial trailed his hands over one of the steel-framed jewelry cabinets as he passed, well aware that Leslie's attention was still on him. He closed the door and handed Rabbit the brown glass vials—blood and tears of the Dark Court. "I need the ink exchanges to work sooner than we'd planned. We're out of time."

"The fey might"—Rabbit paused and rephrased it—"it could kill them, and the mortals aren't recovering well."

"So find a way to make it work. *Now*." Irial tried a smile, softening his expression as he rarely did for the dark fey.

Then he faded to invisibility and followed Rabbit back into the main room of the shop. Unhealthy curiosity made him pause beside Leslie. The others were gone, but she stood looking at the flash on the wall, lesser images than what Rabbit could draw on her skin given a chance.

"Dream of me, Leslie," Irial whispered, letting his wings wrap around them both, enclosing them. Maybe the girl would get strong enough to withstand an ink exchange with one of the chosen faeries. If not, he could always give her to one of the weaker fey. It seemed a shame to waste a lovely broken toy.

CHAPTER 1

EARLY THE FOLLOWING YEAR

Leslie slipped into her school uniform and got ready as quickly as she could. She closed her bedroom door softly, staying quiet so she could get out of the house before her father woke. Being retired wasn't good for him. He'd been a decent father before—before Mom left, before he'd fallen into a bottle, before he'd started taking trips to Atlantic City and gods knew where else.

She headed to the kitchen, where she found her brother, Ren, at the table, pipe in hand. Wearing nothing but a pair of ratty jeans, his blond hair loose around his face, he seemed relaxed and friendly. Sometimes he even was.

He looked up and offered a cherubic smile. "Want a hit?"

She shook her head and opened the cupboard, looking for a tolerably clean cup. *None.* She pulled a can of soda from the meat drawer in the fridge. After Ren had doped a bottle—and thereby doped her—she'd learned to drink only from still-sealed containers.

Ren watched her, content in his chemical cloud, smiling in a perversely angelic way. When he was friendly and just smoking pot, it was a good day. Ren-on-Pot wasn't a problem: pot just made him mellow. It was Ren-on-Anything-Else that was unpredictable.

"There's chips over there if you want some breakfast." He pointed to a mostly empty bag of corn chips on the counter.

"Thanks." She grabbed a couple and opened the freezer to get the toaster waffles she'd hidden. They were gone. She opened the cupboard and pulled out a box of the only type of cereal her brother didn't eat—granola. It was nasty, but his pilfering stopped at the healthy stuff, so she stocked up on it.

She poured her cereal.

"No milk left," Ren mumbled, eyes closed.

Sighing softly, Leslie sat down with her bowl of dry granola. *No fights. No troubles.* Being home always made her feel like she was walking on a high wire, waiting for a gust of wind to knock her to the ground.

The kitchen smelled strongly of weed. She remembered when she used to wake up to the scent of eggs and bacon, when Dad would brew fresh coffee, when things were normal. It hadn't been like that for more than a year.

Ren plunked his bare feet on the kitchen table. It was covered with junk—news circulars, bills to pay, dirty dishes, and a mostly empty bottle of bourbon.

While she ate, she opened the important bills—electric and water. With relief, she saw that Dad had actually paid ahead on both of them. He did that when he had a good run of luck at the tables or a few sober days: sent extra on the big bills so it wouldn't be a hassle later. It didn't help for groceries or the cable bill, which was overdue again, but she could usually cover those when she had to.

Not this time, though. She'd finally decided to go through with it, to get a tattoo. She'd been wanting one for a while but hadn't felt ready. In the last few months, she'd become near obsessed with it. Waiting wasn't the answer, not anymore. She thought about that act far too often—marking her body, reclaiming it as her own, a step she needed to take to make herself whole again.

Now I just need to find the right image.

With what she hoped was a friendly smile, she asked Ren, "Do you have any money for cable?"

He shrugged. "Maybe. What's it worth to you?"

"I'm not bargaining. I just want to know if you can cover cable this month."

He took a long hit off his pipe and exhaled into her face. "Not if you're going to be a bitch about it. I have expenses. If you can't do a guy a favor now and then, make nice with my friends"—he shrugged—"you pay it."

"You know what? I don't need cable." She walked over to the trash and dropped the bill in the can, fighting back the sickness in her throat at the mention of *making nice* with his friends, wishing that someone in her family cared about what happened to her.

If Mom hadn't taken off . . .

But she had. She'd bailed and left Leslie behind to deal with her brother and father. "It'll be better this way, baby," she'd said. It wasn't. Leslie wasn't sure if she'd want to talk to her mom anymore—not that it mattered. She had no contact information at all.

Leslie shook her head. Thinking about that wouldn't help her cope with her current reality. She started to walk past Ren, but he stood up and grabbed her for a hug. She was stiff in his arms.

"What? Are you on the rag again?" He laughed, amused by his crass joke, amused by her anger.

"Never mind, Ren. Just forget I—"

"I'll pay the bill. Relax." He let go of her, and as soon as he let his arm drop, she stepped away, hoping the scent of pot and cigarettes wouldn't cling to her too obviously. Sometimes she suspected that Father Meyers knew exactly how much things had changed for her, but she still didn't want to walk into school reeking.

She put on her fake smile and murmured, "Thanks, Ren."

"I'll take care of it. You just remember it next time I

need you to come out with me. You're a good distraction when I need credit." He looked at her calculatingly.

She didn't reply. There wasn't an answer that would help. If she said no, he'd be a prick, but she wasn't saying yes. After what his druggie friends did—*what* he *let them do*—she wasn't going anywhere near them again.

Instead of rehashing that argument, she went and grabbed the bill out of the trash. "Thanks for taking care of it."

She handed it to him. Right now, it didn't matter if he did it or not: she couldn't pay the cable bill and get ink, and really, she didn't watch cable enough to justify paying for it. Mostly, she paid it because she was embarrassed by the idea of anyone finding out that her family *couldn't* pay a bill, as if by keeping it normal as long as possible maybe it'd get normal. It kept her from facing the inevitable pity and whispers if everyone found out how lame her father had become since Mom left, if they found out just how low her brother had gotten.

By fall she'd be in college, escaped from here, away from them. *Just like Mom did—escape.* Sometimes she wondered if her mother had been escaping something she didn't want Leslie to know about. If so, her mother's leaving made more sense—but her leaving Leslie behind made less sense. *It doesn't matter.* Leslie had already sent out her first-choice applications and applied for a bunch of scholarships. *That's what matters—getting a plan and getting out.* Next year she'd be safe, in a new city, in a new life.

But that didn't stop the wave of terror she felt as Ren lifted his bourbon in a silent salute.

Without another word, she grabbed her bag.

"Catch you later, sis," Ren called, before he turned his attention to packing another bowl.

No. You won't.

By the time Leslie walked up the steps to Bishop O'Connell High School, her fears were safely tucked back in their box. She'd gotten better at watching for the warning signs—the tense calls that meant Ren was in trouble again, the strangers in the house. She worked extra if there were too many warning signs. She'd put locks on her bedroom door. She didn't drink out of open bottles. Her safeguards didn't undo what was, but they helped avoid what could be.

"Leslie! Hold up," Aislinn called out from behind her.

Leslie stopped and waited, schooling her face to be bland and calm, not that it mattered: Aislinn had been lost in her own world lately. A few months ago, she'd hooked up with the all-too-yummy Seth. They'd been practically dating anyhow, so that wasn't so weird. What was weird was that Aislinn had simultaneously developed a very intense relationship with another guy, Keenan. Somehow neither guy seemed to object to the other.

The guys who'd walked Aislinn to school stood watching her from across the street while she caught up to Leslie. Keenan and Niall, his uncle, didn't move from their post, seeming far too serious—and apparently oblivious to the number of people watching them like they were members of the Living Zombies. Leslie wondered if Niall played an instrument. He was sexier than any of the Zombies. If he played or sang too . . . he'd be halfway to success just by looking so delicious. He had a mysterious aura, plus he was a couple years older than Leslie and Aislinn—a college sophomore maybe. Add that oddly sexy responsibility thing—he was one of Keenan's guardians, an uncle, but still young—and he seemed like a perfect package, one she was staring at again.

When he smiled and waved, Leslie had to force herself not to go toward him. She always felt like that when he looked at her. There was an illogical urge to run toward him, like something was coiled too tightly inside her and the only way to ease the tension was to go to him. She didn't. She wasn't about to make a fool of herself over a guy who hadn't shown any genuine interest. *Maybe he would, though.* So far, their only contact had been under the watchful eye of Keenan or Aislinn, and that was usually interrupted by Aislinn's flimsy excuses to go somewhere away from Niall.

Aislinn put her hand on Leslie's arm. "Come on."

And, like they had so often, they walked away from Niall.

Leslie turned her attention to Aislinn. "Wow. Rianne said you were crazy tan, but I didn't believe it."

Aislinn's perpetually pale skin was perfectly tan, as if she'd been living on a beach, as tan as Keenan always was. It hadn't been that way on Friday. Aislinn bit down on her lip—a nervous habit that usually meant she was feeling cornered. "It's some winter thing—SAD, they called it—so I needed to get some sunlight."

"Right." Leslie tried to keep the doubt out of her voice and failed. Aislinn didn't seem depressed at all—or to have reason *to* be depressed lately. In fact, she seemed like she'd become rather flush with money and attention. A few times when Leslie had seen her out with Keenan, both of them had been wearing matching twisted golden necklaces that fit snugly around their throats. The clothes that Aislinn wore, the new winter coats, the chauffeurs, and—let's not forget—Seth's being cool with all of it. *Depressed? Yeah, right.*

"Did you go over the reading for Lit?" Aislinn pulled open the door and they joined the throng of people in the halls.

"We had a dinner thing out of town, so I didn't finish." Leslie gave an exaggerated eye roll. "Ren even dressed with all the required pieces of clothing."

They both continued to steer the conversation away from topics they didn't want to address. Leslie lied easily, but Aislinn seemed determined to direct the conversation toward neutral subjects. Eventually, she glanced behind her—as if there were someone there—and made another random topic switch: "Are you still working over at Verlaine's?"

Leslie looked: there wasn't anyone there. "Sure. It drives Dad mad that I wait tables, and you know, gives me a good excuse if I need to explain my weird hours."

Leslie didn't admit that she *had* to work or that her father didn't have a clue what she did for money. She wasn't sure her father knew she had a job or that she paid the bills. He might have thought Ren was doing it, although he probably didn't realize Ren was dealing—*or selling me*—to get his money. Talking about money, home, and Ren was so not the sort of conversation she wanted to have, so she took a turn shifting the topic. With a conspiratorial grin, she looped her arm around Aislinn's waist and assumed the facade she adopted with her friends. "So, let's talk about Keenan's sexy uncle. What's the scoop on him? Is he seeing anyone?"

"Niall? He's just . . . he's not, but . . ." Aislinn frowned. "You don't want to mess with him. There's prettier . . . I mean, better . . ."

"I doubt that, sweetie. Your vision's clouded by staring at Seth too long." Leslie patted Aislinn's arm. "Niall's top shelf."

His face was as beautiful as Keenan's but in a different way: Niall's had character. One long scar ran from his temple to the corner of his mouth, and he wasn't shy about it. His hair was cut so short that there was no chance of anything detracting from the beauty of that jagged line.

And his body . . . *wow.* He was all sinew and length, moving like he had been training in some long-lost martial art since birth. Leslie couldn't figure why anyone would notice Keenan when Niall was around. Keenan was attractive enough, with his unnatural green eyes, perfect body, and sandy-blond hair. He was gorgeous, but he moved in a way that always made Leslie think he wasn't quite meant for civilization. He frightened her. Niall, on the other hand, was luscious and seemed sweet—kind in a way that Keenan wasn't.

Leslie prompted, "So relationships . . ."

"He doesn't, umm, do relationships." Aislinn spoke softly. "Anyhow, he's too old."

Leslie let it drop for the moment. Although Aislinn was spending much of her time "not-dating" Keenan, she kept her school friends separate from Keenan's crowd as much as possible. When they did intersect, Aislinn clung to Leslie like an extra limb, giving no opportunities for Leslie to have conversations with anyone who hung around Keenan— most especially Niall. For a moment, Leslie wondered if she'd be so intrigued by Niall if it weren't for Aislinn's playing keep-away. The more Aislinn acted as an obstacle, the more Leslie wanted nearer Niall. An older guy with a drool-worthy body and seemingly no bad habits to speak of *and* somehow forbidden: how could that not be appealing?

But Aislinn's plate was overfilled with Seth and Keenan, so maybe she just wasn't getting it. *Or maybe she knows something.* Leslie forced that thought away: if Aislinn had a legitimate reason to think Niall was bad news, she'd say something. They might be in the middle of this weird dance of secrecy, but they were still friends.

"Les!" Rianne shoved through the crowd with her usual exuberance. "Did I miss seeing the dessert tray?"

"Just two of the tasty treats today . . ." Leslie linked her arm through Rianne's as they made their way toward their lockers. Rianne was reliably good at keeping things light.

"So dark-and-pierced wasn't on duty?" Rianne flashed a wicked grin at Aislinn, who blushed predictably.

"No Seth. Today was blond-and-moody along with scarred-and-sexy." Leslie winked at Aislinn, enjoying the brief moments of normalcy, of smiling. Rianne brought that in her wake, and Leslie was ever grateful for it. They stopped in front of Aislinn's locker, and Leslie added, "Our little dessert hoarder was just going to tell me when we're all going out dancing."

"No, not—" Aislinn started.

"Sooner or later, you're going to need to share the wealth, Ash. We're feeling deprived. Weakened." Rianne sighed and leaned heavily on Leslie. "I'm feeling faint with it."

And for a moment, Leslie saw a look of longing pass over Aislinn's face, but then Aislinn caught her watching.

Aislinn's face turned impassive. "Sometimes I wish I could . . . I just don't think it's a good idea."

Rianne opened her mouth to respond, but Leslie shook her head. "Give us a sec, Ri. I'll catch up."

After Rianne left, Leslie caught Aislinn's gaze. "I wish we weren't doing this. . . ." She gestured between them.

"What do you mean?" Aislinn grew so still and silent in the din of the hall, it was like the noise around them vanished for an instant.

"Lying." Leslie sighed. "I miss us being real friends, Ash. I'm not going to encroach on your scene, but it'd be nice to be straight-up again. I miss you."

"I'm not lying. I . . . can't lie." She stared beyond Leslie for a moment, scowling at someone.

Leslie didn't turn to see who it was. "You're not being honest, either. If you don't want me around . . ." She shrugged. "Whatever."

Aislinn grabbed her arms and held her close. Although she tried, Leslie actually *couldn't* pull away.

A jerk passing in the hall called, "Dykes."

Leslie tensed, torn between the once-instantaneous urge to flip him off and the still-new fear of conflict.

The bell rang. Lockers slammed. Aislinn finally said, "I just don't want to see you get hurt. There's . . . people and things . . . and . . ."

"Sweetie, I doubt they're any worse than what—" She stopped herself, unable to say the sentences that would follow. Her heart thunked at the thought of saying those words aloud. She shook her arm. "Can you let go? I've still got to go to my locker."

Aislinn released her, and Leslie left before she had to figure out how to answer the inevitable questions that would follow her almost admission. *Talking won't change it.* But sometimes it was what she wanted most, to tell someone; often, though, she just wanted to not feel those horrid feelings, to escape herself, so there was no pain, no fear, no ugliness.

CHAPTER 2

After school Leslie headed out before Aislinn or Rianne had a chance to catch up with her. She'd spent her free period in the library reading more on the history of tattooing, the centuries-old traditions of marking the body. The reasons—ranging from adopting a totem animal's nature to marking life events to offering visual cues to identify criminals—fascinated her. More important, they resonated with her.

When she walked in the door of Pins and Needles, the cowbell clanged.

Rabbit glanced over his shoulder.

"Be right with you," he called. As the man beside him talked, Rabbit absently ran a hand over his white-and-blue-dyed hair.

Leslie lifted a hand in greeting and walked past him. This week he had left a tiny goatee directing attention to his labret piercing. It was that piercing under his lower lip that had caught her attention the first time Ani and Tish had brought her to the shop. Within a week, she'd had her own piercing—hidden under her blouse—and found herself spending time in the studio.

She felt safe there—away from Bishop O.C., away from the unpleasantness of her father's drunkenness, away from whatever letches Ren brought home to share his drug of the week. At Pins and Needles she could be safe, quiet, relaxed—all the things she couldn't be most other places.

"Yes, always use new needles," Rabbit repeated to the prospective customer.

As Leslie walked around the shop, she listened to the snatches of Rabbit's comments that wound into the silence between songs: "Autoclave . . . sterile as a hospital."

The man's gaze drifted lazily over the flash on the walls, but he wasn't there to buy. He was tense, ready to bolt. His eyes were too wide. His posture was nervous—arms folded, body closed in on itself. Despite the number of people who came through the shop, only a few would actually lay down money for art. He wasn't one of them.

"I have a couple questions," she called out to Rabbit.

With a grateful smile at her, Rabbit excused himself from the man, telling him, "If you want to look around . . ."

Leslie walked over to the far wall, where she flipped through the flash—images that could be bought by and put on as many people as liked them. Flowers and crosses, tribal patterns and geometric designs—many were beautiful, but no matter how long she stared at them, none seemed right. The small rooms branching off the main room had other styles that were less appealing: old-school pinup girls, skeletal figures, cartoon characters, slogans, and animals.

Rabbit came up behind her, but she didn't tense, didn't feel that urge to turn so she couldn't be cornered. It was *Rabbit*. Rabbit was safe.

He said, "Nothing new there, Les."

"I know." She flipped the poster frame board that rested against the wall. One image was of a green vine entwined around a half-human woman; she looked like she was being strangled but smiled as if it felt good. *Idiotic.* Leslie flipped again. Obscure symbols with translations underneath covered the next screen. *Not my style.*

Rabbit laughed, a smoker's raspy laugh, although he didn't smoke and claimed he never had. "With as much time as you've spent looking the past months, you'd have found it by now."

Leslie turned and scowled up at Rabbit. "So design something for me. I'm ready *now*, Rabbit. I want to do this."

Off to the side, the would-be customer paused to look at a couple of the rings in the glass case.

With an uneasy shrug, Rabbit said, "Told you before. You want custom work, you bring me an idea. Something. I can't design without references."

The bell clanged as the man left.

"So help me find an idea. Please? You've had my parental

consent form for weeks." She wasn't backing down this time. Getting ink felt right, like it would help her put her life in order, to move forward. It was *her body*, despite the things that'd been done to it, and she wanted to claim it, to own it, to *prove* that to herself. She knew it wasn't magic, but the idea of writing her own identity felt like the closest she could get to reclaiming her life. Sometimes there's power in the act; sometimes there's strength in words. She wanted to find an image that represented those things she was feeling, to etch it on her skin as tangible proof of her decision to change.

"Rabbit? I need this. You told me to think. I've thought. I need . . ." She stared out at the people passing on the street, wondering if the men who'd . . . if they were out there. She wouldn't recognize them since Ren had drugged her before he gave her to them. She pulled her gaze back to Rabbit and was uncharacteristically blunt, telling him what she couldn't tell Aislinn earlier: "I need to change, Rabbit. I'm drowning here. I need *something*, or I'm not going to make it. Maybe a tattoo isn't the right answer, but right now it's something I can do. . . . I need this. Help me?"

He paused, an oddly hesitant look on his face. "Don't pursue this."

Ani and Tish peeked around the corner, waved, and wandered over to the stereo. The song changed to something darker, with heavy bass and growling lyrics. The volume grew loud enough that Leslie could feel the percussion.

"Ani!" Rabbit shot a frown toward his sister.

"Shop's empty now." Ani cocked her hip and stared at him, unrepentant. She never cowered, no matter how grumpy Rabbit sounded. It wasn't like he'd hurt her, though. He treated his sisters like they were the most precious things he'd ever seen. It was one of the things Leslie found comforting about him. Guys who treated their family well were safe and *good*—guys like her father and brother, not so much.

Rabbit stared at Leslie for several seconds before he said, "Quick fixes aren't what you need. You need to face what you're running from."

"Please? I want this." She felt tears sting her eyes. Rabbit suspected too much, and she didn't want pep talks. She wanted something she didn't have words for—peace, numbness, *something*. She stared at him, trying to figure out what to say to convince him, trying to figure out why he wouldn't help her. All she had was "Please, Rabbit?"

He looked away then and motioned for her to follow him. They stepped through the short hallway to his office. Rabbit unlocked it and led her into the tiny room.

She stopped just inside the doorway, less comfortable but still okay. The room was barely big enough for the things he had crammed into it. A massive dark wood desk and two file cabinets took up the back wall; a long counter cluttered with various artists' tools and media stretched the length of the right wall; the third wall had a matching counter with two printers, a scanner, a projector, and a series of unlabeled jars.

He pulled another key out of his pocket and unlocked a drawer on the desk. Saying nothing yet, he pulled out a thin brown book with words impressed into the cover. Then he sat down in his chair and stared at her until she felt like running, as if everything she knew about him had faded and he were somehow unsafe.

This is Rabbit.

She felt embarrassed by her brief fear. Rabbit was like the older brother she should've had, a true friend. He hadn't ever offered her anything other than respect.

She walked up to the desk and sat on it.

He held her gaze and asked, "What are you looking for?"

They'd talked enough that she knew he didn't mean what sort of picture, but what it represented. A tattoo wasn't about the thing itself, but what it meant.

"Being safe. No more fear or pain." She couldn't look at him when she said it, but she *had* said it. That counted for something.

Rabbit flipped open the book to a section midway through and sat it in her lap. "Here. These are mine. They're special. They're like . . . symbols of change. If the one you need is in here . . . just . . . do any of these feel like what you need?"

Images cluttered the page—intricate Celtic patterns, eyes peering from behind thorny vines, grotesque bodies with wicked smiles, animals too unreal to look at for long, symbols her eyes darted away from as soon as she glanced at them. They were stunning and tempting and repulsive, but for one image that set her nerves on edge: inky-black eyes gazed up from within black-and-gray knotwork surrounded by wings like coalescing shadows, and in the middle was a chaos star. Eight arrows pointed away from the center; four of these were thicker, like the lines of a spiked cross.

Mine. The thought, the need, the reaction were overpowering. Her stomach clenched. She pulled her gaze away, and then forced herself to keep looking. She looked at the other tattoos, but her attention returned to that image as if compelled by it. *That one's mine.* For a moment, some trick of light made it look as if one of the eyes in the image winked. She ran her finger over the page, feeling the slick-smooth plastic sheet covering it, imagining the feel of those wings wrapped around her—somehow jagged and velvety all at once. She looked up at Rabbit. "This one. I need this one."

A strange series of expressions came over Rabbit, as if he weren't sure if he should be surprised, pleased, or terrified. He took the book and closed it. "Why don't you think about it for a few days—"

"No." She put a hand on his wrist. "I *am* sure. I'm past ready, and this image . . . If it'd been on the wall, I'd already have it on me." She shivered, not liking the idea of anyone else having her tattoo—and it *was* hers. She knew it. "Please."

"It's a one-time-only tattoo. If you get it, no one else can, but"—he stared at the wall behind her—"it'll change you, change things."

"*All* tattoos change people." She tried to keep her voice even, but she felt frustrated by his hesitation. He'd been stalling for weeks. This was her tattoo, right there within reach.

Studiously avoiding her gaze, Rabbit slid the book into its drawer. "Those things you were looking for . . . those changes . . . you need to be absolutely positive those are the ones you want."

"I *am*." She tried to get him to look at her, bending down so her face was closer to his.

Ani poked her head in the doorway. "She pick one?"

Rabbit ignored her. "Tell me what you thought when you picked it. Were there any others that . . . called to you?"

Leslie shook her head. "No. Just that one. I want it. Soon. Now."

And she did. It felt like she was looking at a banquet and realizing she hadn't ever eaten, like a craving that she needed to fill immediately.

After another long look, he pulled her into his arms for a quick hug. "So be it."

Leslie turned to Ani. "It's perfect. It's a chaos star and knotwork with these amazing eyes and shadow wings."

Ani took one look at Rabbit—who nodded—and then she whistled. "You're stronger than I thought. Wait till Tish hears." She left, calling out, "Tish? Guess which one Leslie picked."

"No shit?" Tish's shriek made Rabbit close his eyes.

Shaking her head, Leslie told Rabbit, "You realize that you're all being über-weird, even for people who live at a tattoo shop."

Instead of acknowledging her remark, Rabbit brushed her hair back tenderly like he did with his own sisters'. "I'll need a couple days to get the right ink for this one. You can change your mind."

"I won't." She felt the unnatural urge to squeal like Tish had. Soon, she'd have it, the perfect ink. "Let's talk price."

Niall watched Leslie walk out of Pins and Needles. When she walked through the city, she moved with her shoulders squared, pace steady. It was at odds with the fears he knew hid inside her. Today, though, her confidence seemed almost real.

He stepped closer, pushing off the redbrick wall where he'd been leaning while she was in the tattoo shop. As she paused to survey the shadows in the street, Niall brushed his fingers over a lock of her hair that'd fallen forward over her cheek. Her hair—almost as wood brown as his own—wasn't long enough to tie back or short enough to stay back on its own, just right to be intriguing.

Like she is.

His fingers barely grazed her cheek, not enough for her to react. He leaned closer so he could smell her skin. Before work, she had a lavender scent, not perfume, but the shampoo she favored lately. "What are you doing out alone again? You know better."

She didn't answer him. She never did: mortals didn't see faeries, didn't hear them—especially mortals the Summer Queen had insisted be kept unaware of the Faery Courts.

Initially, at his king's request, Niall had taken a few of the shifts guarding Leslie. When she was unaware, he could walk beside her and talk to her as he couldn't when he was visible to her. The way the mortal girl looked at him—like he was better than he'd ever been, like he was attractive because of who he was, not because of his role in the Summer Court—was a heady thing, too much so, in truth.

If his queen hadn't asked it, Niall still would've wanted to keep Leslie safe. But Aislinn did order it. Unlike Leslie, when Aislinn had been mortal, she'd seen the ugliness of the faery world. Since becoming the Summer Queen she'd worked to find a balance with the equally new Winter Queen. It didn't leave a lot of time for keeping her mortal friends safe, but it did give her the power to order faeries to assure the mortals' safety. Such a task would not normally be handled by a court advisor, but Niall had been more family than mere advisor to the Summer King for centuries. Keenan suggested that Aislinn would feel better knowing that her closest friends' safety was under the direction of a faery she trusted.

Although it had been only a few shifts at first, more and more, Niall took extra duty watching over her. He hadn't done so with the others, but they didn't fascinate him as Leslie did. Leslie vacillated between vulnerable and bold, fierce and frightened. Once, when he had collected mortals for playthings, she would've been irresistible, but he was stronger now.

Better.

He forced away that line of thought and watched the sway of Leslie's hips as she walked through the streets of Huntsdale with a courage—*foolishness*—that ran counter to what he knew of her experiences. Maybe she'd go home if home were any safer. It wasn't. He'd seen that the first time he'd stood waiting on her front step, heard her drunken father, her vile brother. Her home might look charming from the outside, but that was a lie.

Like so much of her life.

He glanced down at the heelless shoes she had on, at her bare calves, at her long legs. The unexpectedly early start of summer this year—after ages of oppressive cold—was leading to mortals exposing more skin. Looking at Leslie, Niall wasn't complaining. "At least you have decent shoes tonight. I couldn't believe you went to work in those dainty little things the other night." He shook his head. "They were lovely, though. Well, really, I just liked the glimpse of your ankles."

She headed to the restaurant, where she would put on her fake smile and flirt with the customers. He'd see her to the door; then he'd wait outside, watching the bodies that came and went, making sure they didn't mean her harm. It was the routine.

Sometimes he let himself imagine how things would be

if she could *truly know* him—see him in a true light. Would her eyes widen in fear if she saw the extent of his scars? Would her face crumple in disgust if she knew the horrible things he'd done before he belonged to the Summer Court? Would she ask why he kept his hair shorn? And if she asked, could he answer any of those questions?

"Would you run from me?" he asked in a low voice, hating the fact that his heart sped at the thought of pursuing a mortal girl.

Leslie paused as a group of young men catcalled from their car. One of them hung halfway out the window, displaying his vulgarity as if it made him a man. Niall doubted that she could hear their words: the bass in their car was too loud for mere voices to compete with. Actual words weren't necessary to know threat. Leslie tensed.

The car sped away, the rumbling bass fading like thunder from a passing storm.

He whispered against her ear, "They're just children, Leslie. Come now. Where's that spring in your step?"

Her breathy sigh was soft enough that he would have missed it if he hadn't been standing very close. A little of the tension eased from her shoulders, but the drawn look stayed on her face. It never seemed to fade. Her makeup didn't hide the shadows under her eyes. Her long sleeves didn't hide the purpling bruises from her brother's angry strikes the other day.

If I could step in . . .

But he couldn't, not into her life, not into her home.

That was forbidden to him. All he could do was offer her his words—words she couldn't hear. He still said, "I'd stop anyone from taking that smile from you. I would, if I were allowed."

Absently, she put one hand on her back and glanced in the direction of Pins and Needles. She smiled to herself, the same smile she'd worn when she left the tattoo parlor.

"Aaah, you've finally decided to decorate that pretty skin. What will it be? Flowers? Sun?" He let his gaze drift up her spine.

She paused; they'd reached the restaurant. Her shoulders sagged again.

He wanted to comfort her, but instead he could only give her his nightly promise, "I'll wait right here."

He wished she'd answer, tell him she'd look for him after work, but she wouldn't.

And it's better this way. He knew it, but he didn't like it. He'd been a part of the Summer Court long enough that his original path was almost forgotten, but watching Leslie— seeing her spirit, her passion . . . Once, when he'd been a solitary fey, when he'd had another name, there'd have been no hesitating.

"I agree with Aislinn, though. I want you kept safe," he whispered in her ear. Her soft, soft hair brushed against his face. "I will keep you safe—from them *and* from me."

CHAPTER 3

Irial stood in the early morning light, silent, one of his faeries lying dead at his feet. The faery, Guin, had worn a mortal guise so often that bits of her glamour still clung to her after death—leaving part of her face painted with mortal makeup and part gloriously other. She had on tight blue denims—*jeans*, she and her sisters always reminded him when they spoke—and a top that barely covered her chest. That slip of cloth was soaked with blood, *her* blood, *fey* blood, spilling onto the dirty ground.

"Why? Why did this happen, *a ghrá*?" Irial bent down to brush her bloody hair from her face. Around her were bottles, cigarette butts, and used needles. None of these offended him the way they once had: this area was rough, grown more violent these past years as the mortals settled their territorial disputes. What offended him was the notion that a mortal bullet had taken one of his own. It might not have been intentional, but that changed nothing. She was still fallen.

Across from him waited the tall, thin beansidhe who'd summoned him. "What do we do?" She wrung her hands as she spoke, resisting her natural instinct to wail. She wouldn't resist for long, but Irial didn't—*couldn't*—answer yet.

He picked up an empty casing, turning it over in his fingers. The brass shouldn't hurt a fey, nor should the lead slug that he'd removed from the dead faery's body when he arrived. It had, though: a simple mortal bullet had killed her.

"Irial?" The beansidhe had bitten her tongue until blood seeped from her lips to drip down her pointed chin.

"Ordinary bullets," he murmured, turning the bits of metal over in his fingers. In all the years since mortals had begun fashioning the things, he'd never seen one of his own dead from them. Shot, yes, but they had healed. They'd *always* healed from most everything mortals inflicted—everything but severe wounds made by steel or iron.

"Go home and wail. When the others come to you, tell them this area is off limits for now." Then he lifted the bloodied faery into his arms and walked away, leaving the beansidhe to begin keening as she ran. Her cries would summon them, his now-vulnerable Dark Court faeries, bring them to hear the awful word that a mortal had killed a faery.

By the time the current Gabriel—Irial's left hand—approached mere moments later, Irial's winged shadow had spread like a pall over the street. His ink-black tears dripped onto Guin's body, wiping away the glamour that still clung to her. "I've waited long enough to address the threat of the Summer Court's growing strength," he said.

"Waited too long," Gabriel said. "Keep waiting and war comes on their terms, Iri."

Like his predecessors, this Gabriel—for the name was one of rank, not birth—had always been blunt. It was an invaluable trait.

"I'm not seeking war in the courts, just chaos." Irial paused at the stoop of a heavily shuttered house, one of the many such houses he kept for his faeries in whichever cities they called home. He stared at the house, the home where Guin would be laid out for the court's mourning. Soon, Bananach would hear the news of Guin's death; the war-hungry faery would begin her interminable machinations. Irial was not looking forward to trying to placate Bananach. She grew less patient by the year, pressing for more violence, more blood, more destruction.

"War is not what's best for our court," Irial said, as much to himself as to Gabriel. "That's Bananach's agenda, not mine."

"If it's not yours, it's not the Hounds', either." Gabriel reached out and brushed Guin's cheek. "Guin would agree. She wouldn't support Bananach, even now."

Three dark fey came out of the house; smoky haze clung

to them as if it seeped from their skin. Mute, they took
Guin's body and carried her inside. From the open door,
Irial could see that they'd already begun hanging black mirrors throughout his house, covering every available surface
in the hopes that some lingering darkness would find its
way home to the body, that some trace would be strong
enough to come back to the empty shell, so Guin could be
nurtured and heal. It wouldn't: she was truly gone.

Irial saw them in his street, filthy mortals with so much
lovely violence he couldn't reach. *That will change.* "Find
them, the ones who did this. Kill them."

The previously blank space around the oghams on
Gabriel's forearm filled with scrolling script in recognition
of the Dark King's command. Gabriel always carried out
the king's orders with the intent plainly writ on his skin—
to intimidate and to make clear that the king willed it.

"And send the others to bring some of Keenan's fey for
the wake. Donia's too." Irial grinned at the thought of
sullen Winter Court faeries. "Hell, bring some of Sorcha's
reclusive faeries if you can find them. Her High Court's not
good for anything else. I'll not sanction a war, but let's start
a few fights."

At nightfall Irial sat on his dais looking out at his grieving
faeries. They squirmed, paced, and wailed. The glaistigs
were dripping dirty river water all over the floor; several
beansidhes still keened. The Gabriel Hounds—in their
human guise, skin decorated with moving ink and silver

chains—joked amongst themselves, but there were under-currents of alarm. Jenny Greenteeth and her kin stared at everyone with accusing eyes. Only the thistle-fey seemed calm, taking advantage of the fear of the others, nourishing themselves on the panic that pervaded the room. They all knew that the rumblings of upheaval had already begun. With the reality of a faery death, the inducement to resort to extreme measures was inevitable. There were always factions, murmurs of mutiny: that was status quo. This was different: one of their own had died. That changed the stakes.

"Move away from the streets"—Irial let his gaze slide over them, assessing the signs of disagreement, determining who would sway toward Bananach when she began rallying them to her cause—"until we know how weakened we are."

"Kill the new queen. Both of 'em," one of the Hounds growled. "Summer King too if we need."

The other Hounds took up the cry. The Ly Ergs rubbed their bloodred hands together in glee. Several of Jenny's kin grinned and nodded. Bananach sat silently among them; her voice wasn't ever necessary to know her preference. Violence was her sole passion. She tilted her head in her avian way, not doing anything other than watching. Irial smiled at her. She opened and closed her mouth with an audible snap, as if she'd bite him. She made no other movement. They both knew she disapproved of his plans; they both knew she'd test him. *Again.* If she could, she'd kill him to set the court into discord, but Dark Court faeries could not kill their regents.

The snarls grew deafening until Gabriel held a hand up for silence. When the rest of the room quieted, Gabriel flashed a menacing smile. "Your king speaks. You *will* obey him."

No one objected when Gabriel snarled. After he'd slaughtered one of his own brethren for disrespecting Irial so many years ago, few ever challenged his will. If Gabriel had the political grace to go with the violence, Irial would try to cede the throne to him. In all the centuries Irial'd looked for his replacement, he'd only found one faery fit to lead them, but that faery had rejected the throne to serve another. Irial shoved that thought away. He was still responsible for the Dark Court, and considering what might have been didn't help.

He said, "We are not strong enough to fight one court, much less two or three working together. Can any of you truly tell me that the kingling and the new Winter Queen wouldn't work together? Can you tell me that Sorcha wouldn't side with anyone"—he paused and smiled at Bananach—"*most* anyone who opposed me? War is not the right path."

He didn't add that he had no desire for true war. It would look like weakness, and a weak king wouldn't hold his court very long. If there had been someone who could lead the court without destroying them all in unrestrained excess, Irial would step away, but the head of the Dark Court was chosen from among the solitary faeries for good reason. He enjoyed the pleasure of the shadows, but he understood that shadows needed light. Most of his court had trouble remembering that—or perhaps they never knew it. They certainly wouldn't appreciate hearing it now.

The Dark Court needed the nourishment of the finer emotions: fear, lust, rage, greed, gluttony, and the like. Under the last Winter Queen's cruel regime—before the newly empowered Summer King had come into his strength—the very air had been sustaining. Beira had been a malicious queen, inflicting as much agony on her own faeries as on those who dared to not kneel to her. It had been relaxing, if not always pleasant.

Irial said only, "Smaller conflicts can create the energy we need for sustenance. There are plenty of faeries you can use for nourishment."

In a voice that would disturb the calmest of the winter fey, one of Jenny's kin asked, "So we just feed on whatever random faeries we can find like nothing's happened? I say we—"

Gabriel growled at her. "We *will* obey our king."

Bananach snapped her mouth again; she tapped her talon-tipped fingers on the surface of the table. "So the Dark King is unwilling to fight? To allow us to defend our-selves? To strengthen ourselves? Just wait until we get weaker still? There's an . . . *interesting* plan."

She's going to be true trouble this time.

Another green-toothed fey added, "If we fight, maybe some of us might fade, but the rest . . . a war's apt to be good fun, my king."

"No," Irial said, glancing at Chela, Gabriel's sometimes mate. "No war right now. I'll not have any of you fade. That's not an option. I will find a way." He wished he could explain it to them in a way they'd understand. He couldn't.

"Chela, love? Would you?" Irial inclined his head toward a group of faeries who'd been smiling and agreeing with the green-toothed fey. Talk of disobeying him was intolerable, especially when mutiny was simmering in Bananach's eyes again.

Irial lit another cigarette and waited as Chela sauntered across the room. The knotwork hounds on her biceps snapped at each other as they ran around her arm at a blurring pace. A soft hum emanated from her, somewhere between a growl and a contented murmur. As she approached the table, she grabbed a chair from one of the thistle-fey, dumping him to the floor as she lifted it and settled amidst the grumbling faeries.

Several other Hounds dispersed throughout the crowd. Gabriel had spoken, said that they'd support the Dark King: they'd either need to obey Gabriel or kill him. Had he allied with Bananach, a faery war would be unavoidable, but Gabriel had stood with Irial for as long as he'd held leadership of the Hounds.

Irial resumed: "A mortal has chosen my symbol for her tattoo. She'll be bound to me within days. Through her, I will be able to feed on mortals and faeries both; I'll offset your own feeding until we have another option."

They didn't react for a moment. Then they lifted their

voices in a beautiful cacophony.

He'd never funneled his nourishment out to them, but he'd never needed to, either. He could. The head of a court was tied to each faery who swore fealty to him. His strength gave them strength; it was simply the way of things. It wasn't a permanent solution, but it would keep them alive until a better solution was in reach—one that wasn't full-out war.

He exhaled, watching the smoke writhe in the air, missing the dead queen, hating Keenan for defeating her, and wondering what it would take to entice Donia, the new Winter Queen, to become as ruthless as her predecessor. The alliance between Keenan and Donia had swung the balance too far toward a degree of peace that was detrimental to the Dark Court—but war wasn't the answer either. The Dark Court couldn't survive on violence alone, any more than terror or lust would be enough. Everything was about balance, and in a court where the darker emotions were sustenance, attending to that balance was essential.

Another squabble in the middle of the room caught his attention. Gabriel's growl shook the walls as he ground his boot into a Ly Erg's face, leaving the fallen faery bloody enough that there'd be another stain on the floor. Obviously, the Ly Ergs weren't being as cooperative as Gabriel would like. They enjoyed bloodshed too much, clustering to support Bananach every time she stirred mutiny.

With a gleeful grin, Gabriel watched the Ly Erg crawl

back to his table. Then Gabriel turned to Irial and bowed low enough that his face touched the floor, presumably to hide his grin as much as to show respect. He told Irial, "Once you collect your mortal, we'll ride with you to help evoke fear and confusion in the mortals. The Hounds support the will of the Dark King. *That* won't change." Gabriel's gaze didn't drift to Bananach or the glaring faeries who had gone to her side already, but his message was clear enough.

"Indeed." Irial ground out his cigarette and smiled at his most trusted companion. The Hounds had a lovely ability to induce terror in faery and mortal alike.

"We could get a bit of fear out of the disobedient in this lot . . ." Gabriel murmured, and his Hounds grabbed up some of the faeries who'd smiled in support of the earlier mutinous suggestions. "The Dark Court should show a little respect to our king."

Faeries clambered to their feet and talons and paws, bowing and curtsying. Bananach did not move.

Gabriel caught her gaze and grinned again. There would be no more overt objections or discussions tonight. Gabriel would organize the fey and threaten them if they refused to cooperate with Irial's precautions. They'd be almost perversely obedient. *For now.* Then Bananach would step up her attempts.

But not tonight—not yet.

"Tonight, we'll feast in our fallen sister's memory." Irial made a beckoning gesture, and several of Gabriel's Hounds brought in a score of terrified faeries they'd rounded up

from the other courts. None were from the High Court—
which wasn't surprising, as the High Court faeries so rarely
left their seclusion—but there were both Winter Court and
Summer Court faeries.

Irial folded a trembling Summer Girl into his arms. The
vines that clung to her skin wilted under his touch. She was
so filled with terror and loathing that he briefly considered
sharing her with the others, but he was still selfish enough
to want her to himself. Keenan's special girls were always
such a nice treat. If Irial was careful, he could draw enough
desire and fear out of them to stave off hunger for a couple
of days. A few times, he'd been able to leave them so
addicted that they returned willingly to his arms for regular
visits—and hated him for making them betray their king.
It was quite satisfying.

Irial held the girl's gaze as he told his court, "Their
regents did this, brought us to this when they killed Beira.
Remember that as you offer them your hospitality."

CHAPTER 4

The tattoo shop was empty when Leslie walked in. No voice broke the stillness of the room. Even the stereo was silenced.

"It's me," she called.

She went back to the room where Rabbit would do the work. The paper with the stencil of her tattoo waited on a tray on the counter beside a disposable razor and miscellaneous other items. "I'm a little early."

Rabbit stared at her for a moment but didn't say anything.

"You said we could start tonight. Do the outline." She came over to stare down at the stencil. She didn't touch it, though, strangely afraid that it would vanish if she did.

Finally Rabbit said, "Let me get the door."

While he was gone, she wandered around the tiny room—more to keep from touching the stencil than anything else. The walls were covered in various show and convention flyers—most faded and for events long past. A few framed photos, all black-and-white, and theater-size film posters were intermingled with the flyers. Like every other part of the shop, the room was impossibly clean and had a slight antiseptic scent.

She paused at several of the photos, not recognizing most of the people or places. Interspersed among them were framed pen-and-ink sketches. In one, Capone-era thugs were smiling at the artist. It was as realistic as any photograph, skillful to the degree that it seemed bizarre to see it hanging amidst the snapshots and posters. Rabbit returned as she was tracing the form of a stunningly beautiful man sitting in the middle of the group of gangsters. They were all striking, but it was him, the one leaning on an old twisted tree, who looked almost familiar. The others clustered around, beside, or behind him, but he was obviously the one with power. She asked, "Who's this?"

"Relatives," was all Rabbit said.

Leslie's attention lingered on the picture. The man in the image wore a dark suit like the other men, but his posture—arrogant and assessing—gave him the impression of being more menacing than the men around him. Here was someone to fear.

Rabbit cleared his throat and pointed in front of him. "Come on. Can't start with you over there."

Leslie forced herself to look away from the image. Fearing—*or lusting on*—someone who was either old or long dead was sort of weird anyhow. She went to where

Rabbit had pointed, put her back to him, and pulled her shirt off.

Rabbit tucked a cloth of some sort under her bra strap. "To keep it clean."

"If ink or whatever gets on it, it's not a big deal." She folded her arms across her chest and tried to stand still. Despite how much she wanted the ink, standing there in her bra felt uncomfortable.

"You're sure?"

"Definitely. No buyer's remorse. Really, it's starting to border on obsession. I actually dreamed about it. The eyes in it and those wings." She blushed, thankful Rabbit was behind her and couldn't see her face.

He wiped her skin with something cold. "Makes sense."

"Sure it does." Leslie smiled, though: Rabbit wasn't fazed by anything, acting as if the oddest things were okay. It made her relax a little.

"Stay still." He shaved the fine hairs on the skin where the tattoo would go and wiped her off again with more cold liquid.

She glanced back as he walked away. He tossed the razor into a bin, pausing to give her a serious look before coming behind her again. She watched him over her shoulder.

He picked up the stencil. "Face that way."

"Where's Ani?" Leslie'd rarely been at the shop when Ani didn't show up, usually with Tish in tow. It was like she had some radar, able to track people down without any obvious explanation how.

"Ani needed quiet." He put a hand on her hip and moved her. Then he spritzed something lightly on her back where the ink would go—at the top of her spine between her shoulders, spanning the width of her back, centered over the spot where Leslie thought the wings would attach if they were real. She closed her eyes as he pressed the stencil onto her back. Somehow even that felt exciting.

Then he peeled away the paper. "See if it's where you want it."

She went to the mirror as quickly as she could without running. Using the hand mirror to see her reflection in the wall mirror, she saw it—her ink, her perfect ink stenciled on her skin—and grinned so widely, her cheeks hurt. "Yes. Gods, yes."

"Sit." He pointed at the chair.

She sat on the edge and watched as Rabbit methodically put on gloves, opened a sterile stick, and used it to pull a glop of clear ointment out of a jar and put it on a cloth-covered tray. He pulled out several tiny ink caps and tacked them down to the drop cloth. Then he poured ink into them.

I've watched this plenty of times; it's not a big deal. She couldn't look away, though.

Rabbit did each step silently, as if she weren't there. He opened the needle package and pulled out a length of thin metal. It looked like it was just one needle, but she knew from her hours listening to Rabbit talk shop that there were several individual needles at the tip of a needle bar. *My needles, for* my *ink, in* my *skin.* Rabbit slid the needle bar into the machine. The soft sound of metal sliding across metal was followed by an almost inaudible *snick.* Leslie let out breath she hadn't realized she'd been holding. If she thought Rabbit would let her, she'd ask to hold the tattoo machine, ask to wrap her hand around the primitive-looking coils and angled bits of metal. Instead she watched Rabbit make adjustments to it. She shivered. It looked like a crude hand-held sewing machine, and with it he'd stitch beauty onto her body. There was something primal about the process that resonated for her, some sense that after this she'd be irrevocably different, and that was exactly what she needed.

"Turn that way." Rabbit motioned, and she moved so her back was to him. He smeared ointment over her skin with a latex-clad finger. "Ready?"

"Mm-hmm." She braced herself, wondering briefly if it would hurt but not caring. Some of the people she'd seen complained like the pain was unbearable. Others seemed not to notice it at all. *It'll be fine.* The first touch of needles was startling, a sharp sensation that felt more like irritation than pain. It was far from awful.

"You good?" He paused, taking away the touch of needles as he spoke.

"Mm-hmm," she said again: it was the most articulate answer she could offer in the moment. Then, after a pause that was almost long enough to make her beg him to get back to it, he lowered the tattoo machine to her skin again. Neither spoke as he outlined the tattoo. Leslie closed her eyes and concentrated on the machine as it hummed and paused, lifting from her skin only to touch back down. She couldn't see it, but she'd watched Rabbit work often enough to know that in some of those pauses Rabbit dipped the tip of the needle into the tiny ink caps like a scholar inking his quill.

And she sat there, her back stretched in front of him as if she were a breathing piece of canvas. It was wonderful. The only sound was the hum of the machine. It was more than a sound, though: it was a vibration that seemed to slip through her skin and sink into the marrow of her bones.

"I could stay like this forever," she whispered, eyes still closed.

A dark laugh rolled out of somewhere. Leslie's eyes snapped open. "Is someone here?"

"You're tired. School and extra shifts this month, right? Maybe you drifted off." He tilted his head in that peculiar way he and his sisters had, like a dog hearing a new sound.

"Are you saying I fell asleep *sitting up* while you were tattooing me?" She looked back at him and frowned.

"Maybe." He shrugged and turned away to open a brown glass bottle. It was unlike the other ink bottles: the label was handwritten in a language she didn't recognize.

When he uncapped it, it seemed as if tiny shadows slithered out of it. *Weird.* She blinked and stared at it. "I *must* be tired," she muttered.

He poured ink from the bottle into another ink cap—

holding it aloft so the outside of the bottle didn't touch the side of the ink cap—then sealed the bottle and changed gloves.

She repositioned herself and closed her eyes again. "I expected it to hurt, you know?"

"It *does* hurt." Then he lowered the tattoo machine to her skin again, and she stopped remembering how to speak.

The hum had always sounded comforting when Leslie had listened to Rabbit working, but feeling the vibration on her skin made it seem exciting and not at all comforting. It felt different from what she'd imagined, but it wasn't what she'd call pain. Still, she doubted it was something she could've slept through.

"You okay?" Rabbit wiped her skin again.

"I'm good." She felt languid, like her bones weren't all the way solid anymore. "More ink."

"Not tonight."

"We could just finish it tonight—"

"No. This one will take a couple sessions." Rabbit was quiet as he wiped her skin. He slid his chair back; the wheels sounded loud as they slid over the floor, like a boulder being pushed across a metal grate.

Weird.

She stretched—and almost blacked out.

Rabbit steadied her. "Give it a sec."

"Head rush or something." She blinked to clear her vision, resisting the urge to try to focus on the shadows that

seemed to be walking through the room unattached to anything.

But Rabbit was there, showing her the tattoo—*my
tattoo*—with a pair of hand mirrors. She tried to speak, and
might have. She wasn't sure. Time felt like it was off, speeding and slowing, keeping pace with some faraway chaos
clock, bending to rhythms that weren't predictable. Rabbit
was covering her new tattoo with a sterile bandage. At the
same time, it seemed, his arm was around her, helping her
stand.

She stepped unsteadily forward. "Careful with my
wings."

She stumbled. *Wings?*

Rabbit said nothing; perhaps he hadn't heard or understood. Perhaps she hadn't spoken—but she could picture
them—dark, shadowy swoops, somewhere between feathers and slick-soft aged leather, that tickled the sensitive skin
at the backs of her knees.

As soft as I remembered.

"Rabbit? I feel weird. Wrong. Something wrong."

"Endorphin rush, Leslie, making you feel high. It'll be
okay. It's not unusual." He didn't look at her when he
spoke, and she knew he was lying.

She felt like she should be afraid, but she wasn't. Rabbit
had lied: something *was* very wrong. She knew with a
certainty that seemed impossible—like tasting sugar and
having it called salt—that the words he said didn't taste
true.

But then it didn't matter. The missing hands of the chaos clock shifted again, and nothing else mattered in that moment, just the ink in her skin, the hum in her veins, the euphoric zinging that made her feel a confidence she'd not known in far too long.

CHAPTER 5

Although Rabbit had told him where to find her, Irial hadn't approached the mortal yet; he'd had no intention of doing so until he saw if she really was strong enough to be worth the effort. But when he felt their first tenuous link fall into place, felt her euphoria as Rabbit's tattoo machine danced across her skin, he knew he had to see her. It was like a compulsion tugging at him—and not just him: *all* the dark fey felt it, tied as they were to Irial. They'd protect her, fight to be near her now.

And that urge was a good one to encourage—their being near her would mean they'd taunt and torment the mortals, elicit fear and anguish, appetites and furies, delicious meals to sate his appetites once the ink exchange was complete. Where the girl walked, his fey would follow. Mortals would become a feast for king and court—he'd caught only slight drifts of it so far, but already it was an invigorating thing. *Shadows in her wake, for me, for us.* He drew a deep breath, pulling on that still-tenuous link Rabbit was forging with his tattoo machine.

Irial rationalized it: if he was going to be tied to her, it made sense to check in on her. She'd be his responsibility, his burden, and in many ways a weakness. But despite the reasons he could list, he knew it wasn't logic leading him: it was desire. Fortunately, the king of the Dark Court saw no reason to resist his appetites, so he'd co-opted Gabriel and was on the way to her city, seeking her presence the way he had sought so many other indulgences over the years. He leaned back, seat reclined all the way, enjoying the thrill of Gabriel's seemingly reckless driving.

Irial propped one boot on the door, and Gabriel growled. "She's fresh painted, Iri. Come on."

"Chill."

The Hound shook his shaggy head. "I don't put my boots on your bed or any of those little sofas you have everywhere. Get your boot off there before you scratch her."

Like the rest of the Hounds' steeds, Gabriel's wore the guise of a mortal vehicle, shifting so truly into that form that it was sometimes hard to remember when it had last looked like the terrifying beast it truly was. Maybe it was an extension of Gabriel's will; maybe it was the steed's own whim. All of the creatures mimicked mortal vehicles so well that it was easy to forget that they were living things—except when anyone other than the Hounds tried to ride them. Then it was easy to recall what they were: the speed at which they moved sent the offending faery—or mortal—

hurtling through the air into whatever target the beasts chose.

Gabriel steered his Mustang into the small lot beside Verlaine's, the restaurant where the mortal worked. Irial lowered his foot, scraping his boot on the window as he did so; the illusion of its being a machine didn't waver.

"Dress code, Gabe. Change." As Irial spoke, his own appearance shifted. Had any mortals been watching, they'd have seen his jeans and club-friendly shirt vanish in favor of a pressed pair of trousers and conservative oxford-cloth shirt. His scuffed boots, however, stayed. It wasn't the glamour he usually wore, but he didn't want the mortal to recognize him later. This meeting was for him, so he could watch her; it was not one he'd prefer her to remember.

"A face to meet the faces that we meet," but not my face— not even the mask I wear for the mortals. Layers of illusions . . . Irial scowled, unsure of the source of the strange melancholia that was riding him, and gestured to Gabriel to don a relatively unthreatening glamour as well. "Pretty yourself up."

Gabriel's appearance shift was more subtle than Irial's: he still wore black jeans and a collarless shirt, but the Hound's tattoos were now hidden under long sleeves. His unruly hair appeared to be neatly trimmed, as were his goatee and sideburns. Like Irial's, Gabriel's glamour was not his usual one. Gabriel's face was somehow gentler, without the dark shadows and hollows that he usually left visible for the mortals. Of course, the glamour did nothing for the

Hound's intimidating height, but for Gabriel, it was near conservative.

As they got out of the car, Gabriel bared his teeth at several of the Summer Court's guards in a taunting smile. They were, no doubt, minding the mortal since she was friends with the new Summer Queen. The guards saw him as he truly was and cringed. If Gabriel were to start trouble, they'd inevitably suffer serious injury.

Irial opened the door. "Not now, Gabriel."

After a longing look at the fey who lingered in the street, Gabriel went inside the restaurant. In a low voice, Irial told him, "After the meal, you can visit our watchers. A bit of terror so near the girl . . . It's what she's for, right? Let's see how the initial connection holds up."

Gabriel smiled then, happily anticipating a spot of trouble with the Summer Court guards. Their presence meant that neither Winter nor Summer Court would harm the girl, and no solitary fey would be foolish enough to try to engage in any sport with a mortal who was under such careful watch. Of course, it also meant that Irial would have the great fun of stealing her away without their noticing before it was too late.

"Just the two of you?" the hostess, a rather vapid mortal with a perky smile, asked.

A quick glance at the chart on the hostess station showed him which tables were in his mortal's section. Irial motioned to a table in the far corner, a darkened section fit for romantic dinners or stolen trysts. "We'll take that table in back. The one by the ficus."

After the hostess led them to the table in question, Irial waited until she—*Leslie*—walked up, her hips swaying slightly, her expression friendly and warm. Such a look would work well if he were the mortal he appeared to be. As it was, the shadows that danced around her and the smoke-thin tendrils that snaked from her skin to his— visible only to dark fey—were what made his breath catch.

"Hi, I'm Leslie. I'll be your server tonight," she said as she placed a basket of fresh bread on the table. Then she launched into specials and other nonsense he didn't quite hear. She had too-thin lips for his taste, darkened only slightly with something pink and girlish. *Not suitable for* my *mortal at all.* But the darkness that clung so poignantly to her skin was quite fit for his court. He studied her, reading her feelings now that they were linked even this slightly. When he'd met her she'd been tainted, but now she positively crawled with shadows. Someone had hurt her, and badly, since he'd first seen her.

Anger that someone had touched what was his vied with awareness. What they had done—and how ably she resisted the shadows—these were what made her ready to be his. Had they not wounded her, she'd be inaccessible to him. Had she not resisted the darkness so successfully, she'd not be strong enough to handle what he was about to do to her. She'd been damaged, but not irreparably. Fragmented and strong, the perfect mix for him.

But he'd still kill them for touching her.

Silent now, obviously done with her lists and recommendations, she stood and stared expectantly at him. Aside from a quick glance at Gabriel, her attention was riveted on Irial. It pleased him more than he'd expected, seeing the mortal look at him attentively. He liked her hunger. "Leslie, can you do me a favor?"

"Sir?" She smiled again but looked hesitant as she did so. Her fear spiked, showing in a slight shifting of shadows that made his heart race.

"I'm not feeling very decisive"—he shot a glare at Gabriel, whose muffled laugh turned into a loud cough—"in terms of the menu here. Could you order for me?"

She frowned and looked back at the hostess, who was now watching them carefully. "If you're a regular, I'm sorry, but I don't remember—"

"No. I'm not." He ran a finger down her wrist, violating mortal etiquette, but unable to resist. She was his. It wasn't official yet, but that didn't matter. He smiled at her, letting his glamour drop for a fraction of a moment, showing her his true face—testing her, seeking fear or longing—and added, "Just order whatever you think we'd like. Surprise me. I enjoy a good surprise."

Her waitress facade slipped a little; her heartbeat fluttered. And he *felt* it, the brief surge of panic. He couldn't taste it, not yet, not truly, but almost—like a pungent aroma wafting from a kitchen, teasing hints of flavors he couldn't swallow.

He opened the black-lacquered cigarette case he favored

of late and drew out a cigarette, watching her try to make sense of him. "Can you do that, Leslie? Take care of me?"

She nodded, slowly. "Do you have any allergies or—"

"Not to anything on your menu. Neither of us does." He tapped his cigarette on the table, packing it, watching her until she looked away.

She glanced at Gabriel. "Order for you too?"

Gabriel shrugged as Irial said, "Yes, for both of us."

"Are you sure?" She watched him intently, and Irial suspected that she was already feeling something of the changes that would soon roll over her. Her eyes had dilated ever so slightly when her fears rose and faded. Later tonight, when she thought of him, she'd think he was just an odd man, memorable for that alone. It would be a while until her mind would let her process the extent of her changing body. Mortals had so many mental defenses to make sense of the things that violated their preconceptions and rules. At times those defenses were quite useful to him.

He lit his cigarette, stalling just to watch her squirm a touch more. He lifted her hand and kissed her knuckles, once more being completely inappropriate for the guise he wore and for the setting. "I think you'll bring me exactly what I need."

Terror surged, tangling around an unmistakable blaze of desire and a bit of anger. Her smile didn't waver, though.

"I'll put your order in, then," she said as she took a step backward, pulling her hand free of his grip.

He took a drag on his cigarette as he watched her walk

away. The dark smoky line between them stretched and wound through the room like a path he could follow.

Soon.

At the doorway, she looked back at him, and he could almost taste her terror as it peaked.

He licked his lips.

Very soon.

CHAPTER 6

Leslie slipped into the kitchen, leaned on the wall, and tried not to fall to pieces. Her hands shook. Someone else needed to handle the odd guest; she felt frightened by his attention, his too-intense stare, his words.

"You okay, *ma belle*?" the pastry chef, Étienne, asked. He was a wiry man with a temper that flared to life over the oddest things, but he was just as irrationally kind. Tonight, kind appeared to be the mood of choice, or at least this hour it was.

"Sure." She pasted a smile back on her face, but it was less than convincing.

"Sick? Hungry? Faint?" Étienne prompted.

"I'm fine, just a demanding guest, too touchy, too everything. He wants . . . Maybe you could figure out what to order—" She stopped, feeling inexplicably angry at herself for thinking, even for that brief second, of having someone else order *his* food. *No.* That wouldn't work. Her anger and fear receded. She straightened her shoulders and rattled off a list of her favorite foods, complete with the marquise au chocolat.

"That's not on the dessert menu tonight," one of the prep cooks objected.

Étienne winked. "For Leslie it is. I have emergency dessert for special reasons."

Leslie felt relieved, irrationally so, that Étienne's rum-soaked chocolate decadence was available. It wasn't as if the customer had asked for it, but she wanted to give it to him, wanted to please him. "You're the best."

"*Oui*, I know." Étienne shrugged as if it were nothing, but his smile belied the expression. "You should tell Robert this. Often. He forgets how lucky he is that I stay here."

Leslie laughed, relaxing a bit under Étienne's irresistible charm. It was no secret that the owner, Robert, would do almost anything to please Étienne, a fact that Étienne pretended not to notice.

"The order for table six is up," another voice called out, and Leslie resumed her work, smile sliding back into place as she lifted the steaming dishes.

As the shift wore on, Leslie caught herself looking at the two odd guests often enough that she had a difficult time concentrating on her other tables.

Tips will be low if this keeps up.

It wasn't like touchy guests were unheard of. Guys seemed to think that because she waited tables she'd be easily swayed by a little charm and affluence. She smiled and flirted a bit with male diners; she smiled and listened a few minutes longer with older guests; and she smiled and paid attention to the families with children. It was simply how it went at Verlaine's. Robert liked the waitstaff to treat the guests personably. Of course, that ended at the threshold of the restaurant. She didn't date anyone she met on duty; she wouldn't even give her number.

I would with him, *though.*

He looked comfortable in his skin, but also like he'd be able to hold his own in the shadowy parts of the city. And he was beautiful—not his features, but the way he moved. It reminded her of Niall. *And he's probably just as unavailable.*

The guest watched her in much the same way Niall did, too—with attentive gazes and lingering smiles. If a guy at a club looked at her that way, she'd expect him to hit on her. Niall hadn't, despite her encouragement; maybe this one wouldn't go further either.

"Leslie?" The guest couldn't have spoken loudly enough for her to hear him, but she did. She turned, and he gestured for her to come closer.

She finished taking an order from one of the weekly regulars and just barely resisted the urge to run across the room. She navigated the space between the tables without taking her eyes off of him, stepping around the busboy and another waiter, pausing and moving between a couple leaving the restaurant.

"Did you need something?" Her voice came out too soft, too breathy. A brief flicker of embarrassment rolled over her and then faded as quickly as it had risen.

"Do you—" He broke off, smiling at someone behind her, looking as if he'd laugh in the next moment.

Leslie turned. A crowd of people she didn't know stood in a small circle around Aislinn, who was waving at her. Friends weren't welcome at work; Aislinn knew that, but she started walking across the room toward Leslie. Leslie looked back at the guest. "I'm so sorry. Just one second?"

"Absolutely fine, love." He pulled out another cigarette, going through the same ritual as before—snapping the case shut, tapping the cigarette on the tabletop, and flicking the lighter open. His gaze didn't waver from her. "I'm not going anywhere."

She turned to face Aislinn. "What are you doing? You can't just—"

"The hostess said I could ask you to wait on us." Aislinn motioned at the large group she'd come in with. "There's not a table in your section, but I wanted you."

"I can't," Leslie said. "I have a full section."

"One of the other waitresses could take your tables, and—"

"And my tips." Leslie shook her head. She didn't want to tell Aislinn how badly she needed that money or how her stomach clenched at the possibility of walking away from the eerily compelling guest behind her. "Sorry, Ash. I can't."

But the hostess came over and said, "Can you take the group and your tables, or do I need to have someone pick up your tables so you can take them?"

Anger surged in Leslie, fleeting but strong. Her smile was pained, but she kept it in place. "I can take both."

With a hostile look at the table behind Leslie, Aislinn went back to her party. The hostess left too, and Leslie was seething. She turned to face *him*.

He took a long drag off the cigarette and exhaled. "Well, then. She seems territorial. I suppose that little look was a don't-hit-on-my-friend message?"

"I'm sorry about that." She winced.

"Are you two together?"

"No." Leslie blushed. "I'm not . . . I mean—"

"Is there someone else? A friend of hers you see?" His voice was as delicious as the best of Étienne's desserts, rich and decadent, meant to be savored.

Unbidden she thought of Niall, her fantasy date. She shook her head. "No. There's no one."

"Perhaps I should return on a less-crowded night, then?" He traced a finger up the underside of her wrist, touching her for the third time.

"Maybe." She felt the odd urge to run—not that he was

any less tempting, but he was looking at her so intently that she was certain he wasn't anywhere near safe.

He pulled out a handful of bills. "For dinner."

Then he stood and stepped close enough to her that her instinct to flee flared to life; she felt suddenly sick in the stomach. He tucked the money into her hand. "I'll see you another night."

She stepped backward, away from him. "But your food isn't up yet."

He followed, invading her space, moving so close that it would seem normal only if they were about to dance or kiss. "I don't share well."

"But—"

"No worries, love. I'll be back when your friend isn't around to snarl at me."

"But your dinner . . ." She looked from him to the bills in her hand. *Oh my gods.* Leslie was startled out of her confusion by the realization of how much she was holding: they were all large bills. She immediately tried to hand some of them back. "Wait. You made a mistake."

"No mistake at all."

"But—"

He leaned in so he whispered in her ear, "You're worth emptying my coffers for."

For a moment she thought she felt something soft wrap around her. *Wings.*

Then he pulled back. "Go tend to your friend. I'll see

you again when she's not watching."

And he walked away, leaving her motionless in the middle of the room, clutching more money than she'd ever seen in her life.

CHAPTER 7

When Niall reached Verlaine's, Irial had gone. Two of the guards who'd been outside the restaurant were bleeding badly from teeth marks in their arms. Some embarrassing part of him wished he'd been sent for sooner, but he quashed that thought before it became one he had to consider. When Irial acted against the Summer Court faeries, Niall was always summoned. The Dark King often refused to strike Niall. Gabriel, on the other hand, had no compunction against wounding Niall and often seemed to be more violent toward Niall when Irial was near.

"The Gabriel"—one of the rowan shuddered—"he just walked up and ripped into us."

"Why?" Niall looked around, seeking some clue, some indication of a reason that Gabriel would do so. Niall might've chosen to avoid the Dark King's left hand as often as possible, but he hadn't forgotten the things he'd learned in the Dark Court: Gabriel didn't ever act without reason. It mightn't be a reason that the Summer Court understood, but there was always a reason. Niall knew that. It was part of why he was an asset to the Summer Court: he understood the less gentle tendencies of the other courts.

"Mortal girl talked to the Gabriel and Dark King," a rowan-woman said as she wrapped her bloody biceps. She clenched the end of a strip of spider silk between her teeth as she bound her arm. Niall would offer to help her, but he knew she'd trained with the glaistigs. It made her a great fighter, but it also meant anything that looked like mercy would be summarily rejected.

Niall looked away. He could see Leslie through the window: she smiled at the Summer Queen and refilled a glass of water. It wasn't an unusual task, or an exciting one, but as he watched her, his throat suddenly felt dry. He wanted to go to her, wanted to . . . do things he should not dream of doing with mortals. Without meaning to, he'd crossed the street, stepped close to that window, and rested his hand on it. The cold glass was a thin barrier; he could crack it with just a bit of pressure, feel the edges slice into his skin, go to her, and sink his body into hers. *I could let her see me. I could—*

"Niall?" The rowan-woman stood beside him, staring through the window. "Do we need to go in?"

"No." Niall pulled his gaze away from Leslie, forced his thoughts back to something less alluring. He'd been watching her for months; there was no reason for his sudden surge of irrational thoughts. Perhaps his guard was down from thinking of Irial. Niall shook his head in self-disgust.

"Go home. Aislinn has plenty of guards with her, and I'll watch the queen's mortal," he said.

Without any further comment, the rowan and her companions left, and Niall crossed back to the alcove where he'd waited out so many of Leslie's shifts at Verlaine's. He leaned against the brick wall, feeling the familiar edges press into his back, and watched the faces of the mortals and faeries in the street. He forced himself to think about what he was, what he'd done before he knew who Irial was, before he knew how twisted Irial was. *All things that mean I should not touch Leslie. Ever.*

When Niall had first walked among them, he'd found mortals enthralling. They were filled with passion and desperation, carving out what joy they could in their all-too-finite lives, and most were willing to lift their skirts for a few kind words from his lips. He shouldn't miss their dizzying willingness and mortal touch. He knew better. Sometimes, though, if he looked too closely at what he knew himself to be, he did miss it.

The girl was weeping, clutching Niall's arm, when the dark-haired faery approached. The girl had bared herself when she entered the wood and had innumerable scratches on her flesh.

"She's an affectionate thing," the faery said.

Niall shook her off again. "She's been drinking,
I suspect. She wasn't so"—he grabbed her hand as
she began unfastening his breeches—"aggressive last
week."

"Indeed." The dark-haired faery laughed. "Like
animals, aren't they?"

"Mortals?" Niall stepped closer to him, dodging
the girl's agile hands. "They seem to hide it well
enough at first. . . . They change, though."

The other faery laughed and caught the girl up
in his arms. "Maybe you're just irresistible."

Niall straightened his clothes now that the girl
was contained. She stayed motionless in the other
faery's grasp, looking from one to the other like she
was insensible.

The dark-haired faery watched Niall with a
curious grin. "I'm Irial. Perhaps we could take this
one somewhere less"—he looked up the path toward
the mortals' town—"public." The lascivious look
on Irial's face was the most enticing thing Niall
had ever seen. He had a brief flash of terror at his
tangled mix of feelings. Then Irial licked his lips
and laughed. "Come now, Niall. I think you could
use a bit of company, couldn't you?"

Later he wondered why he hadn't been suspicious at Irial's
knowing his name. At the time all Niall could think of was
that the nearer he got to Irial, the more it felt like stumbling

upon a feast and realizing he'd never tasted anything until that moment. It was an intensity he'd never felt before—and he loved it.

Over the next six years, Irial stayed with Niall for months at a time. When Irial was at his side, Niall indulged in debauched pleasures with more mortals than he'd known he could lie with at one time. But it wasn't ever enough. No matter how many days Niall lost in a blur of yielding flesh, he was never satisfied for long. There were equally dizzying days when it was just them, dining on exotic foods, drunk on foreign wines, touring new lands, listening to glorious songs, talking about everything. It was perfect—for a while. *If I hadn't gone to his* bruig *and seen the mortals there in Irial's domain . . .* Niall wasn't sure who he'd hated more when he realized what a fool he'd been.

"It's been too long, Gancanagh." Gabriel's voice was an almost-welcome interruption of the unpleasant memories. The Hound stood on the edge of the street, just close enough to traffic to be clipped by careless drivers but far enough to be mostly safe. Ignoring the flow of cars, he looked up and down the sidewalk. "The rowan gone?"

"Yes." Niall glanced at the dark faery's forearm, checking to see if there were words he should know, almost hoping Irial'd ordered Gabriel to do something that would allow Niall to strike out.

Gabriel noticed. With a wicked grin, he turned his arms so Niall could see the undersides. "No messages for you. One of these days, I'll get a chance to give you a matching scar on the other side of your pretty face, but not yet."

"So you keep saying, but he never gives you permission." Niall shrugged. He wasn't sure if it was because he was impervious to the terror of the Hounds' presence or because he'd walked away from Irial, but Gabriel brought up old pains every chance he could—and Niall usually let it go. Tonight, however, Niall didn't feel very tolerant, so he asked, "Do you suppose Iri just likes me more than you, Gabriel?"

For several of Niall's too-fast heartbeats, Gabriel simply stared at him. Then he said, "You're the only one who doesn't seem to know that answer."

Before Niall could reply, Gabriel slammed his fist into Niall's face, turned, and walked away.

Blinking his eyes against the sudden pain, Niall watched the Hound saunter down the street and calmly wrap his hands around the throats of two Dark Court fey who'd apparently been lurking nearby. Gabriel lifted the Ly Ergs and choked them until the faeries went limp. Then he slung them over his shoulders and took off in such a blur of speed that small dust devils swirled to life in his wake.

Gabriel's violence wasn't unusual, but the lack of obvious orders on the Hound's skin was enough to make Niall wary. It was inevitable that the semi-peace that resulted from Beira's death would cause ripples in the other courts. How Irial dealt with that should concern Niall only as far as protecting his true court—the Summer Court—but Niall had a residual moment of concern for the Dark King, a twinge that he had no intention of ever admitting aloud.

Leslie was pleasantly surprised that Aislinn was waiting on the curb outside the restaurant when her shift ended. They used to meet up after work sometimes, but everything had changed over the winter.

"Where's"—Leslie paused, not wanting to say the wrong thing—"everyone?"

"Seth's out at the Crow's Nest. Keenan's working on some stuff. I don't know where Carla or Ri are." Aislinn stood up and wiped her hands on her jeans, as if the brief contact with the ground had dirtied them. For all Aislinn's comfort in grungy places that made most people uncomfortable, she still had tidiness issues.

Aislinn glanced at a few unfamiliar guys across the street. When she looked away, one of them shot a grin at Leslie and licked his lips. Reflexively, Leslie flipped him off—and then tensed as she realized what she'd done. She knew better: caution kept a girl safer than provoking trouble did. She wasn't the sort to flip anyone off or speak up, not now, not anymore.

Beside her, Aislinn had finished her survey of the street. She was always cautious, enough so that Leslie had wondered more than a few times what Aislinn had seen or done that made her so careful.

Aislinn asked, "Walk over to the fountain?"

"Lead the way." Leslie waited until Aislinn started walking

before she glanced back to make sure that the guy she'd flipped off hadn't decided to cross the street. He waved at her but didn't follow.

"So did you know that guy tonight? The one you were talking to when I got there?" Aislinn tucked her hands in the oversize leather jacket she had on. She had a nice coat of her own, but she tended to wear Seth's beat-up jacket when he wasn't with her.

"I've never met him before." Leslie shivered at a sudden rush of longing that rolled over her at the mention of the strange guy—and decided not to tell Aislinn that he'd said he'd be back.

"He was kind of intense." Aislinn paused as they waited to cross the poorly lit intersection at Edgehill.

The headlights of a passing bus cut through the shadows, illuminating shapes that for a moment looked like a feather-haired woman and a group of red-tinted muscular men. Leslie's imagination was entirely too active lately. Earlier she'd had the disconcerting feeling that she was looking out of someone else's eyes, that she could see things that were somewhere else.

The bus passed, sending an exhaust-scented gust of air over them, and they crossed into the slightly better lit park. On a bench across from the fountain, four unfamiliar guys and two equally unknown girls nodded to Aislinn. She lifted her hand in a wave of sorts but didn't go toward them. "So did he ask you to meet him or something, or—"

"Ash? Why are you asking?" Leslie sat down on an empty

bench and kicked off her shoes. No matter how long she stretched or how much she walked, there was something about waiting tables that always resulted in sore feet and achy calves. As she rubbed her legs, she glanced over at Aislinn. "Do you know him?"

"You're my friend. I just worry and . . . He looked like trouble, you know? . . . The kind of guy that I wouldn't want near someone I care about." Aislinn moved so she was sitting cross-legged on the bench. "I want you to be happy, Les."

"Yeah?" Leslie grinned at her, suddenly calm despite the swirl of feelings that had been swarming through her tonight. "Me too. And I'm going to be."

"So that guy—"

"Was just passing through town. He talked pretty, wanted to be adored while he ordered his meal, and is probably already gone." Leslie stood and stretched, bouncing a little on the balls of her feet. "It's cool, Ash. No worries, okay?"

Aislinn smiled then. "Good. Are we walking or sitting? We just got here. . . ."

"Sorry." Leslie thought about sitting down for a half second. Then she looked up at the dark sky swallowing the moon. A wonderful rush of urgency filled her. "Dance? Walk? I don't care."

It was as if her months of fears and worries were slipping away. She reached back to touch her tattoo. It was just an outline still, but she already felt better. Believing in a thing—acting to symbolize that belief—really did make her feel stronger. *Symbols of the conviction.* She was becoming herself again.

"Come on." She grabbed Aislinn's hands and pulled her to her feet. She walked backward until they were several feet away from the bench and then spun away. She felt good, free. "You sat around all night while I was working. You have no excuse for sitting still. Let's go."

Aislinn laughed, sounding like her old friend for a change. "The club, I guess?"

"Until your feet ache." Leslie looped her arm with Aislinn's. "Call Ri and Carla."

It felt good to be herself again.

Better, even.

CHAPTER 8

Leslie walked down the hall of Bishop O.C., shoes held in her hand, careful not to swing her arm and smack one of the dingy metal lockers with her heels. It had been three days since she'd had the outline tattooed, but Leslie was unable to stop thinking about that dizzying energy. She had been having strange bursts of panic and joy, emotions that seemed misplaced, out of context somehow, but they weren't debilitating. It was like she'd borrowed someone else's moods. *Odd, but good.* And she felt stronger, quieter, more powerful. She was certain it was an illusion, a result of her new confidence, but she still liked it.

The part she didn't like was how many fights she seemed to notice—or that they didn't frighten her. Instead she caught herself daydreaming of the Verlaine's customer. His name was almost clear when she thought of him, but he'd never told it to her. *Why do I know . . . ?* She shook off that question and hurried to the open door of the supply room.

Rianne was motioning impatiently. "Come *on,* Les."

Once Leslie was in the room, Rianne shut the door with a quiet *click.*

Leslie looked around for a spot to sit. She settled on a pile of gym mats. "Where are Carla and Ash?"

Rianne shrugged. "Being responsible?"

Leslie suspected that she should be doing the same thing, but when Rianne had seen her in the hall that morning she'd mouthed, "Supply room." For all her flakiness, Rianne was a good friend, so Leslie ditched first period.

"What's up?"

"Mom found my stash." Rianne's heavily made-up eyes welled with tears. "I didn't think she was coming home, and—"

"How mad was she?"

"Livid. I have to go back to that counselor. And"— Rianne looked away—"I'm sorry."

Leslie felt like a weight was pressing on her chest as she asked, "For what?"

"She thinks it's from Ren. That I got it from him, so I can't . . . You shouldn't call or come over for a while. It's just . . . I didn't know what to say. I *blanked.*" Rianne caught Leslie's hand. "I'll tell her. It's just . . . she's really—"

"Don't." Leslie knew her voice was harsh, but she wasn't surprised, not really. Rianne never did well with confrontation. "It wasn't from him, right? You know to stay away from Ren."

"I do." Rianne blushed.

Leslie shook her head. "He's a bastard."

"Leslie!"

"Shh. I mean it. I'm not mad at you for letting her think whatever. Just stay clear of Ren and his crowd." Leslie felt ill at the thought of her friend under Ren's influence.

"You're not mad at me?" Rianne's voice trembled.

"No." Leslie was surprised by it, but it was true. Logic said anger made sense, but she felt almost peaceful. There was an edge of anger, like she was about to be mad but wasn't quite able to get there. Every emotion the past three days floated away before it grew intense.

She had the irrational thought that her emotions would settle once she got the tattoo finished—or maybe it was just that she was yearning for it, that bone-melting sensation that she felt when the tattoo needles touched her skin. She forced the thought away and focused on Rianne. "It's not your fault, Ri."

"It is."

"Okay, it *is*, but I'm not mad." Leslie gave Rianne a quick hug then pulled back to glare at her. "I *will* be, though, if you go near Ren. He's hanging with some real losers lately."

"So how are you safe?"

Leslie ignored the question and stood up. She suddenly needed air, needed to be somewhere else. She gave Rianne what she hoped was a convincing smile and said, "I need to go."

"All right. See you in fourth period." Rianne pushed the stack of mats back into some semblance of a tidy pile.

"No. I'm out."

Rianne paused. "You *are* mad."

"No. Really, I'm just—" Leslie shook her head, not sure she could explain or *wanted* to explain the strange feelings compelling her. "I want to walk. Go. I just . . . I'm not sure."

"Want company? I could ditch with you." Rianne smiled, too brightly. "I can catch up with Ash and Carla and we'll meet you at—"

"Not today." Leslie had an increasingly pressing urge to run, roam, just take off.

Rianne's eyes teared up again.

Leslie sighed. "Sweetie, it's not you. I just need air. I guess I'm working too much or something."

"You want to talk? I can listen." Rianne wiped the mascara streaks from under her eyes, making them worse in the process.

"Hold still." With the edge of her sleeve, Leslie rubbed away the black marks and said, "I just need to run it off. Clear my head. Thinking about Ren . . . I worry."

"About him? I could talk to him. Maybe your dad—"

"No. I'm serious: Ren's changed. Stay away from him." Leslie forced a smile to take the sting out of her words. The conversation was becoming entirely too close to topics she didn't like. "I'll catch you later or tomorrow, okay?"

Not looking at all happy about it, Rianne nodded, and they slipped into the hall.

After Leslie left Bishop O.C., she wasn't entirely sure where she was headed until she found herself at the ticket window of the train station. "I need a ticket to Pittsburgh for right now."

The man behind the counter muttered something unintelligible when she slid the money across to him. *Emergency money. Bill money.* She was usually hesitant to spend her money on a few hours' trip to see a museum, but right then she needed to be somewhere beautiful, to see something that made the world feel right again.

Behind her, several guys started shoving each other. People around them began joining in, jostling one another.

"Miss, you need to move." The man glanced past her as he slid her ticket toward her.

She nodded and walked away from the fracas. For a brief moment, she felt like a wave of shadows surged over her, *through* her. She stumbled. *Just fear.* She tried to believe that, to tell herself that she'd been afraid, but she hadn't been.

The actual ride into Pittsburgh and the walk through the city were a blur. Odd things caught her eye. Several couples—or strangers to each other, by the looks of the very disparate clothing styles in one case—were embarrassingly intimate on the train. A beautiful boy with full sleeve tattoos dropped a handful of leaves or bits of paper as he walked by, but for a bizarre moment Leslie thought it was the tattoos flaking from his skin to swirl away in the breeze. It was surreal. Leslie wondered briefly at the oddity of it all, but her mind refused to stay focused on that. It felt *wrong* to question the odd things she'd been feeling and seeing. When she tried, some pressure inside her skin forced her to think of something, *anything*, else.

And then she walked inside the Carnegie Museum of Art, and everything felt right. The oddities and questions slid away. The very world slid away as Leslie wandered aimlessly, past columns, over the smooth floor, up and down the stairs. *Breathe it in.*

Finally her need to run eased completely and she slowed. She let her gaze drift over the paintings until she came to one that made her pause. She stood silent in front of it. *Van Gogh. Van Gogh is good.*

An older woman walked through the gallery. Her shoes clacked in a steady rhythm as she moved, purposeful but not hurried. Several art students sat with their sketchbooks open, oblivious to everything else around them, caught in the beauty of what they saw on the gallery walls. To Leslie, being in the museum had always felt like being in a church, as if there were something sacred in the very air. Today that feeling was exactly what she needed.

Leslie stood across from the painting, staring at the verdant green fields that stretched away, clean and beautiful and open. *Peace.* That's what the painting felt like, a bit of peace frozen in space.

"Soothing, isn't it?"

She turned, surprised that anyone could walk up to her so easily. Her usual hyperawareness was absent. Niall stood beside her, looking at the painting. His button-up was untucked and hanging over the waist of loose-fitting jeans; his sleeves were folded back, giving her a glimpse of tanned forearms.

"What are *you* doing here?" she asked.

"Seeing you, it seems." He glanced behind him, where a lithe girl with vines painted on her skin stood staring at them. "Not that I'm complaining, but shouldn't you be in classes with Aislinn?"

Leslie looked at the vine-girl, who continued to watch them openly, and wondered if she was a living art display. But then she realized that it must've been bad lighting or shadows: the girl had nothing painted on her. Leslie shook her head and told Niall, "I needed air. Art. Space."

"Am I in that space?" he said as he took a step back. "I thought I'd say hello since we never seem able to speak . . . not that we should. You could go. I could go if you have things—"

"Walk with me?" She didn't look away, despite the too-pleased look on his face. Instead of being nervous, she felt surprisingly bold.

He gestured for her to lead the way, acting more gentlemanly than she thought normal. It wasn't quite stiff, but he seemed tense as he glanced around the gallery.

Then Niall looked back at her. He didn't speak, but there was a strange tension in the way he held himself away

from her. He lifted and lowered his right hand like he didn't
know what to do with it. The fingers on his left hand were
curled tightly together; his arm was held motionless against
his body.

She rested a hand on his arm and told him, "I'm glad
you're actually here instead of with Keenan for a change."

Niall didn't speak, didn't answer. Instead he looked away.

He's afraid.

Inexplicably, she thought of the strange guest at
Verlaine's, could almost imagine him sighing as she
breathed in Niall's fear.

Breathed in fear?

She shook her head and tried to think of something,
anything, to say to Niall—and to avoid thinking about the
fact that his fear was a little exciting. She just stood beside
him and let the silence grow until it was uncomfortably
obvious. It felt like the other museum patrons were staring
at them, but every time she glanced at them, her vision
would catch at the edges, as if a filter slid over her eyes and
distorted what she saw. She stared at the painting, seeing
only blurs of color and shape. "Do you ever wonder if what
you look at is the same thing everyone else is seeing?"

He went even stiller at her side. "Sometimes I'm sure it
isn't the same . . . but that's not so bad, is it? Seeing the
world in a different way?"

"Maybe." She glanced over at him, at his nervous posture, and wanted to reach out to him—to frighten or calm
him, she wasn't sure which.

"Creative vision creates art"—he motioned around the gallery—"that shows the rest of the world a new angle. That's a beautiful thing."

"Or some sort of madness," she said. She wanted to tell someone that she wasn't seeing things right, wasn't feeling them right. She wanted to ask someone to tell her she wasn't going crazy, but asking a stranger for reassurance was pretty far from comfortable—even with her feelings skewed.

She folded her arms over her chest and walked away, carefully not looking at the people watching her or Niall, who was following her with an expression of pain on his face. The past few days it seemed like people were behaving oddly—or perhaps she was just starting to pay attention to the world again. Perhaps it was a waking up from the depression she'd been fighting. She wanted to believe that, but she suspected she was lying to herself: the world around her had become off-kilter, and she wasn't entirely sure she wanted to know why.

CHAPTER 9

With a wariness that felt out of place in the museum, Niall watched the fey watch them. Vine-covered Summer Girls wore glamours to seem mortal. One of the Scrimshaw Sisters slid through the room invisibly, peering into mortals' mouths when they spoke. Another faery, whose body was nothing more than wafting smoke, drifted past. The faery plucked invisible traces from the air and brought them to his mouth, tasting mortals' breath, feeding himself with hints of coffee or sweets that they exhaled. None tested others' boundaries. Here was a place where the faeries all minded their manners, regardless of court affiliation or personal conflicts. It was neutral space, safe space.

And Niall was taking advantage of that safety to break his court's rules. He'd appeared to Leslie, spoken to her on his own. He had no explanation for it. It was an irresistible compulsion to be near her, worse than he'd felt at Verlaine's. He'd disobeyed his queen—not a direct order, but her obvious intent. Should Keenan not intercede with Aislinn, the consequences would be severe.

I can explain that . . . that . . . that what? There was nothing he could say that would be true. He'd simply seen Leslie, watched her blind wanderings, and revealed himself to her—stripped his glamour away right there in the gallery where any mortal could have seen, where plenty of faeries *did* see.

Why now?

The pull to go to her, to reveal himself, was like an order he simply could not refuse—nor, truth be told, did he want to. But he knew better. Until today he'd done fine with not approaching her, but that did not undo the embarrassing number of witnesses to his actions. He should excuse himself, turn back before he crossed lines that would result in his queen's anger. Instead he finally asked, "Did you see the temporary exhibition?"

"Not yet." She kept her distance now, after his too-long silence.

"There's a painting from the Pre-Raphaelites I wanted to see. Would you care to join me?" He had made a habit of viewing every Pre-Raphaelite painting he could. The reigning High Queen, Sorcha, had been inordinately fond of them and lent her likeness to a number of their canvases: Burne-Jones had almost done her justice in *The Golden Stairs.* He thought to tell Leslie—and stopped. He was visible to her. He shouldn't be talking to her at all, about anything.

He stepped away. "You're probably not interested, I can—"

"No. I am. I don't know what the Pre-Raphaelites are. I sort of walk around and look at the paintings. It's not . . . I don't know a lot about art history, just what"—she blushed lightly—"moves me."

"That's all you really need to know, isn't it? I remember the term, in part, because I know that their art moves me." He put a hand gently on the small of her back, allowing himself to reach out and touch her. "Shall we?"

"Sure." She walked forward, out of reach, away from his hand. "So who are these Pre-Raphaelites?"

That was something he could answer. "They were artists who decided to disregard the rules at their art academy, to create new art by their own standards."

"Rebels, huh?" She laughed then, suddenly relaxed and free for no obvious reason. And the beautiful paintings and fabulously carved pillars were less stunning with her for comparison.

"Rebels who changed the world by believing they could." He steered Leslie past a group of Summer Girls—invisible to her—whispering and pointing at him with pouts on their faces. "Belief is a powerful thing. If you believe you can . . ." He paused as faeries clustered nearer them.

Keenan will not be happy.

No mortals, Niall. You know better.

Unless Keenan agreed to that one . . .

She's Aislinn's *friend.*

Niall! Leave her alone. This last was delivered with an outrage that bordered on maternal.

"Niall?" Leslie was staring at him.

"What?"

"You stopped talking. . . . I like your voice. Tell me something else?" She wasn't bold like this, not during the months he'd been watching her, not a few moments ago. "The artists?"

"Right. They didn't follow the rules. They made their own." He refused to look at the faeries watching them and chattering their warnings. Their voices were angry and afraid, and although he knew better, he was excited by it. "Sometimes the rules need to be challenged."

"Or broken?" Leslie's breathing was uneven. Her smile was dangerous.

"Sometimes," he agreed.

There was no way she understood what breaking the rules would mean for him, for her, but he wasn't really breaking them. He was just bending them. He offered Leslie his arm as they walked toward the next gallery. Her hand trembled as she laid it on the curve of his arm. *My king sent me here to watch over her. He knows I can do this. I can be careful, stay within the rules.*

It will be fine. More often than not it was Niall who Keenan asked to guard Leslie. Despite the dangerous consequences of mortals being exposed to Niall's embraces, Keenan trusted him. They'd not spoken often of the way mortals lost themselves after they'd been too long with Niall; they'd not discussed how many mortals he'd destroyed under Irial's influence. All Keenan had said was, "I trust you to do what needs to be done."

Niall had intended to keep Leslie safe from the corruption of his affection. *And I will.* But today, all of Niall's good intentions had faded when he saw her looking so lovely and alone. After today, he would resume watching her invisibly.

I am able to do this: walk with her, talk, and be heard. Just this one conversation.

He'd keep himself distant; there was no harm in that. It wasn't like telling her what he was, or how often he walked with her unawares. He could walk next to her without kissing her.

"Do you want to grab a sandwich before we go to the exhibit?" she asked.

"A sandwich . . . I can do that. Yes."

It's still within the rules. Eating with her isn't dangerous. It would be if it were faery food he offered to her, but this was mortal fare prepared and delivered by mortal hands. *Safe.*

Her hand tightened on his arm, touching him, holding on to him. She murmured, "I really am glad I ran into you."

"Me too." He pulled his arm away, though. He could be a friend, perhaps, but anything more—that was forbidden him. *She* was forbidden.

And all the more tempting for it.

After a couple of too-brief hours, Niall excused himself and retreated, uncomfortably grateful when Leslie's evening guard arrived early. The time with her was painful—beautiful but painful in its emptiness—reminding him of what could not be his.

As he left the museum, he encountered several badly injured faeries, all but insensible from whatever drug they'd found in Irial's houses. It wasn't surprising to see such things so close to Irial's currently favored haunts, but it wasn't only the fey who shimmered with the taint of faery bruises. Mortals—far too many mortals—walked by with the ugly colors of healing bruises on their skin. The mortals might not recognize them as the handprints of something with talons where fingers should be, but Niall saw the bruises' true forms.

Why?

Winter fey passed him with uneasy glances. Solitary fey clustered in small groups at his approach. Even the usually implacable kelpies in the city fountains watched him warily. Once, he'd deserved such suspicions, but he'd shunned the Dark Court. He'd chosen to remake himself, to make amends for what he'd done.

But the sight of the wounded mortals and the anxious faeries made Niall's thoughts return to memories best left forgotten: *the glass-eyed awe as a tiny red-haired girl drooped in his arms, exhausted from too many hours in his hands; Irial's delicious laughter as a table crashed under the dancing*

girls; Gabriel's joy at terrorizing the people of another city
while Irial poured more drinks; strange wine and new herbs in
their dishes; dancing with hallucinations; objections from mor-
tals taken out of his embrace . . . And he'd reveled in all of it.

By the time Niall reached Huntsdale and went to the
Summer Court's loft, his depression was far too pronounced for him to join the revelry. Instead he stood at the
large window in the front room staring at the browning
ring of grass in the park across the street. There they cele-
brated the Summer Court's rebirth, rejoicing at the court's
new—albeit uneasy—accord with the Winter Court.
Summer had come unseasonably early this year—a gift
from the Winter Queen, a peace offering or token of affection perhaps. No matter. It was beautiful. It should soothe
him but did not.

He sighed. He'd need to mention the state of the greenery to Keenan. *Think of duties. Think of responsibilities.*
He'd spent a lifetime atoning for what he'd done. Whatever
aberration was making him feel so off the past few days
would pass.

He rested his forehead on one of the tall panes of glass
in the main room. Across the street, faeries danced in the
park. And as always the Summer Girls spun among them,
darting in and out of the throng in that dervish way of
theirs, trailing vines and skirts. Keenan's on-duty guards
watched over them, keeping them safe, and off-duty guards
danced with them, keeping them amused.

It looks like peace.

That's what Niall had fought for, what he'd pursued for centuries, but he stood alone in the loft—a silent watcher. He felt distant, disconnected from his court, his king, the Summer Girls, everyone but one mortal girl. If he could take Leslie to the dance, spin in the revelries with her in his hands, he'd be there.

But the last Summer King had made clear the terms of accepting Niall's fealty. *No mortals, Niall. That's the price of being in my court.* It wasn't so awful. Mortals were still enticing, but between his memories and his vow, Niall had learned to resist. He had not wanted for dancing—in revelries or in his bed—and it had been enough.

Until her. Until Leslie.

CHAPTER 10

By the end of the week, Leslie was more exhausted than usual. She'd taken extra shifts so she could afford to cover the groceries and still have money for the rest of her ink. She'd tucked that ridiculous tip away, not sure if she'd keep it. If it *was* a tip, she'd have a good deal toward getting a place later, enough to get started on her own, get some basic furniture. *Which is why it's not a tip. That much money doesn't come for free.* For now, she'd keep doing what she was doing before—earning her own money, paying her own way. *Which means being broke.* She knew Rabbit would let her do payments, but that would mean admitting she needed credit, and she wasn't keen on that plan either.

Better to be tired than sold, *though.*

But tired meant forgetting to control her words. Her cattiness slipped out after school while she and Aislinn were waiting for Rianne to finish meeting with a counselor. Apparently, a private counselor wasn't quite enough intervention; Rianne's mother had notified the school as well, and Sister Isabel had waylaid Rianne at the last bell.

Aislinn was watching up the street. She had folded her arms, one hand resting over the thick gold band on her upper arm. Leslie had seen it when they'd changed for PE. Now it was hidden under Aislinn's shirt. *What's she doing that she's getting all these baubles?* Leslie didn't think Aislinn was dumb enough to be trading herself for money, but lately it seemed that Keenan's wealth was in Aislinn's hands.

Without thinking it through, Leslie said, "So are you watching for the second-string boy-toy or the starting player?"

Aislinn stared at her. "What?"

"Is it Keenan's or Seth's turn to take you home?"

"It's not like that," Aislinn said. For a brief moment, it looked like the air around her shimmered, like heat rising off the ground.

Leslie rubbed her eyes and then stepped closer. "I'd rather believe it was like that than that you're letting Keenan use you because he's got money." She squeezed Aislinn's arm where the bracelet was. "People notice. People talk. I know Seth doesn't like me, but he's a good guy. Don't screw it up because of blondie and his money, okay?"

"God, Les, why does everything have to be about sex? Just because you gave it away so easily—" Aislinn stopped herself, looking embarrassed. She bit down on her lip. "I'm sorry. I didn't mean it like that."

"Like what?" Leslie had been friends with Aislinn since

almost the moment they'd met, but *friends* didn't mean she told Aislinn everything, not anymore. They were close *before*, but these days Leslie needed barriers. She didn't know how to start the conversation she'd needed to have for months now. *Hey, Ash, do you have the handout from Lit? By the way, I was raped, and I have these hella-awful nightmares.* She was holding it together, planning to move away, to start life all over again—and when she imagined trying to talk about it, about the rape, she felt like something was ripping her apart. Her chest hurt. Her stomach clenched. Her eyes burned. *No. I'm not ready to talk.*

"I'm sorry," Aislinn repeated, gripping Leslie's arm with an almost uncomfortably warm hand.

"We're cool." Leslie forced a smile to her lips and wished these emotions would fade away. Numbness was increasingly appealing. "All I'm saying is that you've got a good thing with Seth. Don't let Keenan ruin it."

"Seth understands why I spend time with Keenan." Aislinn bit down on her lip again and glanced back up the street. "It's not what you're saying, though. Keenan is a friend, an important friend. That's it."

Leslie nodded, hating that they couldn't really talk about their lives, hating that even her closest friendships were filled with half-truths. *Would she look at me with pity?* The idea of seeing that in Aislinn's eyes was awful. *I survived. I am surviving.* So she stood there, waiting with Aislinn, and switched the topic to one where they could both be honest. "Did I tell you? I'm finally getting my tattoo. I got the outline already. One more session—*tomorrow*—and it's done."

Aislinn looked somewhere between relieved and disappointed. "What did you pick?"

Leslie told her. It was easy to remember: she could see the eyes staring out at her, could picture them without trying. The more she thought of her art, the less tense she felt.

By the time Seth strolled up the street to meet Aislinn—looking like a walking advertisement for how hot facial piercings could be—Leslie and Aislinn were having a comfortable conversation about tattoos.

Seth draped an arm around Aislinn's shoulders and gave Leslie a questioning look. One pierced brow raised, he asked, "You got ink? Let's see."

"It's not finished." Leslie was barely able to contain the shiver of pleasure at the idea of getting the rest of it, but the thought of showing anyone felt surprisingly not-appealing. "Show you in a few days."

"Rabbit must have been pleased. Virgin skin, right?" Seth got a faraway smile on his lips and started walking, moving in that easy lope that was the only speed at which he seemed to do anything.

"It was. I got the outline last week." Leslie moved faster to keep up with Seth and Aislinn, who'd kept pace with Seth without pause, seeming as oblivious as he was. They had a synchronicity that came from truly fitting together. *That's how it's supposed to be: relaxed, good.* Leslie wanted to believe that someday life would be like that for her too.

Aislinn held Seth's hand and steered the two of them through the people passing on the street. As they walked, Seth talked a bit about friends' tattoos, about the shops up in Pittsburgh, where Rabbit did the guest-artist gig sometimes. It was one of the most enjoyable conversations Leslie had ever had with him. Until recently, he'd been terse with her. She hadn't asked why, but she suspected it had something to do with Ren. Seth wasn't very tolerant of dealers.

Guilty by association. She couldn't really blame Seth: Aislinn was too gentle to be exposed to Ren's crowd. If Seth thought being friends with Leslie would put Aislinn in danger, he'd have reason to disapprove. She shook off the thought, enjoying the banter with Aislinn and Seth.

They'd only gone two blocks when Keenan and Niall stepped out of a doorway. Leslie wondered how they'd known Aislinn was passing at that moment, but the awkward silence that came with Keenan's arrival made questions feel unwise.

Seth tensed as Keenan held out his hand to Aislinn and said, "We need to go. Now."

Niall stood to the side, watching the street. Aside from a curt hello to Seth, Keenan behaved as if he and Aislinn were the only two people there. He didn't look at anyone or anything other than Aislinn, and the way he looked at her was much the same as the way Seth did: like Aislinn was the most amazing person he'd ever seen.

"Aislinn?" Keenan made a weirdly elegant gesture with his hand, as if to direct Aislinn to walk in front of him.

Aislinn didn't respond or move. Then Seth kissed her briefly and said, "Go on. I'll see you tonight."

"But Niall . . ." Aislinn frowned as she glanced from Niall to Leslie.

"There's a guest in town. We need to find him. . . ." Keenan shoved his hair away from his face, elegance gone as quickly as it had arrived. "We should've gone hours ago, Aislinn, but you had your classes."

Aislinn bit her lip and looked at everyone. Then she started: "But Niall . . . and Leslie . . . and . . . I can't just *leave* them here, Keenan. It's not . . . fair."

Keenan turned to Seth. "You can stay with Niall and Leslie, right?"

"Planned on it. I got it, Ash. Just go with Sunshine"— Seth paused and gave Keenan a friendly grin that seemed at odds with the situation—"and I'll see you tonight. We're cool." He tucked a piece of her hair behind her ear and let his hand linger there, his palm resting around Aislinn's cheek, fingertips against her ear. "I'll be fine. Leslie will be fine. Go on."

When Seth stepped back, Keenan nodded to him and took Aislinn's hand. Whatever those three had going on was decidedly weirder than Leslie wanted to know about, and Niall's studious observation of the street was starting to make her feel angry. He hadn't even acknowledged her presence. The few moments of easy friendship with Aislinn and Seth didn't mean that she wanted to be caught up in whatever their drama was. "I'm out of here, Ash. I'll see you at sch—"

Aislinn put her hand on Leslie's wrist. "Could you hang with Seth? Please?"

"Why?" Leslie looked from Seth to Aislinn and back again. "Seth's a bit old to need a sitter."

But Niall turned toward her, the movement drawing her attention to his scar. Leslie froze, caught between wanting to stare and wanting to look away.

Niall said, "Surely you could join us for a while?"

Leslie turned to stare pointedly at Aislinn; there'd been enough "stay away" messages from Aislinn, but all Aislinn did was look to Keenan. And he smiled approvingly at them. *Maybe* he's *why Ash wanted Niall away from me.* Leslie shivered in a sudden rush of fear. Keenan might be Aislinn's friend, but something about him made her uncomfortable, more so today.

"Please, Les, could you? As a favor?" Aislinn asked.

She's terrified.

"Sure," Leslie said as a wave of dizziness rolled over her, like something in the core of her was being stretched and tugged. The force of it made her unable to move, unsteady to the point that she thought she was going to be sick if she tried. She started cataloguing everything she'd drunk or eaten or touched to her lips in any way. *Nothing unusual.* She stayed motionless, concentrating on breathing until she felt whatever it was recede.

No one else moved either. They didn't seem to even notice.

Seth said, "We're good. Go on, Ash."

Then Aislinn and Keenan got into a long silver Thunder-bird parked at the curb and drove off, leaving Leslie stand-ing there with Niall and Seth. Niall leaned back against the wall, not looking at her or Seth, just waiting on . . . *something.*

Leslie shifted from foot to foot, watching a group of skaters across the street. They were taking advantage of the traffic-less side street and doing tail slides on the curb—not that there weren't other places they could go, but they were content to be where they were. It was appealing, that sense of peace. Sometimes Leslie felt like she was chasing that—at Rabbit's, at her friends' parties. She just needed the right timing to catch it.

Seth started to walk away, and Niall pushed off from the wall, watching Leslie with a hungry expression. Something was different, unleashed. He stepped closer to her, slowly, and she felt sure his caution was to keep her from running.

"Niall?" Seth had stopped and called back, "Crow's Nest?"

"I'd rather go to the club." Niall didn't even glance at Seth. Instead he watched her with a pensive look, as if he were studying her. She liked it far too much.

"I need to bail," she said. She didn't wait for an answer but simply turned and left.

But Niall was standing in front of her before she'd gone more than a half dozen steps. "Please? I'd really like you to join us."

"Why?"

"I like being near you."

And she felt a surge of the confidence she'd been filled with in fleeting moments since she'd been tattooed.

"Come with me?" he prompted.

She didn't want to leave. She was tired of running every time she felt afraid. That fearful girl wasn't the person she'd been before; that wasn't who she wanted to be. She let go of the fear but couldn't answer.

He held her gaze as he lowered his head toward her. He didn't kiss her, though—just leaned kissably close and asked, "Will you let me take you in my arms . . . for a dance, Leslie?"

She shivered, confidence swirling with a surge of longing for the peace she could almost taste, peace she was suddenly sure she'd feel if she slipped into Niall's arms. She nodded. "Yes."

CHAPTER 11

Niall knew better. He knew not to allow himself so very close to temptation. He was to keep the queen's mortals safe while Keenan and Aislinn sought out the Dark King. Protecting Seth was easy: the mortal was the closest thing to a brother Niall had ever had. Leslie was more difficult: Niall knew he shouldn't even be considering seducing a mortal he was to protect.

This is work, just like any other day. Think about the court. Think about vows.

But it was hard to think about the Summer Court—or the Dark Court, for that matter. Niall had been a confidant to both kings, and now he was relegated to caretaker of the Summer Queen's mortals. Everything had changed when Keenan found Aislinn, the mortal who'd been meant to be his queen, and despite the fact that Niall was happy for his king, his friend, there was a sudden absence in his life. After centuries of advising Keenan, Niall was without purpose.

He needed direction. Without it he became . . . not of the sunlight. It frightened him, these too-frequent flashes of the memory of what he had been before he'd been taken into the Summer Court.

Being around Leslie had become a reward—and punishment. His unexpectedly intense longing to be near her the past week or so was complicating an already unstable situation. He was staring at her again, and Seth noticed.

"You think that's a good idea?" Seth glanced pointedly at Leslie.

Niall kept his expression carefully neutral; Seth knew him too well. "No, I don't suppose it would be."

Leslie seemed oblivious, lost in her own thoughts, and Niall wished she would share them with him. He had no one he could truly share such things with. Until he'd seen Aislinn and Seth, he hadn't realized—*admitted*—how he longed for that. Even Aislinn and Keenan had a beautiful bond, while Niall was increasingly disconnected from everyone. If Niall kissed Leslie, pulled her into his arms and let himself lower his guard, they'd be far from disconnected. She'd be his, willing to press her body against his, willing to follow him anywhere.

It was both the temptation and the trouble with mortals. The caresses of some faeries, Gancanaghs like him and like Irial once was, were addictive to mortals. Irial's nature had been altered long before Niall ever drew breath. Becoming the Dark King had changed him, made him able to control the impact of his touch. Niall had no such recourse: he was left with memories of mortals who'd withered and died for lack of his embrace. For centuries, those memories were reminder enough to restrain himself.

Until Leslie.

Niall could hardly look at her as they walked. If Seth weren't with them . . . Niall felt his pulse race at the images in his mind, at the thought of Leslie in his arms. Not for the first time, he was glad he had Seth's company. The mortal's calm seemed to help Niall remember himself. *Usually.*

Niall stepped a little farther away from Leslie, hoping—irrationally perhaps—that distance would bolster his self-control.

Keenan had been suggesting Niall pursue a relationship of his own now that the court was strong—*growing stronger by the day*—but Niall didn't imagine he'd be permitted to do so with a mortal, especially one Aislinn wanted sheltered. His king wouldn't ask him to disobey their queen.

Would he?

And Niall had no intention of betraying his king or queen's trust, not willingly. They'd asked him to keep the mortals safe, and so he would. He could resist the temptation.

But he still had to fold his hand into a fist at his side. The urge to lay his skin against hers was a compulsion he hadn't felt so strongly in centuries. He stared at her, looking for some clue as to why her, why now.

Leslie realized that Niall was staring at her again. "That's sort of creepy, you know?"

He looked amused, the corner of his scar wrinkling as he smiled ever so slightly. "Did I offend you?"

"No. But it's weird. If you have something to say, speak."

"I would if I could figure out what to say," Niall said. He put a hand on the small of her back and nudged her forward gently. "Come. The club is a safer place to relax than out here"—he gestured at the empty street—"where you are so vulnerable."

Seth cleared his throat and scowled at Niall. Then he told Leslie, "The club's right around the corner."

Leslie walked a little faster, trying to move away from Niall's hand on her back. Speeding up didn't help: he kept pace with her.

When they rounded the corner and she saw the dark building in front of them, she felt panic well up. There was no sign, no posters, no people hanging outside, nothing to indicate that the building in front of them was anything other than abandoned. *I should be freaking out.* She wasn't, though, and she couldn't understand why.

Niall said, "Head toward the doorman."

She looked back. Standing at the front of the building was a muscular guy with an ornate tattoo covering one half of his face. Spirals and lines disappeared under hair as black as the ink. The other side of his face was inkless. The only ornamentation was a small black tusklike piercing in his upper lip, the white match of which was in the corner of his mouth on the inked side of his face.

"Keenan cool with her being here?" The man pointed at her, and Leslie realized that she was still staring—in part because she couldn't fathom how she could've missed seeing someone like him standing outside the door.

"She is a friend of Aislinn's, and there are *unpleasant* guests in town. The"—Niall paused and crinkled his face into a wry smile—"Aislinn is with Keenan."

"So are Keenan and Ash good with it or not?" the inked man asked.

Niall clasped the man's forearm. "She is my guest, and the club should be near empty, yes?"

The doorman shook his head, but he opened the door and motioned to a short, muscular guy with the most incredible dreads Leslie had ever seen. They were thick and well formed, hanging like a mane around the guy's face. For a moment, Leslie thought it *was* an actual mane.

"We have a new *guest*," said the doorman as the dreadlocked guy came outside. The door thudded shut behind him.

Dreadlocks stepped closer and sniffed.

Niall quirked his mouth in what looked like a snarl. "*My* guest."

"Yours?" Dreadlocks' voice was low—harsh like he lived on cigarettes and liquor.

Leslie opened her mouth to object to the proprietary tone in Niall's voice, but Seth put a hand on her wrist. She glanced at him, and he shook his head.

Dreadlocks said, "My pride is in—"

Seth cleared his throat.

"Go tell them," the doorman said as he opened the door and motioned Dreadlocks back inside. "Two minutes."

They stood there awkwardly for a moment before the tension felt too unbearable for Leslie. "If this is a bad idea—"

But the door had already reopened, and Seth was stepping into the shadowy building.

"Come on." Niall went inside.

She went only a few steps before she stopped, unable to think what to say or do. The few people inside were all wearing strange and ornate costumes. A woman passed by with vines draped all over her arms; the vines seemed as if they flowered.

Like the living art at the museum.

Another couple wore feathered wigs; still others had blue faces and misshapen teeth, not like the vampire teeth the costume places sold at Halloween—but each tooth jagged, like sharks' teeth.

Niall stood beside her, his hand resting on her back again. In the odd blue lights of the club, his eyes looked reflective; his scar was a black slash on his skin.

"Is it okay that we don't have costumes, too?" she whispered.

He laughed. "Quite. These are their everyday wear."

"Everyday? Are they like one of those reenactment groups? A role-playing group?"

"Something like that." Seth pulled out a tall chair. Like the rest of the furniture, it was a polished wood. Nothing in the low-lit club seemed to be made of anything *other* than wood, stone, or glass.

Unlike the rough-looking exterior, the inside of the club was far from run-down. The floor gleamed like polished marble. Running the length of one side of the room was a long, black bar. It wasn't wood or metal, but it looked too thick for glass. As the rotating club lights hit the bar, Leslie saw streaks of color—purples and greens—shimmering in it. She gasped.

"Obsidian," said a raspy voice beside her ear. "Keeps the patrons calm."

A waitress in a skin-suit with shimmering silver scales all over her legs and arms stood there. She circled behind Leslie and sniffed her hair.

Leslie took a step away from her.

Although neither Niall nor Seth had ordered yet, the waitress handed them drinks—a golden-colored wine for Niall and a microbrew for Seth.

"No drinking age in here?" Leslie's gaze wandered over the room. The people in their odd costumes all had drinks, though some of them looked younger than she was. Dreadlocks was with a group of four other guys with pale brown dreads. They were sharing a pitcher that looked like it was filled with the same golden wine Niall was drinking.

A pitcher of wine?

"Now you see why I prefer to come here. Seth cannot

relax as well at the Crow's Nest, and they do not carry my preferred vintage"—Niall lifted his glass and sipped—"at any other club."

"Welcome to the Rath, Leslie." Seth leaned back in his chair and motioned to the dance floor, where several almost normal-looking people were dancing. "Weirder than anywhere else you'll ever see . . . if you're lucky."

The music grew immediately louder, and Niall tipped back his glass one more time. "You could relax more fully, Seth. Some of the girls—"

"Go dance, Niall. If we don't hear from Ash within the next couple hours, we'll need to get Leslie to work."

Beside her, Niall stood. He sat his half-full glass on the table and gestured to the dance floor. "Come join the dance."

At his words, Leslie felt a whispering need to refuse and a simultaneous tug of impatience to go toward the small group of costumed people who were dancing almost manically. The music, the movement, his voice—they all beckoned her, pulled her as if she were a marionette with too many strings. Out there in the throng of swaying, shifting bodies, she'd find pleasure. A sea of lust and laughter floated in the air around the dancers, and she wanted to swim in it.

To buy a moment to steady her nerves, she grabbed for Niall's glass. When she lifted it to her lips, it was empty. She stared at it, turning it in her hand by the fragile stem.

"We don't drink this in anger or fear." Niall put his hand over hers so that they were both holding on to his glass.

It wasn't anger or fear she felt; it was longing. But she wasn't telling him that. She couldn't.

The waitress stepped from somewhere behind them. Silently, she tilted a heavy bottle over the glass Niall and Leslie both held. From this close the wine looked thick as honey. Spirals of iridescent color shimmered as it filled the cup. It was tempting, smelling sweeter and richer than anything she'd ever known.

Her hand was still under his when Niall lifted the glass to his lips. "Would you like to share my glass, Leslie? In friendship? In celebration?"

He watched her as he sipped the golden drink.

"No, she wouldn't." Seth slid his beer across the table. "If she wants a drink, it'll be from my glass or my hand."

"If she wants to share my cup, Seth, it's her choice." Niall lowered the glass, still holding her hand over the stem.

The drink, the dance, Niall—too many temptations were in front of Leslie. She wanted them all. Despite how weirdly Niall was acting, she wanted that tumble into pleasure. The fears that had been binding her since the rape were loosening lately. *The decision to get tattooed did that. Freed me.* Leslie licked her lips. "Why not?"

Niall lifted the glass until the rim was touching her lips, close enough that her lipstick smudged the glass, but he didn't tilt it, didn't pour that strange-sweet wine into her mouth. "Indeed, why not?"

Seth sighed. "Think for a minute, Niall. Do you really want to deal with the consequences?"

"Right now, more than anything I can think of, but"—Niall pulled the glass away from Leslie's lips and curled their hands until her lipstick smudge was against his mouth—"you deserve more respect than this, don't you, Leslie?"

He drained the glass and set it on the table but kept hold of her hand.

Leslie wanted to run. His hand still held hers on the glass, but his attention was no longer intense. Her confidence faltered. Maybe Aislinn had good reasons to keep Keenan's family away from her: Niall alternated between fascinating and bizarre. She licked her suddenly dry lips, feeling denied, rejected, and angry. She shook off his hand. "You know what? I'm not sure what game you're playing, but I'm not interested in it."

"You're right." Niall lowered his gaze. "I don't mean to . . . I don't want . . . I'm sorry. I'm not myself lately."

"Whatever." She backed up.

But Niall took both of her hands in his, gently so that she could pull away if she wanted. "Dance with me. If you're still unhappy, we'll see you home. Seth and I both."

Leslie looked back at Seth. He sat in a club that she hadn't known existed, surrounded by people in extreme costumes and bizarre behavior, yet he was calm. *Unlike me.*

Seth tugged at his lip ring, rolling it into his mouth as he did when he was thinking. Then he motioned toward the floor. "Dancing's fine. Just don't drink anything he offers you—or that anyone else offers you, okay?"

"Why?" She forced the question out, despite her instant

aversion to asking, to knowing.

Neither Niall nor Seth answered. She thought to press the matter, but the music was beckoning her, inviting her to let go, to forget her doubts. The blue lights that came from every corner of the club spun across the floor, and she wanted to spin with them.

"Please dance with me." Niall's expression was one of need, of longing and unspoken offers.

Leslie couldn't think of any question—or answer—worth refusing that look. "Yes."

And with that Niall spun her into his arms and onto the floor.

CHAPTER 12

Several songs later, Leslie was thankful for the long hours of waitressing. Her legs ached, but not as much as they would have if she'd been out of shape. She'd never met anyone who could dance the way Niall did. He led her through moves that made her laugh and taught her strange steps that required more concentration that she thought casual dancing could ever need.

Through it all, he was curiously careful with her. His hands never strayed out of the safe zones. Like at the museum, he was almost distant as he held her. If not for a few flirtatious remarks, she'd suspect she'd imagined that delicious look when he'd invited her to dance.

Niall finally paused. "I need to check in with Seth before I"—he burrowed his face into the side of her neck, his breath almost painfully warm on her throat—"give in to my unconscionable desire to put my hands on you properly."

"I don't want to stop dancing. . . ." She was having fun, feeling free, and didn't want to risk that pleasure ending.

"So don't." Niall nodded to one of the dreadlocked guys who'd been dancing nearby. "They would dance with you until I return."

Leslie held out her hand and the dreadlocked guy pulled her into his arms and spun her across the room. She was laughing.

The first guy passed her to another dreadlocked guy, who spun her toward the next. Each of them looked identical to the last one. There were no pauses in their movements. It was as if the world had begun spinning at a different rate. It was fabulous. At least two songs passed, and Leslie wondered how many guys there were—or if she was dancing with the same two over and over. She wasn't sure if they really were identical or if the illusion was a result of being spun so impossibly fast. But then she stumbled to a halt. The music hadn't ended, but the dizzying movement had.

The dreadlocked guys stopped moving and she realized there were five of them.

A stranger walked across the floor toward her, moving with languid grace like he heard a different song than she did. His eyes were surrounded by dark shadows. *He* looked like he was surrounded by shadows, as if the blue lights glanced away without touching him. A silver chain glinted against his shirt. Dangling from the chain was a razor blade. He waved a hand dismissively at the dreadlocked guys and said, "Shoo."

She blinked when she realized she was staring. "I know you. You were at Rabbit's once. . . . We met."

Her hand drifted to the top of her spine, where her not-yet-complete tattoo was. It suddenly throbbed like a drumbeat caught under her skin.

He smiled at her as if he could hear that illusory beat.

Two of the dreadlocked quints had bared their teeth. The others were growling.

Growling?

She looked at them and then back at him. "Irial, right? That's your name. From Rabbit's . . ."

He stepped behind her, slid his hands around her waist, and pulled her back to his chest. She didn't know why she was dancing with him, why she was still dancing at all. She wanted to walk off the dance floor, find Niall, find Seth, leave, but she couldn't walk away from the music.

Or him.

Her mind flashed odd images—sharks swimming toward her, cars careening out of control in her path, fangs sinking into her skin, shadowy wings curling around her in a caress. Somewhere in her mind she knew she needed to step away from him, but she didn't, couldn't. She'd felt the same way when she'd first seen him: like she'd follow him wherever he wanted. It wasn't a feeling she liked.

Irial spun her against his chest, holding her firmly to him as he matched his movements to hers. She didn't want to like it, but she did. For the first time in months, the humming fear that was always just under the surface quieted completely, as if it had never been there. The stillness was enough to make her want to stay next to Irial. It felt good—natural, as if the rush of ugliness she was constantly fighting not to feel had drifted away when he took her into his arms. His hands were on her skin, under the edge of her shirt. She didn't know him, but she couldn't find any words to make him stop. *Or start.*

Laughing softly, he slid his hands over her hips, his fingers bruisingly tight on her skin. "My lovely Shadow Girl. Almost mine . . ."

"I'm not sure who you think I am, but I'm not her." She pulled back with a ridiculous amount of effort. She felt like a cornered animal. She shoved at him. "And I'm *not* yours."

"You are"—he put his hand over hers, capturing it as she pushed angrily at him—"and I'll look after you well."

The room felt like it was shifting, tilting, and she wanted to run. She shook her head with effort, and she said, "No. I'm not. Let go."

Then Niall was beside them, saying, "Stop."

Irial pressed his lips to Leslie's in a lingering open-mouth kiss.

She didn't like him, but she wouldn't have pulled away for anything. Her anger shifted into something territorial. The dual desire to resist being claimed as property and to claim him as hers surged through her. Irial stepped back, staring at her as if they were the only two people there. "Soon, Leslie."

She stared at him, not sure if she wanted to shove him again or pull him closer. *This isn't me. I'm not . . . what?* She didn't have words for it.

Niall was watching, and standing behind him were all of the dreadlocked guys and a larger group of people she'd not noticed earlier. *Where had they all come from?* The club had seemed mostly empty before; now it was filled. And no one looked friendly.

Niall tried to move her behind him, murmuring, "Come away from him."

But Irial slid his hands around Leslie's waist. His thumbs slipped under the edge of her shirt to stroke her skin. Her eyes blurred at the pleasure of that casual touch—not anger, not fear, just *want.*

Irial was asking Niall, "You didn't think she was yours, did you? Just like old times. You find them, and I take them."

Leslie blinked, trying to focus, trying to remember what she should be doing. She should be afraid. She should be angry . . . or something. She shouldn't be watching Irial's mouth. She stumbled as she tried to back away from him.

Niall bristled. Leslie could swear his eyes actually flashed. He stepped closer to Irial, hand clenched like he'd strike him. He didn't. He just ground out, "Stay away from her. You're—"

"Mind your place, boy. You have no authority over me or mine. You made your feelings on *that* quite clear." Irial pulled Leslie closer until she was right back where she'd been when they danced, in his arms and frighteningly unable—*unwilling*—to move.

Her face was flame red, but she couldn't move for several heartbeats.

"No," she said, forcing the word out. "Let go."

Then Niall stepped forward. "Leave her alone."

His eyes did *flash.*

"She's a friend of *our* court, of Aislinn's, of mine." Niall moved as close as he could to Irial without touching him.

Court?

"My girl claimed by your family?" Irial pulled her up so they were face-to-face and gazed at her as if there were secrets written on her skin. "She's not been claimed by yours."

Claimed? Leslie looked at him, at Niall, at the strangers around her. *This is not my world.*

"Let go of me," she said. Her voice wasn't strong, but it was there.

And he did. He let go of her and stepped away so suddenly, she had to grab his arm to keep from falling to the floor. She was mortified.

"Get her out of here," Niall said. From somewhere in

the crowd behind him, Seth stepped forward. He reached out for her hand, an uncharacteristically friendly move for him, and pulled her away from Irial.

"Soon, love," Irial said again as he bowed from the waist.

Leslie shivered. If her legs had been working, she would've run from the club. Instead the best she could do was stumble alongside Seth.

CHAPTER 13

Leslie and Seth had gone several blocks before she felt able to look at him. They weren't friends—by his choice—but she still trusted him more than she trusted most guys. She still valued his opinion.

They were almost at the Comix Connexion before she spoke. "I'm sorry."

She'd glanced at him as she said it but turned away at the sight of the anger on his face. His hands were held in loose fists. He wouldn't hurt her—Seth wasn't like that—but she still flinched when he reached out and caught her wrist.

"Sorry for what?" He quirked his eyebrow.

She stopped walking. "For making a scene, for acting like a big slut in front of you and Niall, for . . ."

"Stop." Seth shook his head. "That was not your fault. Irial's trouble. Just . . . just get away from him if you see him coming your way, okay? If you can, just go. Don't run, but get out."

Mutely, she nodded, and Seth pulled his hand away from her wrist. Like at the Rath, Leslie was sure he knew things he wasn't saying. *Is it a gang thing?* She hadn't heard of any real gangs in Huntsdale, but that didn't mean there weren't any. Whatever it was that Seth knew, he wasn't talking, and she didn't know how to ask. Instead she said, "Where are you going?"

"*We* are going to my house."

"We?"

"You have somewhere else safe to go before work?" His voice was gentle, but she felt certain that it wasn't a real question.

"No," she said, turning away from the too-knowing look on his face.

He didn't say anything else, but she'd seen the understanding in his eyes. And in that instant, she was sure that he—and therefore Aislinn—knew how ugly things were at home. They knew that she'd been lying to them, to everyone.

She took a deep breath and said, "Ren's probably there, so . . . you know, not exactly the safest place to be."

Seth nodded. "You're always welcome to crash at the house if you need."

She tried to laugh it off. "It's not . . ."

He raised an eyebrow.

And she sighed and stopped lying. "I'll remember that."

"You want to talk?"

"No. Not today. Maybe later." She blinked back the tears in her eyes. "Ash knows, then?"

"That Ren hits you or about what happened with his dealer?"

"Yeah." She felt like throwing up. "Both, I guess."

"She knows. She's been there, in a bad place, you know? Not the same, not as—" He stopped. He didn't offer her a hug or do any of those touchy-feely things that a lot of people would do, things that would make her fall apart.

"Right." Leslie folded her arms over her chest, feeling her world unraveling from somewhere inside, and knowing she couldn't fix it.

How long have they known?

Seth swallowed audibly before adding, "She'll hear about Irial too. You can talk to her."

"Like she talks to me?" Leslie held his gaze then.

"Not my business either way, but—" He bit his lip ring and rolled it into his mouth. He stared at her for several heartbeats before saying, "You'd both be better off if you started being straight with each other."

Panic welled up inside of her, a black bubble that made her throat feel tight. *Like it had when their hands . . . No.* She wasn't thinking about that, wouldn't think about it. Lately, the awful feelings had been so distant. She wished they would stay that way. She wished numbness would settle over her. She started walking faster, almost running, feet hitting the sidewalk with a steady *thunk*ing noise.

If I could outrun the memories . . . She couldn't, but it was better to think her heart raced from running than from the terror hidden in the memories. She ran.

And Seth ran steadily beside her, not behind or in front, keeping his pace measured to hers. He didn't try to stop her, try to make her talk. He just sprinted alongside her like running through the streets was perfectly normal.

They were at the edge of the railroad yard where he lived before she could bear to stop. Breathing deeply, she stared at one of the fire-blackened buildings across the street. Standing there in the patch of grass that shouldn't thrive in the dirty lot, she braced herself for the conversation she didn't want to have. She asked, "So how . . . what . . . how much do you know?"

"I heard about Ren setting you up to get out of trouble."

Hands, bruising, laughter, the sickly-sweet smell of crack, voices, Ren's voice, bleeding. She let the memories wash over her. *I didn't drown. I didn't break.*

Seth didn't look away, didn't flinch.

And neither did she. She might scream when the nightmares found her, but not by choice, not when she was awake.

She tilted her head back and forced her voice to stay steady. "I survived."

"You did." Seth's keys clinked together as he shook them

to find the door key. "But if everyone had known how bad things were before Ren let—" He stopped himself, looking pained. "We didn't know. We were so caught up with . . . things, and—"

Leslie turned away. She didn't—*couldn't*—say anything. She kept her back to him. The door creaked open but didn't slam closed, which meant he was standing there waiting.

She cleared her throat, but her voice sounded as tear-filled as it was. "I'll be in. I just need a sec."

She darted a glance his way, but he was staring into the empty air behind her.

"I'll be in," she repeated.

The only answer was the sound of the door closing gently.

She sat down on the ground outside Seth's train and let her gaze follow the murals that decorated it. They ranged from anime to abstract—dizzying, blurring as she tried to follow the lines, concentrate on the colors, the art, anything but the memories she didn't want to face.

I did survive. *I still am. And it won't happen again.*

It hurt, though, knowing that her friends, people she respected, knew about what *they* had done to her. Logic said not to be embarrassed, but she was.

It hurts. But she didn't want to let it. She stood up and ran a hand over one of the metalwork sculptures that sprouted like plants outside the train. She squeezed it until the sharp metal edges dug into her palm, until blood started to ooze between her fingers and drip onto the ground, until the pain in her hand made her think about *now*, not then, not other pains that left her curled into herself sobbing.

Think about this feeling, this place. She uncurled her hand, looking at the big cut in her palm, the smaller ones in her fingers. *Think about* now.

Right now she was safe. It was more than she could say some days.

She opened the door and went inside, fisting her hand again so the blood didn't drip on the floor. Seth was sitting in one of the weird curved chairs in the front of the train. His boa constrictor was coiled in his lap, one thick loop trailing toward the floor like the hem of a blanket.

"Be right out," she said as she walked past him to the second train car, where the tiny bathroom and his bedroom were. She almost believed he hadn't noticed the way she held her hand.

Then he called out, "There's bandages in the blue box on the floor if you need one. Should be some antibiotic junk too."

"Right." She rinsed her hand in the cold water and grabbed some toilet paper to hold. She didn't want to wipe her still-bleeding hand on Seth's towels. After she'd bandaged herself, she went back out.

"Feel better?" He was toying with his lip ring again.

Aislinn had said that the lip-ring bit was a stalling thing—not that Aislinn had been spilling secrets, but she seemed to find everything about Seth fascinating. Leslie smiled a little, thinking about them. Aislinn and Seth had something real, something special. It might not be easy to find, but it was possible.

"Some," Leslie said, sitting back on Seth's battered sofa. "I should probably rinse the, umm, sculpture off."

"Later." He motioned to the blanket he had put on the end of the sofa. "You should catch a nap. Here or back there"—he gestured toward the hallway that led to his room—"wherever you feel comfortable. There's a lock on the door."

"Why are you being so nice?" She stared at him, hating that she had to ask, but still needing to know.

"You're Ash's friend. *My* friend now." He looked like some freaky wise man, sitting in the weird chair with a boa in his lap and a stack of old books beside him. It was partly an illusion made by the surreality of the details, but not entirely. The way he watched her, watched the door. He knew about what sort of people waited out there.

She tried to make light of it all. "So we're friends, huh? When did that happen?"

Seth didn't laugh. He stared at her for a moment, stroking the boa's head as it slithered toward his shoulder. Then he said, "When I realized that you weren't a loser like Ren, but his victim. You're a good person, Leslie. Good people deserve help."

There wasn't any way to make light of that. She looked away.

Neither of them spoke for a few moments.

Finally, she picked up the blanket and stood. "You sure you don't mind if I crash back there?"

"Lock the door. It won't hurt my feelings, and you'll sleep better."

She nodded and walked away. In the hallway, she paused and said, "Thank you."

"Get some sleep. Later, you need to talk to Ash. There's other things. . . ." He paused and sighed. "She should be the one to tell you. Okay?"

"Okay." Leslie couldn't imagine what sorts of things Aislinn could say that would be any more awful or weird than what Leslie already knew, but she felt nervous at the tone in Seth's voice. She added, "Later. Not tonight."

"Soon," Seth insisted.

"Yeah, soon. I promise." And then she closed the door to Seth's room and turned the lock, hating that she felt compelled to do so but knowing that she'd feel safer with it in place.

She stretched out on top of Seth's bed, not pulling back the covers but wrapping up in the blanket he'd given her. She lay there in the darkened room and tried to focus on thoughts of Niall, of how carefully he'd held her when she was dancing with him, of his soft laugh against her throat.

But it wasn't Niall she dreamed of when she fell asleep: it was Irial. And it wasn't a dream. It was a nightmare to rival the worst ones she'd had: Irial's eyes staring back at her from the faces of the men who'd raped her, the men who'd held her down and done things that made the word *rape* seem somehow tame.

It was his voice that echoed in her head as she fought to wake and couldn't. *"Soon, a ghrá," he whispered from those other men's mouths. "Soon, we'll be together."*

CHAPTER 14

Since the Summer King was looking elsewhere for him, Irial had gone to the place where the court's darlings were most likely to be, the Rath and Ruins. *Better to let Keenan stew a bit longer before meeting.* The more the Summer regents panicked, the more emotional they'd be, and Irial could use a good meal. In the interim, he'd had the fun of watching Niall snarl over Leslie with a possessive streak that was quite unlike the Summer Court.

It made sense that the Gancanagh was already drawn to Leslie. Her growing bond with Irial was enough to make her tempting to everyone in the Dark Court. While Niall might have rejected the Dark Court so very many years ago, he was still connected to them. It was his rightful court, where he belonged whether or not he chose to accept it.

As does Leslie. She might not know it, might not realize it, but something in her had recognized Irial as a fitting match. She'd chosen him. Not even riding with Gabriel's Hounds was as satisfying as knowing that the little mortal was soon to be his, as knowing that he'd have her as a conduit to drink down emotions from mortals. The hints and teasing tastes he'd already been able to pull through her were a lovely start to how it would soon be. The Dark Court had fed only on fey for so long that finding nourishment from mortals had been lost to them—until Rabbit had started doing the ink exchanges. So much would be better once this exchange was finished. *And she might be strong enough to handle it.* Now he just had to wait, bide his time, fill in the hours until she was fully his.

Idly, Irial needled Niall, "Shouldn't you have a keeper or something, boy?"

"I could ask the same of you." Niall's expression and tone were disdainful, but his emotions were in flux. Over the years, the Gancanagh had continued to worry over Irial's well-being—though Niall would never say it aloud—and something had made that worry far more pronounced than usual. Irial made a note to ask Gabriel to look into it.

"A wise king has guards," Niall added. His concern had an edge of genuine fear now.

"A weak king, you mean. Dark Kings don't need to be cosseted." Irial turned his attention to finding a new distraction: Niall was too easily provoked just now, and Irial felt too much affection for him. At best, it was a bittersweet indulgence to taste Niall's emotions.

One of the waitresses, a wraith with crescent moons glowing in her eyes, paused. *One of Far Dorcha's kin.* Death-fey didn't usually linger in the too-cheerful Summer Court. Here was another lovely distraction. He beckoned her closer. "Darling?"

She glanced at the cubs, the rowan guards, and at Niall's glowering face—not in anxiety, but to track where they were. Wraiths could handle their own in almost any conflict: no one escapes death's embrace, not if death truly wants you.

"Irial?" The wraith's voice drifted over the air, as refreshing as a sip of the moon, as heavy as churchyard soil on his tongue.

"Would you fetch me some nice hot tea"—Irial made a pinching gesture with his first two fingers—"with just a kiss of honey in it?"

After a low curtsy, she floated around the assembled fey and headed behind the bar.

She'd be lovely at home. Perhaps she'd be willing to wander.

With a lazy smile at the scowling group, Irial followed her. None of them stepped in his way. They wouldn't. He might not be their king, but he was a king. They wouldn't—*couldn't*—assault or impede him, no matter how many of their delicate sensibilities he offended.

The little wraith set his tea on the slick slab of obsidian that made up the bar.

He pulled out a stool and angled it so he had his back to the Summer Court's guards. Then he turned his attention to the wraith. "Precious, what are you doing with this crowd?"

"It's home." She brushed his wrist with grave-damp fingers.

Unlike the rest of the faeries in the club or on the streets, the wraith was immune to him: he'd not provoke any fear in her. But she would pull it from others: hers was a sort of unpleasant beauty that they all feared—and sometimes longed for.

"By anchor or choice?" he prompted, unable to resist pursuing her—not when she'd be such an asset to his fey.

She laughed, and something quite close to the feel of maggots sliding into his veins assailed him.

"Careful," she said in that moon-sliver voice. "Not everyone is unaware of your court's *habits*."

He tensed briefly, watching her across the rainbow of color flaring in the obsidian bar. Between the purple streaks reflecting from the stone and the blue lights of the bar, she looked more terrifying than many of his own fey on their best days. And she brought fear to him with her intimation of knowledge. During the centuries of Beira's cruelty, the Dark Court's particular appetite wasn't hard to hide. Violence, debauchery, terror, lust, rage—all their favorite meals were amply available, floating in the very air. These new days of growing peace ruined that, required more careful hunting.

The wraith leaned forward and pressed her lips to his ear. Though he knew better, images of serpents coiled over his skin as she whispered, "Secrets of the grave, Irial. *We* aren't so forgetful or oblivious as the merry ones." Then she pulled back, taking the slithering sensation with her and offering a genuinely disturbing smile. "Or so chatty."

"Indeed. I shall remember that, my dear." He didn't look behind him, but he knew everyone there had watched, just as he knew that none would ask the wraith what she said. To learn a death-fey's secrets was to risk paying a price too high for any fey. He merely said, "The offer is there, should you ever want to wander."

"I'm content here. Do what you need before the king arrives. I've business to tend." She wandered away to wipe down the bar with a rag that looked like a remnant of a shroud.

She truly would be a lovely prize.

But the look she gave him made clear that she found the whole situation more amusing than persuasive. Far Dorcha's kin might not be organized within a court, but they didn't need to be. Death-fey walked freely in any house, separate from the squabbles and follies of the courts, seeming to laugh at all of them. If he amused her enough, she might deign to visit his house someday. That she chose to linger among Keenan's court spoke well of the young kingling.

However, it didn't change what Irial needed, what he'd

come to find—sustenance. He lingered, teasing the other waitresses, inciting the glares of the cubs and the rowan-men. Finally, the waitresses watched him through heavy-lidded gazes; the guards stood tense and angry, glaring at him. The combined dark temptations—to violence and lust—of the group still weren't enough to offer a proper meal, but it took the edge off his hunger.

He sighed, hating that he missed the last Winter Queen—not *her* but the sustenance she'd given him all those years. Her price had been painful, even by dark fey standards, but he'd rarely had a decent meal since her death. The ink exchange with Leslie would change that.

Maybe get a decent bit of chaos with the Summer Court too.

On that happy note, he stood and bowed his head to the wraith, who was now waiting attentively. "My dear."

Face as emotionless as when he'd arrived, she curtsied.

Irial turned to Niall and the scowling guards. "Tell the kingling I'll catch him on the morrow."

Niall nodded, bound by his fealty to his king to pass on the words, bound by law to tolerate the presence of another regent unless it threatened his own regents.

And hating it.

Irial pushed in his chair and stepped up to Niall. With a wink, he whispered, "I think I'll see if I can find the little morsel that was in here dancing. Pretty thing, isn't she?"

Niall's emotions flared, jealousy tangling with posses-siveness and yearning. Although it didn't show on Niall's face, Irial could taste it. *Like cinnamon.* Niall had always been such fun.

Laughing, Irial sauntered out of the club, feeling almost satisfied with how unexpectedly well the day had turned out.

CHAPTER 15

By the time Irial left, Niall was sure that the Dark King would try to see Leslie again—if for no other reason than to provoke Keenan. *Or me.* Irial might not actively strike out at Niall for refusing the offer to succeed him, but they both knew it was an unforgiven insult. Leslie was doubly vulnerable for being Aislinn's friend and for being Niall's . . . *what?* Not his paramour, but perhaps his friend—that was something he could be. He could enjoy her company, be near her; he could have all of the things he wanted—save one. *If she's safe from harm . . .* The best Niall could hope for was that Leslie wouldn't ever cross paths with Irial again. *Hope isn't enough.*

A commotion at the door heralded Aislinn and Keenan's arrival.

"Where's Seth?" Keenan hadn't crossed the length of the room before he asked the question that was of utmost importance to the court. "Is he safe?"

Aislinn was not beside Keenan. She had been waylaid by the cubs to allow Keenan to speak to Niall first. It was a weak ruse, but it would buy the king a brief moment.

"I sent him away with Leslie. Well guarded, but—" Niall paused as the Summer Queen approached, her skin glowing with obvious pique. "My queen."

He bowed briefly to her.

She ignored him, her gaze only on Keenan. "That's getting old, Keenan."

"I . . ." The Summer King sighed. "If Seth was in peril, I wanted to protect—"

She turned to Niall. "Is he?"

Niall kept his face unreadable as he told them, "Fortunately, Seth did not attract the Dark King's attention, but Leslie did."

"Leslie?" Aislinn repeated. She blanched. "That's the third time he's met her, but I didn't think . . . he didn't pay any attention to her at Rabbit's, and he was dismissive at Verlaine's, and she said he wasn't . . . I'm a fool. I . . . never mind." She shook her head and refocused on the topic at hand. "What happened?"

"Seth took Leslie away. The guards followed, but—" He looked not at Aislinn but at Keenan, hoping that their centuries of companionship would weigh in his favor. "Let me stay nearer her until Irial leaves again. I can't touch him, but he has . . ."

Niall couldn't say it, even now with everything that had

passed; he wasn't sure how to finish that statement. Irial's random moments of kindness weren't something Niall liked to acknowledge.

A look of brief understanding passed over Keenan's face, but he did not ask the obvious questions. He did not point out that Niall was treading on unsafe ground. He merely nodded.

Aislinn spoke softly, "She is already interested in you, Niall. I don't want her to lose her mortal life because of a fleeting crush."

It was a warning. He knew it, but he'd been fey longer than his queen had drawn breath. Hoping Keenan wouldn't interfere, he asked, "What are your terms?"

"My terms?" She looked at Keenan.

"Terms under which he can go to her," Keenan clarified.

"Nothing's ever simple, is it?" Aislinn shoved at the gold-and-shadow streaks of her hair, looking like the sort of omnipotent deity mortals once believed the court fey to be.

"I will agree to whatever you ask of me if you let me keep her safe." Niall looked at Aislinn, but he spoke to Keenan as well. "I don't ask for many considerations."

Aislinn paced several steps away from them. For a newly fey monarch, the queen did exceptionally well, but Keenan and Niall had been together in the courts for centuries. There were habits, laws, traditions that Aislinn couldn't begin to understand so soon.

Niall looked at his king while Aislinn had her back turned.

Keenan didn't offer assurances. Instead he spoke softly to Aislinn. "You can set terms to Niall's presence in her life. He wants to protect the girl, to keep her safe. I would allow him to go to her."

"So I just need to figure how much he can get involved in her life?" Aislinn looked from Niall to Keenan, her observant gaze letting on that she knew there were nuances to the conversation that she was missing.

"Exactly," Keenan said. "None among us would willingly place a child in the Dark Court's hands, but if Irial's done no affront to our court, it's not our concern by law. I cannot act, not directly, unless he violates the laws."

Then his king walked away, having told Niall what he needed to know, what he'd already known: Keenan wasn't going to act. The Summer King didn't approve of Irial's predilections, his cruelties, or anything that happened in the shadows of the Dark King's court, but that didn't mean he was willing to enter a fight with the other court unless he could justify it by law. Those were *his* terms, whether he'd spoken them into the negotiations or not.

The Dark Court—like any of the courts—had volition. If Leslie belonged to the Summer Court, things would be different. But she was unattached, and thus fair game for any fey who wanted her. Years ago, Keenan had forbidden his fey from collecting mortals. Donia had made the same ruling when she took the Winter Queen's throne. The Dark Court, however, had no such compunction. Musicians who were particularly tempting "died young" to the mortal world. Artists retired to

unknown locales. The striking, the unusual, the enticing—
they were stolen away for the pleasures of the dark faeries. It
was an old tradition, one Irial had always permitted his court
fey. If he wanted her for himself, Leslie had no defense.

Niall dropped to his knees in front of his queen. "Let me
tell her about us. Please. I'll tell her, and she will swear fealty
to you. She'd be safe then, out of his reach."

The Summer Queen bit her lip. She almost flinched
away from him. "I don't want my *friends* under my rule. I
didn't want any of this. . . ."

"You don't know what the Dark Court is like. I do,"
Niall told his queen. And he didn't want Leslie to know.
Self-consciously he touched the scar on his face. Irial's fey
had done that to remind him of them every day.

"I want her to be free of all of this." Aislinn gestured at
the fey cavorting in the Rath. "To have a normal life. I don't
want this world to be her life. She's already been so hurt—"

"If he takes her with him, he'll hurt her worse than you
can begin to fathom." Niall had seen the mortals the Dark
Court had taken into their *bruig*, seen them after they left
the faery mound—comatose in mortal hospitals, muttering
and afraid in every city, shrieking in sanatoriums.

Aislinn looked across the room, unerringly finding the
Summer King where he stood waiting. She bit her lower lip
nervously, and he knew she was considering it.

Niall pressed her, "If Irial has decided to claim her, you
and Keenan are the only ones who can stop him. I can't
touch him. He's a king. If you invite her to our court first,

ask her to swear loyalty to you—"

"She's doing better lately," Aislinn interrupted. "She seems happier and more herself, stronger. I don't want to stop that and introduce all of this mess into her life. . . . Maybe he's just toying with us."

"Would you risk that?" Niall was aghast that his queen was being so foolhardy. "Please, my queen, let me go to her. If you won't bring her to you, let me try to keep her safe."

Keenan didn't approach—staying at a distance, making clear that it was the queen who was in charge—but he did speak. "Perhaps there is something to her we do not know, some reason for Irial to pursue her. And if not, Niall would still be there to try to keep her out of his reach, perhaps to distract her so she doesn't go willingly to Irial."

Keenan caught and held Niall's gaze. Although Aislinn could not see it, Keenan nodded at Niall; the king offered permission, consent to act. But Niall still needed Aislinn to assent. "She is *your* friend, but I am . . . grown fond of her as well. Let me keep her safe until he leaves. Remember how hard it was for you when Keenan pursued you. And she does not See him, not like you saw us."

"I want her safe from Irial"—Aislinn looked back at Keenan then, staring at the Summer King with some trace of the old fear in her eyes—"but I don't want her caught up in this world."

"Do you truly think there's a choice?" Keenan asked, his voice making clear that he did not. "You wanted to keep your ties to the mortal world. With that come risks."

"There are *always* choices." The Summer Queen straightened her shoulders. The wavering in her voice, the glint of fear in her eyes—they were gone now. "I won't make her choices for her."

Keenan did not disagree, although Niall knew him well enough to realize that he too thought Leslie's choices were growing limited. The difference was that Keenan didn't care; he simply couldn't involve himself in the life of every mortal who was plagued by a faery. This one didn't matter to Keenan, not really.

To Niall, however, she mattered more than any mortal ever had. He asked, "What terms, my queen?"

"You cannot tell her—about me or the fey or what you are. We need to learn more before we do that. . . . If there's a way to keep her safe from our world, to keep her unaware, we will." Aislinn watched his face, obviously looking for reactions, trying to gauge the wisdom of her terms.

Niall had centuries of experience, however. He stared unblinkingly at her. "Agreed."

"You may distract her, spend time with her, but no sex. You may *not* sleep with her. If Irial's interest is fleeting, you will be out of her life," Aislinn said.

Keenan did intervene then. "Don't start any wars without my accord. She might be important to you and to Aislinn, but I'll not go to war over one mortal."

She's more than just a mortal. Niall wasn't sure why that was or if it mattered. He nodded, though.

Then Keenan, half smiling, added, "Just be true to

yourself, Niall. Remember who and what you are."

Niall almost gaped at his king, but he'd spent too long practicing hiding his emotions. He merely let out his breath. Keenan's intimations were directly in conflict with Aislinn's expressed wishes.

He knows what I am. Addictive to mortals, leaving them willing to say or do anything to have another touch, another fix . . .

Oblivious to this, Aislinn peered down at Niall, shining so brightly that no mortal could've faced her without pain. Small oceans shimmered in her eyes; dolphins breached within them, breaking the blue surface. "Those are my terms. Our terms."

Niall took Aislinn's hand, turning it over to press a kiss into her palm. "You are a generous queen."

Aislinn let him hold her hand for a moment, and then she pulled him to his feet and asked, "Why do I feel like I've left out something important?"

"Because you are also a wise queen, m'lady." He bowed his head to her so she couldn't see his expression.

Then he left the Rath, not wanting to waste precious time to list all of the other terms she could have set upon him: time limits; alliances he could make with other courts and with solitary fey; vows he could make to Leslie that wouldn't reveal what they were yet would protect her more fully; renouncing the Summer Court to swear to another court for Leslie's safety; bartering his own person in her stead.

Keenan should've spoken some of those into the negotiation. He should've bound Niall more tightly. *Why hadn't
he?* He should've supported Aislinn's intent; instead he'd
suggested Niall seduce Leslie. Niall could pretend he hadn't
understood the import of Keenan's words and gesture;
Keenan could pretend he hadn't suggested such a thing. It
all added up to a kind of lie, though, a deceit that made
Niall uneasy.

CHAPTER 16

When Leslie woke with the nightmares still riding her, she had that awful first moment of not knowing where she was. Then she heard Seth talking, presumably on the phone since there were no answering voices.

Safe. At Seth's, and safe.

After stopping in the tiny bathroom, she went out into the front room.

Seth closed his phone and looked at her. "Sleep okay?"

She nodded. "Thanks."

"Niall's coming over."

"Here?" She raked a hand through her hair, attempting to unsnarl it. "Now?"

"Yes." Seth wore a bemused expression, not unlike the look he'd given her when she had sought his advice at the Rath. "He's a good . . . someone you can trust in the important things. He's close to a brother to me—a *good* brother, not like Ren."

"And?" She hated it, but she was embarrassed. Just thinking about the fiasco with Irial and Niall made her anxious.

"He likes you."

"Maybe he *did*, but after what happened—" She forced herself to meet Seth's gaze. "It doesn't matter. Ash has been pretty clear about the 'stay away' message."

"She has reasons." He motioned to a chair.

"Thought he was a good person?" she asked, ignoring the offer to sit.

"He is, but he's"—Seth toyed with one of the studs in the curve of his ear, a contemplative expression on his face—"in a complicated world."

Leslie didn't know what to say. She sat in silence with Seth for a few minutes, thinking over the day, the weirdness. Regardless of Seth's remarks, she wasn't keen on seeing Niall, not right now. It didn't matter, either: she needed her work clothes and they were at home. "I need to go home."

"Because Niall's coming here?"

"No. I'm not sure. Maybe."

"Wait for him. He'll walk you." Seth kept his tone casual, but the disapproval of her leaving was there all the same. "There doesn't have to be strings, Les; he can just be a person to get you safely to where you need to be."

"No." She scowled.

"Would you rather I walk with you?"

"I *live* there, Seth. I can't just not go home or take people with me all the time."

"Why?" He sounded far more naive than she knew him to be.

Leslie bit back her irritated reply and said only, "It's not realistic. Not everyone has the good luck to—" She stopped, not wanting to argue, not wanting to be unpleasant when he was only trying to be a friend. "It doesn't matter why. It's home for now. I need to change for work."

"Maybe Ash has clothes here that—"

"They wouldn't fit me, Seth." She stood up and grabbed her bag.

"Call me or Ash if you need anything? Put my number in your cell, too." He waited until she pulled out her cell, and he recited his number.

Leslie punched the digits in and slipped the phone back into her pocket. Forestalling any more objections, she said, "I need to go, or I'll be late for work."

Seth opened the door and stared out at the empty rail-yard. It looked as if he waved at someone, a sort of 'come here' gesture, but she saw no one.

"Are you all eating 'shrooms or something, Seth?" She tried to make her voice teasing, not wanting to fight, not after he'd shown her such kindness.

"No 'shrooms." Seth grinned. "Haven't licked any toads, either."

"So the staring off into space thing everyone's doing?"

He shrugged. "Communing with nature? Connecting with the unseen?"

"Uh-huh." Her tone was sarcastic, but she smiled.

In a brotherly gesture, he put a hand on her shoulder—not restraining her but holding on to her firmly. "Talk to Ash soon, okay? It'll make a lot more sense."

"You're freaking me out," she admitted.

"Good." He gestured toward the edge of the yard again and back at her. "Remember what I said about Irial. Get away from him if you see him."

Then he went back inside his train house before she could think of what to say.

When she walked into her house, Leslie wasn't really surprised to see the grungy crowd in the kitchen with Ren.

"Baby sister!" Ren called in a way that told her he was in the up part of his high.

"Ren." She acknowledged him with as friendly a smile as she could muster. She didn't look long at the people with him. Not for the first time she wished there were an easier way to determine whether they were just getting-high friends or if one was a dealer—not that it mattered. When people were high, they could be unpredictable. When they weren't high but jonesing for whatever they used, they were worse.

Her brother complicated things by dabbling with too many drugs and therefore too many circles of druggies. Today, though, there was no need to guess what they were using: the sickly-sweet smell of crack filled her kitchen the way the scents of home-cooked meals once had.

A skinny girl with lank hair grinned at Leslie. The girl

was sitting astride a guy who didn't seem to be high at all. He didn't share her pinched look, either. Without looking away from Leslie, he took the pipe out of the scrawny girl's hand and put the girl's hand on his crotch. She didn't hesitate—or look away from the pipe he held out of her reach.

He's the one to fear.

"Want a hit?" He held the pipe out to Leslie.

"No."

He patted his leg. "Want a seat?"

She glanced down, saw the skinny girl's hand moving there, and started to back away. "No."

He reached out as if to grab Leslie's wrist.

She turned, ran up the stairs to her room, and closed the door against the laughter and crude invitations that rang through her house.

Once she was ready for work, Leslie slid open the window and slung a leg out. It wasn't a huge drop, but when she landed wrong it hurt pretty badly. She sighed. She couldn't waitress with a sprained ankle.

I could go back in, just run down the stairs and out.

Carefully, she dropped her bag to the ground.

"Here goes."

She sat with both legs dangling from the window, then twisted so her stomach was on the wood and she was facing the house. Slowly she backed out, bracing herself with her feet on the siding and gripping the wooden window frame with her hands.

I hate this.

She pushed off, bracing herself for the impact. It didn't come. Instead she was caught in someone's arms before she touched the ground.

"Let go of me. Let *go.*" She was facing away from the person who held on to her. She kicked backward and made contact.

"Relax." The guy holding her lowered her gently to the ground and stepped back. "You looked like you could use help. It's a big drop for a little thing like you."

She turned to face him and had to crane her neck to see his face. He was an utterly unfamiliar older man, not grand-father old, but older than most of the people who hung around Ren. He had a different look, too. Heavy silver chains dangled from both of his wrists. His jeans were faded and ripped in the calves to reveal the tops of scuffed combat boots. Tattoos of zoomorphic dogs covered his forearms. She should be afraid, but she wasn't: instead she felt still, calm, like whatever emotions churned inside had ceased to connect with the world around her.

She motioned to the tattoos on the man's arms. "Nice."

He smiled in what seemed to be a friendly way. "My son did that. Rabbit. He has a shop—"

"You're *Rabbit's dad*?" She stared. There was no family resemblance that she could see, especially when she realized that this meant he was also Ani and Tish's father.

The man smiled wider still. "You know him?"

"And his sisters."

"Look like their mothers. All of them. I'm Gabriel. Nice to meet . . ." He scowled then, causing her to step backward and stumble—not in fear, not even then, but in wariness.

But his scowl wasn't directed at her. The creepy dealer from the house had stepped around the corner. He said, "Come back inside."

"No." She collected her bag from the grass where it had fallen. Her hands shook as she clutched it and tried not to look at the dealer walking toward her or at Gabriel. Fear surged. Delayed and dulled as it was, it still made her feel like running.

Is Gabriel here to see Ren? Rabbit never talked about his dad; neither did Ani and Tish. *Is he a drug dealer too? Or just an addict?*

Gabriel stepped in front of the dealer. "Girl's leaving."

The dealer reached out toward Leslie. And without thinking, she grabbed his arm, wrapped her fingers around his wrist and held it immobile and away from her body.

I could crush him. She paused at her thoughts, at the weird calm settling back over her, at the weird confidence. *I could do it. Break him. Bloody him.*

She tightened her grip just a little, feeling bone under the skin, fragile, in the palm of her hand. *Mine to do with as I want.*

The dealer wasn't fazed by her grip, not yet. He was talking, telling Gabriel, "It's cool, man. She lives here. It's not a—"

"Girl's *leaving now*." Gabriel looked at Leslie and smiled. "Right?"

"Sure," she said, looking dispassionately at her hand curled around the dealer's wrist. She squeezed harder.

"Bitch. That hurts." The dealer's voice grew shriller.

"Don't cuss in front of the girl. It's rude." Gabriel made a disgusted noise. "No manners these days."

Something's wrong here.

Leslie tightened her grip again; the dealer's eyes rolled back in his head. She felt bones splintering and saw white through broken skin.

I'm not strong enough to do that.

But she stood there, holding the dealer's wrist in her hand, still squeezing. He'd passed out from the pain, dropped to the ground. She let go.

"Where you headed?" Gabriel handed her a dark rag.

She wiped her hand, watching the immobile man at her feet. It wasn't sadness or pity she felt. It wasn't . . . anything. *It should be, though.* She knew that, even if she didn't feel it.

"Why are you here?"

"To rescue you, of course." He grinned, baring teeth that looked like he'd filed some of them to points. "But you didn't need rescuing, did you?"

"No." She nudged the dealer with her foot. "I didn't. Not this time."

"So let me give you a lift, since my rescue services weren't needed." He didn't touch her, but put a hand behind her as if he'd rest it on the small of her back.

Not lying. His words felt true, not whole, not all there, but not lying.

She nodded and walked away from her house.

Some part of her thought she should be angry or frightened or ashamed, but she couldn't feel those things. She knew that somehow she had changed, as surely as she knew Gabriel hadn't truly lied.

He led her around the side of the house to a screaming-red Mustang, a classic convertible with black and red seats and vibrant detailing on the exterior.

"Get in." Gabriel opened the door, and she saw that what she'd initially thought were flames on the sides of the car were actually a throng of racing animals, stylized dogs and horses with odd musculature and what looked like smoke writhing around them. For a brief moment, the smoke seemed to move.

Gabriel followed her gaze and nodded. "Now *that* I did myself. Boy might look like his dam, but he's got my art."

"It's gorgeous," she said.

He slammed the door behind her and went around to the driver's side. After he slid the key into the ignition, he gave her a smile that was the exact same look she'd seen on Ani's face before she did something inevitably unwise. "Nah. Gorgeous is how fast she moves. Hook your belt, girl."

She did, and he took off with a scream of tires that could barely be heard over the roar of his obviously modified engine. She laughed at the thrill of it, and Gabriel gave her another Ani-ish grin.

She let the rush roll over her and whispered, "Faster."

That time it was Gabriel who laughed. "Just don't tell the girls you got to go for a ride before they did, okay?"

She nodded, and he accelerated until he topped out the speedometer and delivered her to work remarkably early—and laughing.

CHAPTER 17

"Leslie? Leslie!" Sylvie waved her hand in front of Leslie's face. "Damn. What are you smoking?"

"What?" Leslie tilted the glass of soda, pouring a little out so it wouldn't spill. Thoughts of Niall, of her nightmares of Irial, of her promise to talk to Aislinn, of the weirdly costumed crowd, of the surreal encounter with Rabbit's father, of her assault on the dealer at the house—they tangled and spun in her mind until she wasn't sure of what had really happened at all. *Did I break his arm?*

"Get some sleep or something tonight. You're a mess." Sylvie made a disgusted sound. Then she pointed to the main room. "The couple in section three need their check. Now."

"Right." Leslie set the drinks on her tray and headed back into the din of the restaurant.

The rest of the shift passed in a blur. Leslie smiled and kept herself on autopilot. *Bring the drink. Inane chitchat.*

Smile. Always remember to smile. Sound sincere. She was tired, exhausted really, but she got it done. Table by table, order by order, she got it done. That's how life worked: just keep moving, and it'll pass.

When her shift ended, she cashed out her tips and folded the money—*my ink fund*—into her pocket and made a mental note not to leave it out where her father or Ren could see it. She walked down Trestle Way, too tired to bother seeing who was out and about. *I just want to crash.* She'd gone a few blocks when she bumped into Ani and Tish.

"Leslie!" Ani squealed. She was terminally incapable of speaking at a reasonable volume. "Ohmygods, you look awful."

Tish shoved her sister. "Tired. She meant you look *tired*. Right, Ani?"

"No. She looks, you know, like she needs to go relax." Ani was unapologetic as always. "We're going to the Crow's Nest. You in?"

Leslie summoned up a smile. "I'm not sure I could walk that far tonight. . . . Hey, I met your father earlier. He's nice."

As they walked, Leslie filled them in on select details—omitting Gabriel's giving her a ride to work and her own impossible violence. Leslie felt her knees go wobbly when they turned on Harper. *Too tired for this.* She drew a few breaths, stopped moving. Near her were several people cowering in terror, backs to the wall as if something horrid were leering at them. One wept, begging for mercy. Leslie couldn't move.

"Just vagrants, Les. Bad drugs or something. Come on." The sisters kept walking, propelling her along with them.

"No." Leslie shook her head. It was something else. She tried to see it, sure something was there, like a shadow that lay atop the other shadows.

She started to walk toward the shadows, as if a string had found its way into the middle of her belly and she were being reeled in. A man was dancing manically on a stoop, which was weird enough, but he also seemed to be covered in thorns like shimmering green rose stems.

Ani looped an arm around Leslie's waist. "Come on, sleepy girl. Let's go play. You'll catch your second wind once you get moving again."

"Did you see him?" Leslie stumbled again.

Tish clapped her hands. "Oooh, wait until you see the new dartboards Keenan bought for the club. I heard that all his girlfriend said was that she wanted to try darts, and boom, there were three new boards the next day."

"She's not his girlfriend," Leslie murmured, glancing back behind them at the doorway. The thorn man waved at her.

"Whatever." Ani tugged Leslie forward. "There's new boards."

Leslie hadn't been at the club more than a half hour when Mitchell—her loudmouthed ex—showed up. Not surprisingly, he was ripped.

"Lezzie, girl!" He gave her a cruel smile. "Where's tonight's toy? Or"—he lowered his voice—"do you just take care of that with battery power these days?"

His dumbass friends laughed.

"Back off, Mitchell," she said. Dealing with him was never pleasant. After her mother had left, Leslie and Ren had both made some stupid choices, chasing a fix. Ren's fix had cost Leslie a lot, but even before that, she'd made a few choices that'd cost her. She'd tried to forget where she was, how wrong things were. It made her do stupid things. Mitchell had been one of those stupid things.

From out of nowhere, Niall was there. "Are you okay?"

"I will be." Leslie turned to walk away from Mitchell, but he grabbed her arm. Unbidden, the image of the dealer crumpling to the ground with her hand on his wrist rose up. *It would be wrong.* She stared at Mitch's hand on her skin. *So? He's wrong.*

"Don't touch Leslie," Niall said. He didn't move, but the tension in his body was obvious enough that people were backing away.

"Niall? It's cool. I've got it." She pulled her arm away from Mitchell, but when she turned around, Mitchell slapped her ass. His friends laughed again, but this time they sounded a little nervous.

Leslie swung back, hand curled into a fist, angry to a degree that felt obscenely good. For a moment, her vision was off. People all through the club were watching her, but they didn't look like people. Claws, thorns, wings, horns, fur, misshapen features, so many people looked *wrong*. It made her pause.

Niall stepped in front of her and asked, "Are you well?"

She was anything but well. Her pulse was racing like she had been chasing caffeine pills with espresso shots. Her vision was a mess; her emotions were a mess; and she wasn't about to say any of that aloud. Instead, she said, "I'm fine. It's fine. Everything's . . . fine. You don't need to—"

He cut her off. "He shouldn't disrespect you like that."

Leslie put her hand on Niall's shoulder. "He's no one. Come on."

Mitchell rolled his eyes. She hoped he'd leave it at that, but he was too drunk to have the sense to keep his mouth shut. He leaned in toward Niall. "You don't need to act all heroic to get in her pants, man. She'll spread those scrawny legs for anyone. Won'tcha, Lezzie?"

The sound that came out of Niall's mouth was more animal than human. He started forward, his body at an odd angle as if something were physically holding him back. Mitchell backed up. Leslie followed. She reached out then and gripped Mitchell's face with both hands. She pulled him toward her like she'd kiss him. When he was close enough to feel her words on his lips, she whispered, "Don't. Not tonight. Not ever again." She squeezed his face until tears came to his eyes. "I'll eat you alive. Got it?"

Then she let go, and he stumbled backward. The people who were watching her, those who'd looked just a moment ago feathered and oddly proportioned and otherwise not right, grinned. Some nodded at her. Others applauded. She pulled her gaze away from them. They didn't matter. What mattered was that her heartbeat was calm again.

A few steps away, Mitchell stood stuttering. "She . . . she . . . did you see . . . bitch threatened—"

Right then, Leslie felt invincible, like she could walk into a fight and not be touched, like there was some extra energy humming in her bones. It made her want to move, roam, see how far she could push it. She started to walk away, but Niall touched her arm gently.

"There's all sorts of dangers out there." He caught and held her gaze. "It would be safest if I walk with you."

Safe wasn't quite what appealed to her right then. *Safe* wasn't how she felt. Invincible, in control, *powerful*— those words felt closer to true. Whatever this fearlessness, this strength, this difference was, she was starting to like it. She laughed. "I don't need protecting, but I'd take the company."

Although Niall was mostly quiet as they walked through the dim streets, it didn't feel awkward or uncomfortable.

Her bad feelings, her usual worries and fears, seemed to be absent. It felt good; she felt good. The choice to change herself, to get her skin decorated, had been a turning point.

Niall caught her hand in his as they walked. "Will you stay at Seth's tonight? I have a key."

She wanted to ask why he cared where she slept, but the chance to stay somewhere safe was reason enough not to ask. She might feel invulnerable, but she wasn't entirely without logic. So she asked, "Where's Seth?"

"At the loft with Aislinn."

"And where are you planning to stay?" she asked.

"Outside."

"So you're going to sleep in the yard?" She looked away, and in doing so saw him out of the corner of her eye. Gone was the face she recognized. His eyes weren't just brown: they were shimmering with the patina of well-aged wood, the sheen of something caressed too often. His scar was red, like a still-tender wound, jagged as if an animal had slashed one long claw over his face. But it wasn't these things that made her draw her breath in so suddenly: he glowed faintly, as if he were being illuminated from some brazier inside.

As at the Crow's Nest, what she'd seen a moment ago and what she saw now weren't the same at all. She shivered, staring at him, reaching her hand out to touch the thick black shadows that lingered alongside his skin. Those dark shadows surged toward her hand, as if she were a magnet.

"Leslie?" He whispered her name, and it was the voice of wind racing down an alley, not a sound made by a person.

She blinked, hoping he wasn't one of those people who asked, "What are you thinking?" She wasn't sure what she'd say. The shadows pushed against her outstretched fingers, and she had a flash of the ink at Rabbit's shop: those shadows had wanted to crawl toward her from the uncapped ink bottle.

Niall spoke again. "I want to stay with you, but I can't."

Hesitantly she faced him, immeasurably relieved that he looked normal again. She looked at the street. Everything looked fine. *What just happened?* She was about to turn her head again, to see if he'd look different again, but he lifted her hand to his lips and pressed a kiss to the underside of her wrist.

She forgot about looking at him in her peripheral vision, forgot about the shadows that crept toward her. It was a choice. She could look at the ugliness, the oddities, the wrongness, or she could let herself enjoy life. She wanted that, pleasure instead of ugliness. Niall was offering it to her.

He leaned closer, his face hovering over the pulse of her throat now. It sounded like he said, "Do you know what I would trade to be with you?" But then he pulled away and distance returned to his voice. "Let me take you to Seth's tonight. I'll sit with you until you sleep if you want, if you'll let me."

"Okay." Leslie felt dizzy, swaying into him.

Niall put a hand on either side of her face. "Leslie?"

"Yes. Please." She felt high, blissed out. It was lovely—and she wanted more.

His lips were close enough that she felt his breath with each word. "I'm sorry. I shouldn't—"

"I said yes."

And he closed the slight distance between them and kissed her. She felt the same rush of fierce winds that she thought she'd heard in his voice. She felt it wrap around her like the air had grown solid and touched her everywhere at once, soft and unyielding at the same time. The ground felt different, like there would be thick moss under her feet if she looked. It was euphoric, but somewhere inside, panic was trying to force itself to the surface. She started to push him away, opened her eyes.

He tightened his hold and whispered, "It's okay. It'll be okay. I can stop. We can . . . stop."

But it felt like she was at the edge of a chasm, a swirling mass of tastes and colors she hadn't known could exist. The panic fled, and all she could think of was finding a way to reach that chasm, to slide down the slope into it. There was no pain there. There was nothing but ecstacy, mind-numbingly good and soul sating.

"Not stop," she murmured and pressed closer to him.

It isn't okay. She knew that, but she didn't care. Tiny slivers of shadows danced at the edges of her vision, gyrating like they'd stretch up to consume the moon. *Or me.* And in that moment, she hoped they would succeed.

CHAPTER 18

As Niall led Leslie through the street toward Seth's train, he wondered just how long he could handle being surrounded by that much steel. This part of the city was painful for any fey other than a regent to visit. It was why he wanted Leslie there, safe from the prying eyes of Irial's fey. It wouldn't stop Irial himself, but it would keep Leslie safe from the rest of the Dark Court—even as it would sicken Niall.

I deserve it, though, the sickness. He'd pushed her boundaries, crossed lines he knew not to broach. After all of this time, he'd come perilously close to giving in to what he was—and she'd die from it if he did.

"Are you still with me?" she asked.

"I am." He turned to look at her and saw them— Bananach and several of Irial's less-obedient faeries. They weren't near enough to see Leslie, but they would be if Niall didn't move her. He pulled her into a shadowed doorway and put his back to the street, keeping her out of their sight.

She didn't resist. Instead she tilted her head up so he could kiss her again. *Just one more kiss.*

When he pulled away he was more careful this time, enjoying the glazed look in her eyes, enjoying the knowledge that he made her feel so close to tumbled, but keeping his glamour firmly in place. He wanted to ask her what she had heard, what she had seen earlier, but that wasn't a conversation he could begin—not with Aislinn's rules still in place, and not with Bananach in the streets behind them.

That's what he should be concentrating on—the threat Bananach posed. Niall turned his head to better see the war-hungry faery, trying to think about safe retreat options. His mind was fuzzy, though. Bananach looked deadly beautiful as always, the raven-feathered head of her true image vying with her glamour of sleek black hair. She was one of the least-mannered faeries who lingered in Irial's court; she was the one who had once unseated Irial and continually sought to do so again—not to hold the court, but to create war within it. That she was prowling the streets with several Ly Ergs in tow did not bode well.

We should go. Now. We should—

Leslie pressed closer to him. He drew another deep breath of the curiously sweet scent that was uniquely her. Mortals always smelled so different. He'd almost forgotten how much he'd enjoyed that. He kissed her neck so she didn't find it odd that he was resting his face there. *Bananach hasn't seen us. We have a few more moments.*

Between kisses, he told Leslie, "I would stay with you always if I could."

And he meant it. Right then, he truly meant it. He'd been too long a part of the Summer Court to mean it for always, and before that he'd been even less capable of fidelity, but in that moment, as he stood pressed against her mortal body, he meant it as fervently as he was able.

Where's the harm in letting her linger with me for a while? If I am careful . . . She'd only sicken if he left her. He could stay with her for a few decades.

Behind him, he felt the street shiver as Gabriel and several of his Hounds came into it. Niall tensed. He wasn't able to stand against Bananach, Ly Ergs, and Gabriel.

And how do I explain to Leslie?

But when he glanced back, Gabriel and the others were all invisible. Leslie would not see or hear them.

Gabriel dispatched several Hounds whose names Niall did not recall—or care to—and they gleefully went after the Ly Ergs. Then he said, "Get going, boy, unless you want to help."

Niall held Gabriel's gaze, as answering was impossible.

"Take her out of here, Gancanagh." Gabriel leaned left as Bananach flew at him. She was glorious, moving with an elegance that few faeries could equal. Rather than step out of her path, though, Gabriel stayed between Bananach and Niall.

The raven-woman ripped a strip of flesh from Gabriel's forearm where Irial's orders were written.

Gabriel's snarl was wall shaking as he swung at Bananach. "Go."

Niall turned around as Leslie swayed into him, her eyes unfocused. She closed them and leaned forward like she'd topple over. Shame rose in him. Their kisses had injured her and distracted him beyond reason. If Gabriel hadn't been there, Bananach would've been on them in moments.

What's happening to me? He should be able to resist one mortal girl, especially in the presence of a fatal threat. He'd always been addictive to mortals, but they hadn't been addictive to him. They made him drunk, made him so intoxicated that he could barely stand, but they were never impossible to resist. He looked at Leslie. She was pretty, but he'd seen plenty of pretty girls over the years. Pretty wasn't reason enough to lose himself as he was doing. Nothing made sense. He needed to step away. He wasn't keeping her safe from Irial's faeries—or from himself.

He steadied her with his arm as they walked. Behind them, he could hear the horrific sounds of the tussle among the dark faeries. It had been a long time since Gabriel's snarls and growls were welcome sounds, but tonight the Hound had saved him and Leslie both.

Why?

A gleeful shriek from Bananach made him spin Leslie into a doorway. He felt the ominous rush of Bananach's movement toward them.

Leslie's back was pressed against a tall iron fence. She stared at him with the openness of so many mortals over the years, her lips parted for a kiss he knew not to give her. "Niall?"

"Just . . ." He had no words that he could say. He looked away, counting each measured breath, concentrating on not touching her. Behind them he heard Gabriel's Hounds catch up. Bananach no longer crowed with pleasure. Instead she hurled curses at the Hounds. Then there was only silence in the street.

And he could hear Leslie's uneven breathing, matching his own, proof that they were both more excited than either of them should be. *She shouldn't be that drunk on just a couple of kisses.* It wasn't as if he'd touched her in any intimate way. *Yet.* He wanted to, more than he could remember ever wanting a mortal. He put his hands against the iron fence behind Leslie: the pain of it helped chase away his irrational thoughts.

He looked behind him to assess the safety of moving. Bananach was gone. The Hounds were gone. No other faeries lingered in the street. It was only the two of them. He let go of the fence and opened his mouth to find an excuse to explain why he'd pushed her into the wall and kissed her so—an excuse that would stop things before they went further.

Is there such a statement?

But Leslie's hand slipped under his shirt, tentative but there nonetheless. He could feel the edges of the cuts on her palm and fingers as she slid her hand up his spine.

He pulled back.

Unable to keep her hand on his back as he stepped away, she slid it to his chest, lingering under his shirt. Her fingers traced upward to his heart.

Neither of them spoke or moved for several moments. Leslie's pulse had slowed back to normal. Her passion had abated. His guilt, on the other hand, wasn't leaving so quickly. There was nothing he could say to undo where they were, but he couldn't move forward either. His plan to be near her as a friend was failing horribly. He said, "We should go."

She nodded, but her fingers continued to trace lines on his skin.

"You have a lot of scars," she said, not asking but leaving the comment hanging there for him to answer or not.

Answering that implied question was something he didn't do, not when his king had been too young to realize that it was an awful question, not when he took any of the fey to his bed, not when his new queen had first seen him at guards' practice and looked at him with tears in her eyes. But Leslie had scars of her own, and he knew what had caused hers.

He kissed her eyelids carefully and told her, "It was a very long time ago."

Her hand stilled where it rested over his heart. If she thought anything of his erratic heartbeat, she didn't say.

Finally she asked, "Was it an accident?"

"No. It was very much on purpose." He brought her free hand up to the scar on his cheek. "None of these were accidental."

"I'm sorry." She leaned up and kissed his cheek. Her gentleness was even more dangerous than her passion had been.

If he thought on it, he could remember the pain as vividly as when it had happened. The memory of the pain cleared his head, helped him focus on where he was, and what he needed to be like for Leslie: strong, careful, a *friend*. He said, "I survived. Isn't that what matters? Surviving?"

She looked away. "I hope so."

"Do you think less of me?"

Her expression was aghast. "No. Gods no."

"Some would."

"They're wrong. Whoever hurt you . . ." She shook her head, her look murderous now. "I hope they suffered for it."

"They did not." He looked away then. If she knew how badly they'd broken him, would she pity him? Would she think him less a man for not being strong enough to escape them? He had, afterward. At the time he would've happily become a shade—faded rather than endure another moment of that pain, those memories. It would've been easier to give up, to end. Instead the last Summer King had found him, taken him into the Summer Court, and given him the space to recover his pride, to rebuild his mind.

"It's awful to think they're out there somewhere." She looked past him to the darkened streets, looking for faces in the shadows as he'd seen her do so many nights when he'd walked invisibly at her side. "I never know. I don't remember some of their faces . . . I was drugged when they . . . you know."

"Raped," he said gently. "And yes, I know exactly."

Her hand traced over one of his scars again, more hesitantly this time. The stunned look on her face confirmed that she understood. "You?"

He nodded. "It was forever ago."

Her eyes welled with tears. "Does it ever go away? The panic?"

And she looked at him with such hope he wished that fey could lie. He couldn't. He said, "It gets better. Some days, some years, it's almost gone."

"That's something, right?"

"It's almost everything some days." He kissed her gently, just a brush of lips, not seeking passion but offering comfort. "And sometimes you meet someone who doesn't see you any differently if you tell them. *That* is everything."

Silently she rested her face against his chest, and he held her and admitted the truth to himself: *For this mortal I would disobey my queen, abandon my king, the court that has protected me all these years. All of it.* If he took her into his arms, he would keep her. He wouldn't let her suffer the way the other mortals had when he'd left them. He would keep her, with his court's permission or without it. Irial wouldn't take her, and Keenan wouldn't stand between them.

CHAPTER 19

Leslie woke in the middle of the night to see Niall lying next to her, feverish, his skin damp with a sheen of sweat. He wasn't thrashing; he was perfectly still. His chest didn't appear to be moving at all.

She grabbed his shoulder and shook him. "Niall?"

He blinked at her, but it didn't take long for him to sit upright and look around. "Are you injured? Is someone here?"

"No." The skin under her hand was hot to the touch, far hotter than seemed possible. "You're sick, Niall. Stay here."

She went to the bathroom and grabbed a hand towel. After soaking it with cold water, she came back. Niall had closed his eyes and was lying back on Seth's enormous bed. If he hadn't looked like he was near passing out, it would have been a lovely sight to see. She knelt on the bed and wiped his face and chest with the icy cloth. He didn't react at all. His eyes stayed closed. His heartbeat thudded rapidly enough that she could see the pulse in his throat.

"Do you think you can walk to the front room? I can call a taxi," she murmured, glancing around the room to find her cell phone.

"Taxi to go where?"

"To the hospital." The wet cloth was already warm to the touch, and his body wasn't any cooler.

"No. We're not going there. Stay here or go to the loft." He opened his eyes and looked at her. There was no mistaking that look for anything remotely reasonable.

She sighed but kept her voice gentle as she said, "Sweetie, you're *sick*. Do you know what's wrong?"

"Allergic."

"To what? Do you have one of those pens for a shot?" She picked up his shirt from the floor and looked in the front pocket. There wasn't anything. She dropped it. *Where else?* There was nothing on the bedside tables. She reached down and felt inside the pockets of his jeans—which were still on him.

Niall grabbed her hand. "I did not bring you here to have sex, and I feel far from well enough to do so, but"— he pulled her forward until she was sprawled on his chest— "that doesn't mean I'm immune to your touch."

Using one hand on the wall to steady himself, he stood. "Help me get outside. I need air. Clear my head before I say something I can't."

"Something you *can't*?" She came to stand beside him,

though, offering him her support. He draped an arm over her shoulders; she put her arm around his waist.

Mostly talking to herself, Leslie said, "Seth. Ash. Everyone's keeping secrets." She looked up at Niall. "I ought to keep asking you questions until I get a few answers out of somebody."

She concentrated on getting him through the train and to the door. He hissed when he reached a hand out and brushed the door. They both stumbled when he recoiled.

"Are you okay?"

"No," he said. "Not so much. But I will be."

Not knowing what to say or do, Leslie looked around. She saw one of Seth's wooden chairs. "Come on," she said.

Niall leaned heavily on her as she dragged the chair far away from the train into the shadows of the yard. It was awkward, but she had plenty of practice maneuvering her drunken father into his room. Niall sat in the chair. She had just stepped away from him when Keenan appeared. He seemed to materialize out of the shadowed lot. He hadn't been anywhere in sight, and then suddenly he was in front of them—and angry.

"What were you thinking?" Keenan asked.

Niall didn't reply.

Leslie tensed, feeling an urge to run when he approached. She wasn't sure where he'd come from or why he was here. She *couldn't* wonder how he'd arrived so unexpectedly or why she felt so disquieted by his presence. All she knew was that he frightened her and she wanted him gone.

"I didn't know he had an allergy to"—Leslie glanced at Niall—"what are you allergic to?"

"Iron. Steel. He's allergic to iron and steel. We all are." Keenan scowled. "This serves no purpose, Niall."

Leslie stepped closer to Niall, decidedly uncomfortable with the hostility in Keenan's voice. *Salt for fury, like briny water in my mouth.* She touched Niall's shoulder and found his skin much cooler now.

"This is not the place," Niall muttered.

But Keenan continued, "If Irial wants her—"

Leslie lost her temper. "I'm standing right here, asshole. And where do you get off talking to him like that? You'd think—"

"Leslie." Niall laid his hand over hers.

"No. Why are you putting up with that?" She turned her glare briefly on Niall and then back to Keenan. "Don't talk about me like I'm not standing here. Don't act like some psycho friend of yours hitting on me means—"

"Just be silent for a change, would you?" Keenan stepped closer to her; his eyes seemed to glow with tiny flames. "You have no idea what you're talking about."

"Piss off." Leslie tried to raise her hand to slap the condescending look off his face, but Niall was now clutching both of her hands.

"I'm not sure why he wants this one, but"—Keenan shrugged—"if she's important to him, I want to know why. Your injuring yourself for her would upset Aislinn and serve no purpose for me."

Leslie's mouth gaped open as Keenan spoke: he sounded nothing like he did when he was with Aislinn, nothing like he had when he'd attended Bishop O.C. for those few weeks in the fall. He sounded old, far older than he could possibly be, and callous.

"Be more careful and enjoy your time, my *Gancanagh friend.*" Then, after giving Leslie a brief once-over that made her feel so exposed that she wanted to hide her body, Keenan walked away.

Leslie stared at the shadowed yard. Despite the darkness, she could see the faint outline of Keenan's body as he strode off.

Beside her, Niall watched the shadows in silence.

Leslie stood next to him. She touched his forehead, his neck, his chest: the fever had broken. He seemed physically fine—tired, but fine.

"Keenan means well, but he has worries—"

"He's rude. He's demeaning. He's not the person he pretends to be when Ash is around. He—" She stopped herself and adjusted her tone. "If there's a reason to be nice to him, now might be a good time to tell me what it is."

"I can't. He's under a bit of stress. Aislinn helps, but there's so much I can't tell you. I would if I could. I'd tell you everything. You might not want to see me afterward, but . . ." He pulled her into his lap and stared at her.

"But what?" She wrapped her arms around him. And her anger at Keenan, her distrust, her unease—they all slid away.

Niall said, "I hope you do want to see me after our secrets are spilled. It'll be *your* choice, but I truly hope you still want to be near me."

She wasn't sure she wanted to know, but she *needed* to. She liked Niall, far more than she should after so short a time, but she wasn't interested in getting further involved if he was mixed up in something criminal. She'd had enough of that in her life already. "Are you involved in anything illegal?"

"No."

"No drug deals?" Her body tensed as she waited.

"Not me. No."

"Keenan?"

Niall snorted in laughter. "Aislinn would never tolerate that, even if he had inclinations that way—which he doesn't."

"Oh." She thought about it: the fact that Keenan rarely went anywhere alone, the weird club, the strange allergy, the secrecy Aislinn and Seth were somehow a part of. None of it fit together right; it didn't add up, no matter how she looked at it.

Which should terrify me. But her emotions weren't quite cooperating with that thought. *Which should also frighten me.*

She held Niall's gaze and asked, "What did he call you?"

"Gancanagh. It's a sort of family name. But I can't explain beyond that right now." Niall sighed and pulled her close. "Tonight I'll do my best to answer your every question, but Aislinn . . . She needs to speak with you before I can. No more questions until tonight. I'll explain to her, that we, that you . . . She'll understand. Meet me at the Crow's Nest? We'll talk to her."

She wanted to push him to tell her immediately, but she could tell by his tension and his worried tone that he wasn't going to. She turned so she was facing him. "Promise you'll tell me everything? Tonight."

"Promise." Niall smiled then.

Leslie kissed him cautiously. She knew he would tell her, felt certain of it, of him.

But he pulled back from their kiss almost immediately and asked, "So can I see what you have so far of the tattoo? Or is it somewhere improper?"

She laughed. "It's up by my shoulders. . . . Subtle topic shift."

It had worked, though—or maybe it was his kiss that made her feel so relaxed. Even though he was holding back, she felt her body responding in a way she hadn't thought she ever would again.

"So can I see the tattoo?" He started to tilt her forward, still holding her.

"Tonight. Rabbit is finishing it tonight after work. Then you can see it—when it's all done." She wasn't sure why, but from the moment she'd walked out of Rabbit's shop, she'd had a strong aversion to showing anyone her ink. *Not yet.*

"Another reason to look forward to our date, then. Talking, looking at your art, and"—he gave her a look that sent her pulse racing—"anything else that makes you happy."

He gently kissed her forehead, her cheeks, her eyes, her hair.

"I don't want you to go away," she whispered, finding it easier to admit in the darkness. "But Keenan's comments. The way he . . . I want you with me right now. I've wanted you with me for months."

He kissed her for real then, not gently as he had before, but fiercely.

Afterward he told her, "I'll leave Keenan and Aislinn's side if I need to. I'll walk away from everything, everyone, just for the chance to be with you. . . ."

While she didn't understand much of what was going on, she did understand that he was offering to give up his family for her. *Why? Why would being with me mean that?* She traced her fingertips over his face.

He said, "If you want me in your life, I'll be here. As long as you want. Remember that. It'll be okay. I'll stay with you, and we'll be fine. No matter what else happens or what you learn, remember that."

She nodded, though she felt like she'd wandered into a weird world where everything she thought she knew had faded away. But even with all the weirdness, being in Niall's arms made her feel safe, loved, like the world wasn't awful. She couldn't stay in Huntsdale, though, not living with Ren and her father, not where everything had gone so horribly wrong. "I can't ask you to give up everything when I'm not even sure where I'll be next year. College. And we don't know each other, not really. And—"

"Do you want to get to know each other?" he asked gently.

"Yes."

"Then we'll find a way." He stood then, with her in his arms, and walked toward the train. A yard or so away from it, he put her down. "Go in and sleep. I will be here when you wake. Tonight Aislinn will talk to you . . . or I will."

And when Leslie curled up in bed, she felt herself believing in Niall, believing in them, believing it really could be okay. Those dreams of finding someone who cared about her, who saw her as a person—maybe they weren't as impossible as they'd seemed.

CHAPTER 20

The morning was barely upon him when Irial walked into Pins and Needles, watching the mortals outside the shop with a new interest. Leslie would give him enough of her mortality that he'd be able to feed on them, to grow stronger. It had worked for a few of the thistle-fey, had worked for Jenny Greenteeth and her sisters. He couldn't grow weak. He couldn't allow his fey to grow weak and be ended by mortals. That wasn't an option. He'd have his mortal, nourish himself—through her—to feed his court. If they were strong enough, he and his mortal, they could survive it. If she was not as strong as he thought, she would die or slip into madness; he'd starve, fade, or worse—fail his court.

But she's a strong mortal. He hoped they would both survive. He'd never cared for one of them; there were a few halflings, like Rabbit, who'd mattered—but no true mortals.

"Iri." Rabbit's face lit with the inexplicable happiness he seemed to feel when Irial visited.

"Bunny-boy."

Rabbit scowled. "Man, you really need to stop calling me that. Ani and Tish are around somewhere. You know how they are."

"I know." Irial grinned. He couldn't see Rabbit as a grown man, despite the proof in front of him. "How are the pups?"

"Troublesome."

"Told you. It's all in the blood." Irial pulled out the book he'd brought with him. "Gabriel sends his best."

"He has a best? Been nice if they'd inherited it." Rabbit took the book, flipping it open as eagerly as he had the first time Irial had given him images of the more reclusive fey. The symbols and crude sketches were the start of what would be tattoos tying mortals to the Dark Court. Rabbit would re-create them in ways that faeries could not, capturing the flaws and beauties until they were pulsing on the page, seeking the mortal who could wear them. It was a disquieting skill—one neither of them spoke of.

Then Ani and Tish flew into the room, squealing in that eternally hyper way they had. "Iri!"

"How's Dad?"

"Did he send anything? He was here."

"He met Leslie."

"Rabbit won't let me go to the square anymore."

"Have you seen the new queens? We know the one, the Summer Queen."

"We don't *know* her. We *met* her. It's different."

"Isn't."

"Let Irial talk." Rabbit sighed. He might scowl a bit, but he watched the girls with a care their father wouldn't have. Halflings were typically too fragile to live in the Dark Court, too mortal, but the High Court would've broken their spirits—impeded their natural passions with unnatural restraints. Sorcha's court took the Sighted ones and all of the halflings—unbeknownst to the Winter and Summer Courts—but the Dark Court tried to keep their mortal offspring out of that rigid realm. Rabbit had repaid that secrecy by looking after the other halflings Irial'd found.

"There's trinkets from the Hounds." Irial held out the bag. "And one of Jenny's kin sent those garments you wanted."

The girls snatched the bag and scurried away.

"Exhausting beasts." Rabbit rubbed a hand over his face, then called out, "No clubs tonight, you hear me?"

"Promise," Tish yelled from somewhere in the back.

Ani ran back in. Grinning madly, she skidded to a stop a hairsbreadth away from Irial. "Did you like Leslie? I bet you did. Very hot." Her words all tumbled together. Then she stuck her tongue out at Rabbit. "We'll get to go tomorrow, then. Promise?"

As Rabbit put a hand over his eyes, Irial found himself offering, "I'll take them."

Rabbit made a shooing motion at Ani. Then he

flipped the sign on the door to CLOSED. "Now, let's give this a try."

The room was exactly as it had always been, immaculate and unchanging. Rabbit had aged some, not as fast as mortals, but he looked closer to early twenties than teens now.

Rabbit motioned to the black chair where his clients sat. "You okay?"

Irial squeezed Rabbit's forearm and admitted, "Tired."

After he handed Rabbit the cords Gabriel had sent, Irial sat down in the chair and stretched his legs out in front of him.

"I heard about Guin." Rabbit pulled out three needles and as many vials.

"Gabriel's got the Hounds patrolling; they think they're immune still. The leannan-sidhe are to stay out of sight." Irial leaned back in the tattoo chair and closed his eyes while Rabbit bound him with the cords. Irial always found himself talking freely with Rabbit. In a world of careful deceit, there were so few people Irial could trust without reservation. Rabbit had inherited all of his father's loyalty, but also the mortal sense to think things through, to talk rather than fight.

"I think the ink exchange will help." Rabbit rolled up Irial's sleeve. "It's going to hurt."

"Hurt *me* or the girl?" Irial opened his eyes briefly. "I saw her, the mortal."

"You. Leslie will just feel the tattoo. I think. She did well with the outline. The court's tears and blood are an easier adjustment for a mortal. Her emotions will be volatile, fleeting by now. She's coping, though. Your blood will be harder for her. . . ." His words drifted off. He picked up the brown glass bottle that held the strange ink he'd mixed for the exchanges. "I'm not sure how she'll do, since it's *you*. She's good people."

"I'll look after her," Irial promised. She'd be bound to him, but he'd make sure she was well cared for, satisfied. He could do that.

Rabbit tied another cord around Irial's arm to help raise a vein. Unlike the cords that bound him to the chair, this was a simple thing—a length of rubber like those in mortal hospitals.

"It'll be fine." Irial tested his bonds, then nodded to Rabbit. There were few creatures he'd trust to hold him immobile.

Silently, Rabbit located the vein on the inside of Irial's elbow.

"She's stronger than you know, or she wouldn't have picked me."

Rabbit jabbed a thick, hollow tube into Irial's arm. "Ready?"

"Yes." It was barely a sting, not anywhere near as painful as he'd feared.

Then Rabbit added the tiny filter only he could make to the tube.

Irial's spine bowed; his eyes rolled back. *It'll make me*

strong. Feed my court. Protect them. But the extraction of blood and essence was nightmarishly awful, as if tiny incisors were set to roam inside his body, ripping and tearing at places where sharp things should never enter.

"Keep the pups out of my reach," he gasped as his vision began to blur. "Need." Irial's stomach cramped. His lungs tightened, as if all the air he'd ever breathed were being sucked out all at once.

"Irial?" Ani's voice was in the doorway. Far enough away that he couldn't reach her; too close, though.

His hands clenched. "Rab . . ."

"Ani, go." Rabbit stepped in front of Irial then, blocking her from view.

"It'll pass, Iri. It always passes. Tell him, Rabbit, tell him he'll be okay." Ani's voice faded as she walked away.

"She's right."

"Starving." Irial dug his finger into the chair until the leather ripped. "You're destroying me. My court."

"No. It passes. Ani's right. It passes." Rabbit pulled out the tube with a *schluck*. "Rest now."

"Food. Need. Call Gabriel."

"No. Not until I finish the tattoo. Nothing until then. Else it won't work." Then Rabbit left, locking the door behind him, leaving Irial unable to move from the chair.

CHAPTER 21

Half afraid last night had been a dream, Leslie looked out the window. *He's still here.* Niall was doing some sort of stretching in the yard. Either he'd been awake for a while and was bored or he was just going about his routine. He'd shed his shirt, and in the light of day the spiderweb of scars that covered his torso was difficult to look at. Thin white lines crisscrossed thicker, uneven raised marks, as if something had clawed his skin. Seeing the full extent of it made her want to cry for him. *How is he even alive?* He was, though. He was a survivor, and it made him all the more beautiful.

With as little noise as she could, Leslie opened the door. "Hey."

He paused in midstretch, standing so still that he seemed frozen, as if he were carved of some rare dark stone. Only his voice proved that he was a living being. "Shall I take you to the school?"

"No." She shook her head as she walked toward him. Until then she hadn't decided, but looking at him—knowing that whatever happened next would mean they'd be changed from what they were in that moment—she knew that wasting the day was foolish. Spending the day at Bishop O.C. . . . it simply didn't make sense to her.

"What are you doing today?" she asked when she was standing beside him. Without conscious thought, she lifted her hand, letting her fingertips graze the scars on his chest, like following a map of chaos, lines bisecting lines, furrows branching into ridges and ripples.

He hadn't moved yet, staying as still as when he'd seen her walking toward him. "Taking a long swim in the cold river?"

She stepped slightly closer. "No."

He swallowed. "If I keep suggesting things, will you keep saying no?"

"Maybe." She smiled, feeling brave, confident with him in a way she hadn't felt with a guy in longer than she wanted to consider. "Do you want me to?"

"Yes. No. Maybe." He gave her a shaky smile. "I'd almost forgotten how much fun this dance was, the wanting without having."

"Is it okay if I lead?" She actually blushed when she said it. She was far from innocent, but he made her feel like this mattered, like *they* mattered.

"I'm rather liking it." He cleared his throat. "Not that pursuing you—"

"Shh."

"Okay." He watched her curiously. He still hadn't moved, feet and hands in precisely the same position as when she'd approached. It was odd.

"Did you go to military school or something?" she asked before she could stop herself. *What a dumb question!*

But he wasn't laughing at her or acting like she ruined the moment. He answered seriously, "Not like you're thinking, but I've had to learn a number of things because Keenan's father needed me to do so. Training . . . It's good to know how to protect yourself and those you care for."

"Oh."

"I can teach you how to defend yourself some. Not"— he held her gaze—"that it will always keep you safe. There are times when no amount of training will stop what others would do."

"So why . . ." She let the question drift away.

"Because it helps me sleep at night, because it helps me focus, because sometimes I like knowing that maybe if I were in danger again it would help." He kissed her forehead. "And sometimes because it gives me hope that it'll make me strong enough to be loved and protect the one I would try to love."

"Oh." She was at a loss once more.

He stepped back. "But you were going to lead this dance, so I'll work on following . . . after I ask if we could pause at the loft so I might bathe."

And just like that he eased her fears and brought the tension back to that comfortable zinging feeling they'd shared before he started talking about violence and love.

An hour later, Leslie walked through Huntsdale with Niall—sure that once she stepped away from him, the near illusory connection they had would end. It was so different from their walk the night before, when they'd stopped to kiss in alcoves and dark doorways.

Eventually he gestured at a tall old building in front of them. "We're here."

They stood at the edge of a small park that felt forbidden, as if the air before her had taken form and made a barricade around the greenery. Trees of all sorts bloomed in a riot of contrasting colors and scents; the grass, though, was trampled flat, browned as though by a fair or concert. The park was clean, too; there was no litter or debris at all. It was also empty of people: not even a vagrant lay on any of the odd wooden benches that were scattered throughout the park. Old stone sculptures glistened like they belonged in a museum, and the water in a fountain rose and fell as if a song controlled its flow. Leslie stared at it, the curiously enticing park, wondering how something so beautiful could be here and unused.

"Can we go there?"

"The park?" Niall looked from her face to the park, where she'd been staring. "I suppose."

"It's not private?" She watched as the flow of water shimmered like a girl undulating in some dance that she should remember, that her bones once knew.

There is *a girl.* The woman danced, hands lifted over her head, face tilted upward like she was speaking to the sun or moon. Leslie stepped closer, leaning into the weighty air that seemed to prevent her passing, to stop her from reaching the fountain. Without looking for traffic or for any conscious reason why, Leslie went toward the park. She paused, caught between longing and fear and not sure she truly felt either one.

"Leslie? Are you with me?" Niall took her hand, stopping her from entering the park.

She blinked. The image of the dancing girl vanished. The statues looked dim, and there weren't nearly as many as she'd thought. Nor were the trees all blooming: there weren't even as many trees as she'd thought. Instead, there were people she somehow hadn't seen: girls, many of whom seemed to be watching her and Niall, wandered around the park in small groups, giggling and talking to the guys who stood where she had thought there were only trees.

"Nothing makes sense, Niall." Leslie felt the edge of panic push against her, but it was less than real—more a murmur of an emotion that rose and faded before it found form. "I feel like . . . I don't know what I feel lately. I don't get scared, can't stay angry. And when I feel it, it's like it's not mine. I see things that aren't right—people with thorns on their faces, tattoos that move, horns. I keep seeing things that aren't real; I should be afraid. Instead I look away. Something's wrong with me."

He didn't offer her empty promises that it would be okay or that she was imagining it; instead he looked pained, leading her to believe that he knew something more than she did.

Which should make me angry.

She tried to summon it up, but her growing emotional instability had become so pronounced that it was like being a visitor in her own body. Calmly, as if the question didn't matter, she asked, "Do you know what's wrong with me?"

"No. Not really." He paused. "I know someone awful is interested in you."

"That should scare me." She nodded, still calm, still not frightened. *He* was, though.

"You taste afraid, jealous, and"—she closed her eyes for a moment, savoring some strange thread of emotion that she could almost roll on her tongue—"sad."

She opened her eyes. "Why do I know that, Niall?"

Confusion filled him then; she tasted that too. If his emotions were true, he didn't know any more than she did about her new ability.

"You can—"

"Taste your feelings." She watched him, *felt* him try to be still, like his emotions were being sorted into boxes she couldn't open. Glimmers of tastes—chicory and honey, salt and cinnamon, mint and thyme—drifted by like shadows.

"That's an odd choice of words." He waited, not quite a question, but close enough.

So she told him more of the things she'd been feeling. "There are bursts and absences. There are so many things I feel and see that I can't explain. It should frighten me. It should've made me talk to someone. But I haven't been able to . . . until now."

"Do you know when it started?" He was worried. Her tongue was heavy under a lingering lemony flavor, and she knew that *worry* was the feeling that went with that flavor.

"I'm not sure, not really. . . ." She tried to focus. There was a tumble of words—*the restaurant, the tattoo, the Rath, the museum, when, why*—but when she tried to speak, all the words were gone.

"Irial," Niall said.

His briny anger and cinnamon jealousy surged back until her throat burned with it. She gasped, nearly choking. But as she thought of Irial, everything felt better. She felt calm again. The tastes faded from her tongue.

Niall hurried her back across the street and into the old building. "We'll still spend the day together. He won't come here. Tonight we'll talk to Aislinn and Keenan. After that you'll be safe. Can we do that?"

His worry stretched inside her, filling her up, and then it slithered away as if it had found a tunnel to escape her. In its place she felt calmness. Her body felt as languid as when she was in Rabbit's chair. *Talking about this isn't necessary.* She shrugged. "We didn't have a plan yet anyhow, right? Hang out, work, see Rabbit, then more hanging out? Sure."

"Just a few hours, then, and it'll all be fine." He took her hand and started up a spiraling stone staircase.

"No elevators?" She looked around. The outside had been rather nondescript, worn down like most things in Huntsdale, but the inside of the building was beautiful. As at the Rath, obsidian, marble, and wood seemed to replace what would usually be metal.

"No steel allowed in here," he said distractedly.

She followed him until he stopped at a door that was too beautiful to be exposed to casual passersby. Stones—not cut jewels, but raw stones—were embedded in the wood to create a mosaic. She reached out, hand hovering in the air in front of the door. "It's gorgeous."

Niall opened the mosaic door. The inside was no less lovely. Tall, leafy plants dominated the room. Innumerable birds swooped through the air, nested in nooks in tall columns that supported vine-covered ceilings.

"Be welcome in our home, Leslie," he said.

The words felt strangely formal, setting off warnings that this was not the right place for her, that running would be wise. But Leslie could still feel Niall's emotions—he was happy, honored—and in the middle of it all was a thin cord of genuine love for her. So she stepped farther into the room, breathing the summer-sweet scent of flowers that bloomed somewhere in the loft.

"Make yourself at home while I bathe." Niall motioned

to an overstuffed chair. "Then I'll make us breakfast. We'll stay here. We'll figure it out."

She thought about answering, but he seemed to be talking to himself more than to her. She settled in the cozy chair, watching the birds dance through the air over their heads. *With Niall or with Irial, that's where I should be.* She wasn't sure why, but it was clear to her then. Every day her feelings had become further skewed from normal, and other people's emotions had been growing identifiable. She heard the excuses she'd been using to explain the changes away—and knew they were lies and self-deceits. She could see it all with a peculiar clarity. Something, the same source as the changes, was preventing her from thinking too much about the reasons why she was changing; it was somehow forbidden. *But why worry?* Whatever was changing made her feel good, better than she had in a very long time. So she closed her eyes and enjoyed the languor that had filled her during her conversation with Niall.

CHAPTER 22

They'd spent the day together playing video games, talking, and just being near each other. By the time Leslie had to go to work, she'd begun completely tuning out his worries and murmured warnings. She simply didn't *feel* those things. He was worried—she could taste that—but *she* felt good.

Niall left her at the door of Verlaine's with another reminder not to go anywhere with Irial or any strangers.

"Sure." She kissed his cheek. "See you later tonight?"

"I don't think you should be walking alone. I'll meet you and walk you to Rabbit's, and then I can walk you to the Crow's Nest after."

"No. I can call Ani or Tish or Rabbit to come meet me, or I'll take a cab." She gave him a reassuring smile before she went inside.

Work passed in a blur. They were busy enough that she had a nice amount to add to the money already in her bag. At the end of her shift, she cashed out and went over to Pins

and Needles. Between finally getting her ink and the promise of seeing Niall—*again*—later, she was almost giddy.
Everything was going better than it had in a very long time.

When she walked through the door of the tattoo shop,
all but one of the doors to the rooms adjoining the waiting
area were already shut. From the one open room came
Rabbit's voice, "Shop's closed."

"It's me." She went inside.

Rabbit sat on his stool. His expression was guarded.
"You could change your mind still. We could do something
else with—"

"Change the design midway?" She scowled. "That's
stupid. Honestly, Rabbit, your art is beautiful. I never took
you for insecure."

"It's not that. . . ."

"What then?"

"I just want you to be happy, Les." He tugged at his
goatee, seeming more nervous than she'd ever seen him.

"Then finish my tattoo," she said softly. She slipped off
her shirt. "Come on. We already had this conversation."

With an unreadable look on his face, he motioned to the
chair. "You chose this. You'll be all right. . . . I want you to
be all right."

Grinning, she sat down with her back to him again.
"And I will. I'll be wearing the prettiest, most perfect art on
my skin—my choice, my skin. How could I not be all
right?"

Rabbit didn't answer, but he was often silent as he

went about setting up his supplies. This routine was meticulous. It made her feel good, knowing that he was concerned about his clients' safety. Not all tattooists were so responsible.

She glanced back to watch Rabbit open a strange bottle. "What's that?"

"Your ink." He didn't look at her.

She stared at the brown glass: for a moment, she could swear black smoke danced like small flames above the lip of the bottle. "It's beautiful, like bottled shadows."

"It is." He glanced her way, briefly, face as expressionless as she'd ever seen it. "If I weren't so fond of the shadows, I wouldn't be doing this."

"Tattooing?"

He lifted the bottle and tipped it into a series of caps. Some of the caps already had a crystalline liquid in the bottom. In the dim light, it looked as if the ink separated into variations of darkness as Rabbit poured a little into each cap.

Tiny black tears, like a cup dipped into the abyss. She shook her head. *Too many weird events, making me think strange things.* She asked, "Is it the other liquid in there that changes the colors? Like two inks mixing?"

"They mix into what I need for your work. Turn." Rabbit motioned for her to look away.

She did, moving her body until her back was to him. He wiped her skin, and she closed her eyes—waiting.

Soon the machine hummed, and then the needles were on her skin. They barely pierced the surface, but that slight piercing changed everything. The world blurred and sharpened; colors bloomed behind her closed lids. The darkness grew and split into a thousand shades of light, and each of those shades was an emotion, a feeling she could swallow and cherish. Those emotions would make her live, make them all so much stronger.

Nourish us, save us, the body for the soul. Her thoughts were tangled with waves of feelings that fluttered through her and drifted away, like the strands of a lost dream after waking. She grasped at them, her mind struggling to hold the emotions in place, to identify them. These weren't just her emotions: she could feel the yearnings of strangers outside on the street—a montage of fears and worries, lusts and angers. Then cravings too bizarre to visualize washed over her.

But almost as soon as they touched her, each feeling skittered away, spiraling out onto some cord that led away from her into the shadows, into the abyss from which the ink in her skin had been collected.

Irial drifted in uneasy slumber. He felt her—his Leslie—being stitched closer to him with each brush of Rabbit's needles, tying her to him, making her *his,* far more truly than any of his fey were, than anyone had ever been.

And it felt like Rabbit's needles were puncturing Irial's

heart, his lungs, his eyes. She was in his blood as surely as his blood was in her skin. He felt her tenderness, her compassion, her strength, her yearning for love. He felt her vulnerabilities and hopes—and he wanted to cosset and love her. It was decidedly unfit for the king of the Dark Court to feel such tender emotion. *If I'd known, would I have done the exchange?*

He wanted to tell himself he wouldn't, but he'd allowed far worse to be done to him to ensure the safety of his fey.

In his nightmares, she was the girl he'd carried down the street, his Leslie, bleeding from wounds done to her by men whose faces came slowly into focus. He wasn't sure what was real and what was fear-distorted. She'd tell him, though. He'd walk through her memories as they drew closer. He'd comfort her—and kill the men who'd hurt her.

She'd make him stronger, nourish him by feeding him human emotions he couldn't touch without her. And he'd learn to hide how much she suddenly meant to him, how sickeningly mortal he felt. *What've you done to me, Leslie?* He laughed at the realization of his new weaknesses: by making himself strong enough to lead them, he'd simultaneously made himself far less of the Dark Court than he'd ever been.

What have I done?

As Leslie sat there—eyes closed and waiting—she heard the laughter again, but it didn't bother her this time. It felt good—welcome, even. She smiled. "It's a nice laugh."

"Stay still," Rabbit reminded her.

Then he went back to work, the hum of the machine sounding louder, as if her hearing had shifted. She sighed, and for a moment she could almost see the dark eyes that were now etched on her skin—except they seemed to be looking at her from beyond the room, just close enough that she wondered if she'd see them when she opened her own eyes.

She noticed the hum stop but couldn't quite open her eyes as Rabbit cleaned her back again.

Sleep now. It was just a whisper, but she felt certain that there was a real person talking to her—not Rabbit.

Who?

And he answered, her imaginary speaker. *You know who I am, Leslie. You might not like the answer just yet, but you know me, love.*

Beside her, she heard the bandage package rip, felt pressure as the pad was put over her tattoo.

"Just rest for a few minutes, Leslie," Rabbit murmured as he helped her stand, directed her onto the chair again, reclined now like a bed. "I'll be right back."

Listen to Bunny-boy. I need to wake up, and you don't want to be awake for it. Trust me, love. I want to keep you safe.

"Listen to who?"

"You're strong, Leslie. Just remember that. You're stronger

than you think," Rabbit said as he draped a blanket over her. "I'll be back in a few minutes. Just rest."

She didn't have much of a choice: she was suddenly more exhausted than she'd ever been. "Just a few minutes. Going out dancing, then."

CHAPTER 23

Irial woke with a scream half formed on his lips. He was unbound but still on Rabbit's chair. Red welts crossed his arms and legs. A bruise stretched across his arm where the tube had been. He tried to sit up, sending paroxysms of pain through his whole body.

Ani sealed her lips to his, swallowing his scream—and the ones that followed.

When she pulled back—lips blood red, pupils dilated, cheeks flushed—he gaped at her. Halflings didn't, couldn't, feed on faeries. Mortal blood overcame most of their fey traits. The traits that remained had never included this one.

More troubles.

"How?" he asked.

She shrugged.

"Ani, you can't stay here if you need to—"

"Feed?" she prompted with a smile that was all Gabriel, wicked and predatory.

"Yes, *feed*, like your father. No wonder Rabbit's had so much trouble with you." Irial concentrated on keeping his focus, on not trying to go check on Leslie, on dealing with Ani first. *Leslie's not ready to talk to me. Not here. Not when I'm so weak.*

"Your pain's like a big sundae. Didja know that?" Ani licked her lips. "Cherry. With extra sugar."

"What about Tish?" He pulled on the shirt Ani had given him. *Business first. Then Leslie.* Somehow she didn't seem like business anymore.

"Nope. Just me." Ani leaned closer. "Can I have another taste?"

She bit his chin, drawing blood with her sharp canines.

He sighed and pushed her away. *No violence in disciplining Gabriel's daughter.*

"I can feed off mortals without the ink exchange. No exchange. Just me." She sighed dreamily. "If they're rolling, it's like drinking rainbows. Rainbows. Big, sugary rainbows."

"Mortals?"

She swayed into him. "If I find a strong one, it's okay. It's only when I pick the wrong ones that they get all stupid. Not so different than what you're doing, is it?" She plopped down beside him. "She's fine, you know. Leslie. Resting and all that."

"Rabbit!" he yelled. Then he sent a mental message out to Gabriel. They'd need to take Ani with them for a while.

"What's she done?" Rabbit leaned in the doorway.

"Fed."

He nodded once. "I wondered if that's why—"

"You *wondered*? Why didn't you tell me? Warn me? She could've gotten hurt, could've gotten in trouble." Irial stared at him. "And she could have been what we needed to forestall . . ." He let his words drift away. The idea of finding Ani earlier, of not being with Leslie, made his stomach tighten in unfamiliar panic. Here was a solution that was too little, too late, and he was perversely glad of it.

Beside Irial, Rabbit was still, cautious, all the things Irial wasn't feeling. Rabbit said, "She's my sister, Iri. I wasn't going to turn her over for testing, not when you had a plan that might work."

Ani swayed and tried to step around Rabbit to leave. He scooped up his sister, holding her aloft and away from his body like she was feral, but looking at her with the same affection he'd had when Ani was just a newborn pup.

He pointedly changed the subject. "Leslie's leaving now."

To hide just how confused he was about the feelings he was having for Leslie, Irial focused on Ani, who was kicking her feet in the air and giggling. "Ani can't stay here," he said.

"I know." Rabbit kissed Ani's forehead. His eyes twinkled as he added, "Dad's going to have an awful time with her."

Irial felt the Hounds approach, a skin-prickling roll of terror that he let wash over him like soothing balm. Fey outside—not his, but summer fey—cringed as the Hounds passed. He let himself take nourishment from the horror they wrought by their presence.

"Daddy!" Ani squealed, kicking her feet again.

The Hounds stayed outside—all but Gabriel. He nodded at Rabbit. "Pup."

Rabbit rolled his eyes at his father and turned to Irial. "You ought to go after Leslie soon. *Daddy* can handle Ani." He grinned then, looking every bit like Ani's sibling. "In fact, I'll get Ani's bag together first so she'll be ready to leave with the pack."

Ignoring the look of panic that flashed over Gabriel's face, Irial answered, "Don't let Ani roam while you do."

After Rabbit carried the giggling Ani away, Irial brought Gabriel up to speed.

"What do I do with her?" Gabriel, the Hound who led some of the most terrifying creatures to walk the earth, sounded utterly intimidated. "How do I . . . She's female, Irial. Don't they have different *needs*?"

"She can't be worse than you were when you were younger. Ask one of your females for advice." Irial drew as much nourishment as he could from Gabriel's mingled panic and excitement and pride. Irial needed to be stable before he went to find Leslie, needed to be well fed so he didn't pull too many human emotions through Leslie just yet. *Let her get used to me first, talk to me.* He felt worry for his mortal. If the other dark fey had felt this weakness when they did the ink exchanges, they hadn't admitted it to him.

Gabriel was still talking; Irial forced himself to listen to the Hound.

". . . and they're just not good examples for my pup.

Have you seen them lately? Chela and her litter all but slaughtered the representatives of Sorcha's court the other moon."

"Month, Gabriel. The other *month*."

Gabriel waved a hand, utterly uncowed by his king. "They're too rough for Ani. She's so tiny." He started pacing as he rambled on about the female Hounds.

They were truly fierce, but Irial had trouble objecting to anything that kept Sorcha's court away from him.

"Can she *run*?" Gabriel stopped on the verge of a burst of pride that was almost chokingly sweet.

Irial closed his eyes and savored the orange-sugar rush of Gabriel's emotions. "Ask her."

"You need anything first?" Gabriel paused, as still as a wave before it breaks.

"No. Just take Ani home. Get Rabbit's telephone number so you can reach him if you need advice on her."

Gabriel snarled, but only once.

Irial glared, relieved to deal with the familiar challenge of Gabriel's pride. "He's raised her. You don't know her. Get his number."

The look on Gabriel's face would stop almost any fey or mortal. Accepting orders—even from his king—went against his instincts. Irial softened his tone. "If *you* don't need it, fine, but they should keep in touch. They're a pack of their own."

Gabriel bowed his head slightly. "Do you need someone else for your strength?"

Irial held out a hand to the once more visibly uncomfortable Hound. "After seeing you? Why?"

Gabriel straightened his shoulders. "Then I'll go fetch the pup. My daughter"—he had another burst of tangled emotions then—"it is just the one, right?"

Irial bit back his smile. "Just Ani."

"Right then. I'll get her."

"Be sure to say hello to Tish, though," Irial reminded him. "Then send her to me. We're going out."

I need to find Leslie. My *Leslie, my mercy, my strength, my Shadow Girl . . . mine.*

He drew a deep breath, pleased to realize that he knew exactly where she was, could see her if he tried. She had left the shop and now walked down the street, her step sure, her lips curved in the most enchanting smile he'd ever seen.

Soon. I'll be there soon. He pulled his hands through his hair, brushing it back, and checked that he hadn't any blood on his shirt. He didn't, but his pants were a total loss. He opened the door and called, "Tish! Five minutes."

Then he went to find his bag. *My mortal seeing me like this . . . no, not the best way to entice her, covered in blood.*

CHAPTER 24

Leslie felt a compulsion riding inside her, leaving her with an inexplicable need to move. Her skin felt tight and tingly. She reached back and tore away the bandage that Rabbit had put over her tattoo. The bandage was wet, not with blood but with plasma and traces of ink. Her shirt stuck to her damp skin, its fabric probably getting stained, but she couldn't stand having her beautiful tattoo trapped.

She tossed the bandage in the trash and headed down Crofter Avenue toward the Crow's Nest, grinning to herself when she saw the club's red neon sign. A few guys were hanging out in the shadowed alley alongside the building; it was a shortcut over to the railroad yard, but most people used it as a spot to smoke. As she approached, she saw one guy punch another. She smiled, feeling a pleasant jolt of adrenaline as the two men began hitting each other unreservedly.

At the door of the club, Glenn, the doorman, stopped her. His attention flicked to the fight in the alley, and the bars in his face glittered as the red light from the sign hit them. He shook his head at the fight. Then turned his attention back to her. "Five-dollar cover tonight."

"Least they're fighting outside." She pulled a crinkled bill out of her pocket and held her hand out for the stamp.

"They're staying out, too." He grinned at her. "You bringing trouble in your wake these days?"

She laughed, but privately she wondered if he was right. Inside the club the lead singer of the band all but screamed his lyrics; Leslie winced. "They don't sound like they're worth it."

"Could be worse." Glenn put the money in the box and leaned back on his stool. They listened to the guitar-heavy music for a minute; then he grinned again. "Or not."

"Anybody around?" She couldn't see far into the crowd.

"Seth and Ash are over by the wall." He inclined his chin toward the most shadowed part of the club.

"Is Keenan with them?"

"Yeah, he's there too." Glenn scowled, but he didn't say more.

The door opened behind Leslie. Glenn turned to the newcomer. "Ten-dollar cover."

Leslie leaned in and asked, "Inflation?"

"Nah. Doorman's prerogative." He quirked his mouth in a crooked smile.

She shook her head and started to walk off, but Glenn put a hand on her arm.

"Watch yourself. All sorts of freaks in town tonight."

Glenn shot a glance over the crowded room. The usual familiar faces were there, but a lot of strangers were in the crowd too. Maybe that's what all the fights were about: maybe gangs *were* moving in.

No. It felt weird to think it, but somehow she suspected that the fights were tied to her. It seemed solipsistic to consider it, but the idea felt true.

Or I'm losing it.

"You okay?" Glenn raised his voice to be heard over the increasing din, and she felt a wave of something—*protectiveness*—roll from him. "I could get Tim to watch the door and—"

"No, I'm cool." She didn't feel nervous, not tonight, not anymore. Her hand strayed to her tattoo, hidden under her shirt. "Thanks, though."

She squeezed her way through the crowd to Seth and Aislinn. They sat as close together as they could while still remaining on separate chairs.

Aislinn looked up. "Hey."

Beside her, Seth nodded and looked meaningfully at Aislinn and then back at Leslie. "You should talk."

"Sure." Leslie slid into the chair Seth pushed toward her. She leaned toward Aislinn. "Seth says you have something to tell me. Secret spilling and all that."

"I'm sorry about not telling you; I just wanted to keep you safe"—Aislinn bit her lip—"from things. When I heard about Ren's—"

"Don't," Leslie interrupted, waiting for the panic to hit,

but it was just a dull roar. "You know my secrets. Got it."

"You're right." Aislinn took a deep breath before looking at Seth for assurance.

Keenan approached the table with sodas for Aislinn and Seth and a glass of wine for himself. He handed Seth the drinks and turned to her. "Niall's not here yet. What shall I get you?"

"Nothing." She didn't have much cash on her, and accepting anything from Keenan made her uncomfortable, especially after the other night.

He scowled briefly at the crowd between him and the bar. "Soda? Tea? Water?"

"Nothing."

"Would—"

"Nothing," she interrupted in a firm voice. She stood back up. She *needed* to get away from Keenan. *Now.* She told Aislinn, "Come find me when you figure out what you're trying to say."

But Keenan came closer, beside Aislinn, putting himself between her and Leslie.

Get away from him. He's danger. Enemy. Not us. Leslie stared out at the throng of bodies. The band was awful but she wanted to move, burn some energy, ride out whatever rush she had going from the ink.

"We need to talk, Leslie." Aislinn sounded so serious, so worried.

Leslie forced herself to look at Aislinn. "Sure. I'll be on the dance floor when you're ready."

Leslie stepped away from the table, feeling the increasing pressure to get away from Keenan, to run. Her hands trembled from trying to stay still.

"Leslie, stop," Keenan said as he grabbed the bottom of her shirt.

Aislinn took hold of his wrist but couldn't push him away. "What are you doing?"

Keenan put his other hand on Leslie's hip and turned her. He lifted her shirt, baring Leslie's whole back to Aislinn and anyone who was near. "Look."

Aislinn gasped. "What have you done, Les?"

"Got a tattoo. You knew that." Leslie pulled out of Keenan's grasp. "Lots of people have them. Maybe you should be asking your idiot boyfriend here what *he's* doing. I don't appreciate being treated like—"

"She doesn't know, Aislinn." Keenan sounded weirdly gentle, soothing as if warm breezes were riding on his voice.

But Leslie felt her anger rising with each word that fell from his lips. This anger was not fleeting or fading.

Danger. He's dangerous to us. She paused. *Us?*

Keenan looked inhuman as he stepped closer to her. Some trick of the club lights made him glow like a golden effigy come to life. His voice burned her skin when he demanded, "Who did it?"

She crossed her arms, half-hugging herself, refusing to give in to the urge to run. Fear vied with anger, but she tilted her head to glare at him. "Why? You want one?"

"Tell me." Keenan gave her a look so predatory, she felt

her stomach twist in fear. It was a terrifying look—but no one else saw it. Aislinn and Seth were watching her, not Keenan.

She'd had enough. Her anger and fear fled again; she smiled with a cruelty she didn't remember owning. "Back off, Keenan. I'm not yours to command. Not now. Not ever. Don't cross me, kingling."

Kingling?

They weren't her words. They didn't make sense. But she felt better for saying them. She walked away and wiggled through the crowd until she reached the front of the stage. She felt like she was looking for someone, the one who would make it all better. *Where are you?* The thought repeated like a chant in her mind, so much so that she must have said it aloud.

He answered, "I'm right here."

And she knew who it was without looking. "Irial."

"How are you tonight, my love?"

"Furious. You?" She turned to face him, letting her gaze rake over him the way he'd looked at her at the Rath. He looked good, like sin in a suit. From the tips of his soft leather boots to the silk of his shirt, he was gorgeous, but a pretty package wasn't reason enough to forgive his near assault, to forgive anything. She summoned up her anger, her embarrassment, her fear. Then she looked him straight in the eye and said, "Not impressed *or* interested."

"Liar." He smiled then, and traced his finger down her wrist. He inhaled deeply, like he was trying to catch and hold an illusive scent, and she was suddenly calm. She wasn't afraid, wasn't anxious, none of the things she should feel. Instead she felt something uncoiling inside of her, a shadowy shape stretching and writhing under her skin.

Her eyes started to close; her heart fluttered. *No.* She stepped backward and told him, "You should go away."

"And leave you to fend for yourself?" He shook his head. "Now, why would I do that? I'll look after you when the kingling comes prowling this way in a moment. The boy's a nuisance."

"I have a date," she said, although she wasn't entirely sure how well that would go right now. *Focus on that.* Niall lived with Keenan, was his guardian, and right now the idea of crossing paths with Keenan made her want to strike someone. She froze then, as something pieced together. "Kingling?"

"The boy. But let's not talk about him." He took her hands. "Dance with me, Leslie. I'll be nice. Proper, even. Let's enjoy our moment before business interferes."

I should just go. But walking away from Irial didn't appeal to her. Everyone had warned her that he was trouble, but he didn't frighten her, not right now. It was *Keenan* who terrified her. Having Irial beside her felt right, natural. She didn't move—or answer him.

In the most enticing voice she'd ever heard, Irial said, "Come now, Leslie, would Niall really mind if we had one dance? More important, do *you* really mind?"

"I should." She didn't, though. Briefly she gave in to the

urge to close her eyes against the spiraling ecstasy that had begun to make her body hum.

"Call it an apology? I frightened you at the Rath, didn't I?" His voice seemed so inviting, easing her further into calm. "One song and then we'll sit and talk. I'll stay politely back if you but tell me to."

She swayed toward him like a cobra weaving to a snake charmer's songs. His arms slid around her.

The music was still fast, something suited to thrashing about manically, but Irial seemed oblivious to it. "See, love? Where's the harm, hmm?"

They danced, but she wasn't feeling trapped. She felt dizzy but confident, stepping away when the song ended.

Irial didn't touch her. He walked beside her. In the darkest corner of the room, he snagged two bottles of water from a waitress.

"So, how are you feeling after Bunny-boy's work?" He stood between her and the rest of the club.

She cracked the seal on the bottle of water and leaned against the wall, reveling in the feel of the bass thumping inside her skin. "What?"

Slowly, he reached out toward her. He slid his right hand up the back of her shirt along her spine to rest atop her still-tender skin. "The ink. Our tattoo."

"*Our* tattoo?"

He leaned in closer and whispered, "I know you heard me, saw me watching when Rabbit drew on that delicate skin."

He pressed his fingers over the tattoo until she winced. Her heart raced as if she'd been running for hours, as if the things in her nightmares had stepped into the room. *He's lying. Crazy . . . He's . . . not.* His words tasted true, felt right as they seeped into her mind.

"I felt each touch of the needle, drawing us closer and closer together. My eyes, Leslie, on your skin. My essence, love, buried inside you." Irial leaned back, giving her a scant bit of space, making it possible for her to look into his eyes. "You're my Mercy, my Shadow Girl, my banquet. Only mine."

She slid partway down the wall and would have hit the floor if he hadn't pulled her closer.

"That terror you feel right now"—he spoke softly, lips hovering over hers. "I can make it stop, just like that."

As he said *that*, he inhaled, and she felt perfectly calm, as if they'd been discussing nothing special.

Her mind couldn't process it—*refused* to attempt to make sense of what he'd said. Clarity filled her: all the weirdness of the past few days had brought her here. *He's what's changed. He's why I'm . . . wrong.*

"It's not possible," she said to him, to herself.

"You picked me. Rabbit told you it would change you."

"So Rabbit drew your eyes, my bad luck." She slid to the side, moving a little bit away from him. "That doesn't tie us together. It's just ink."

With sinuous grace, he turned to lean on the spot she'd

just vacated, putting them side by side. He didn't look at her but watched the dancers instead as he said, "You don't believe that. You know better. Somewhere inside, you *feel* different. I know that, as clearly as I know that you're watching for Niall, hoping he'll actually strike me this time."

She turned to look at him. "What?"

"He won't. Can't. There are only a few who can touch me, and he's not one of them. But"—he drew a deep breath and let it out in a long sigh, stirring tendrils of her hair— "I do like that you're wishing it. Healthy feelings, those ones—rage, dismay, fear, and a bit of guilty temptation. They taste good."

He laughed, a smoky sound curling around her like shadows taking form, like the shadows she'd imagined—*not imagined, but truly seen*—hovering over the bottle of ink at Rabbit's shop. She looked then, and saw shadows flowing through the room, crawling toward her from the bodies on the dance floor, stretching themselves out like they had hands that would stroke her skin—and she really didn't want them to. *Do I?* She licked her lips, tasting honey— *longing*—and pushed away from the wall.

Coming through those shadow-draped bodies were Keenan, Aislinn, and Seth. None of them looked happy, but it was Seth's worried expression that made her falter. She didn't want them to reach her any more than she wanted the shadows to. Rage at Keenan spiked, matching the cloud of salt-soaked anger that came through the air in front of him like fog coming in from the sea.

Irial twirled her into his arms and gave her a look that made her shiver with longing.

"Mmmm, I like that one, but"—he kissed her forehead tenderly—"I need to deal with business now. We'll have plenty of time for that soon enough."

She stepped away from him, stumbling into the crowd, where Keenan caught her without looking away from Irial. But being in Keenan's grip made anger flare purer than she'd thought she could feel, replaced the blood in her veins with salt. "Don't touch me," she hissed. "Don't you *ever* touch me, kingling."

"I'm sorry, Les. I'm so sorry," Aislinn whispered to her. For a moment it looked like golden tears slid down her cheeks, but then she turned away and said, "Seth?"

"I got her." Seth pulled her away from Keenan and tucked her under his arm protectively. "Come on, Les."

Keenan put a hand on Seth's shoulder. "Take her to Niall."

"I'm not going anywhere," she told the assembled group. "I don't know what's going on, but I'm—"

"Go home. You'll be safer away from this rabble." Irial inhaled again, and Leslie thought she could actually see shadows crawling across a twisting vine of ink—with feathers where leaves should be—that grew from her skin and vibrated in the air between them. When that shadow vine stilled, she suddenly felt calm again, at peace, quiet.

And she didn't want to be there any longer.

She didn't speak to any of them as she turned her back and left.

CHAPTER 25

Irial watched Leslie walk away with the Summer Queen's mortal. *What would he tell her?* It didn't truly matter, not now; she was his. Whatever they said or did wouldn't undo that.

"If anyone tries to take her from me, to come between us"—he pulled his gaze from Keenan to look at the Summer Queen—"*you* understand, don't you?"

She looked reluctant to answer.

"Aislinn?" Keenan took her hand in his.

She didn't react to either faery. "She's my friend. Leslie is not just some mortal; she's *my friend*. I should've acted when I saw you at the restaurant."

"It wouldn't have changed anything. She was already mine. That's why I was there." He reached out as if he'd touch her cheek, hand hovering by her sun-kissed face, and whispered, "What would you do to keep your mortal safe, Ash? Your Seth?"

"Anything."

"Exactly. You don't want to try to take Leslie from me. Your little kingling *did* tell you who it was that bound him, didn't he?" Irial waited for the flood of worry, of anger, of despair, and was surprised to find that the Summer Queen was in reasonable control of her emotions.

Looking rather like Gabriel's daughters, the Summer Queen cocked her head. "He did."

She stepped forward. Keenan didn't move to stop her. Instead he watched her with confidence, his emotions calmed. The Summer Queen let a trickle of sunlight seep into her voice, a tiny reminder of what she was, what she was capable of. She was close enough that the desert heat of her breath scorched Irial's face when she whispered, "Don't threaten me."

Irial held his hands up. "I'm not the one starting quarrels. I had business here: she's my business now." He felt ill at ease talking about her that way, his Leslie, his vulnerable mortal. So he changed the subject. "Thought I'd pay my respects to you while I was in the area . . . and check in on our Gancanagh. I find myself missing him lately."

Neither of the summer regents moved.

"To think of all the years he's wasted with you . . ." Irial shook his head. "What do you suppose it'd take to call him home to me?" Then he waited, looking forward to sating his hungers well enough to buy Leslie a few more hours to adjust before he started funneling the full weight of his appetite through her.

As the burst of Keenan's emotions seeped into Irial, the Dark King walked toward an open table. Keenan and Aislinn followed, as he knew they would, and sat down across from him. He traced a finger over the names—signs of mortals trying to leave a mark of their passing—that were carved into the surface. A waitress paused to offer them drinks, calling Aislinn and Keenan by name.

Irial accepted. "Whatever they usually have and coffee for me. Dark black."

The girl left, smiling a little longer than necessary at him.

If I could feed on them without an intermediary, like Gabriel's daughter had . . . He paused at that thought. *Had I known about Ani sooner . . .* But he hadn't. He was on this path, had found a solution. He'd look closer at Ani later.

First he'd get things with Leslie settled. If she was strong enough, she'd survive awhile, but in the end . . . in the end mortals always expired before faeries. They were such finite creatures. Their first heartbeat and memory were but a blink from death. To add the weight of nourishing his insatiable court in a time of peace was to hasten that unconscionably. Peace would kill his Leslie too soon, but war was never wise. It was a balance he needed. Being on the edge of violence but not down in it was what the Dark Court needed.

Irial returned his attention to the pair across from him. Aislinn was murmuring to Keenan, soothing him. "Calm down. Niall's not going anywhere . . . especially not to the Dark Court. He's safe—"

"Precious, you wound me." Irial laughed, immensely pleased by such naive belief, a true rarity in the courts. "Niall and I were *close*, if you will, before the young kingling was alive."

Keenan's anger flared. His fists were clenched so tightly, he was hurting himself. "And he's spent centuries suffering for it."

Irial leaned across the table. "Do you know how he struggles to deal with his yearning for Leslie? How very difficult . . ." He paused, pleased to see the tightening expression on Keenan's face. "But perhaps there's a reason he didn't tell you? Perhaps he's still more *my* court than yours. Perhaps he's been mine all along. . . ."

"Stay away from Niall," Keenan said. Waves of desert heat radiated from him, pulsing against them all.

Beside him, Aislinn absorbed that heat as quickly as Keenan released it. "Keenan. Damn it. We need to discuss Leslie's situation. Calm down or take a walk."

What a nice idea. Irial smiled at Aislinn. Then he turned back to Keenan, holding his gaze as he said, "He could reign in my court. What do you offer him? Servitude? Faeries? He's a *Gancanagh*, Keenan. He needs mortal touch or some focus to assuage the yearning. He has denied himself for centuries to protect you. What's he to do without a cause? Play nursemaid to the Summer Girls?"

Keenan struggled—and failed—to hide a flash of despair. A tiny rain shower began on the dance floor. The patrons squealed and laughed, no doubt explaining it away with a mundane answer—a faulty sprinkler head or leaky pipe.

"Niall is better off with me. His loyalty is to *my* court; that's cause enough," Keenan said.

"Did you know that he has seen Gabe of late?" Irial lowered his voice conspiratorially and added, "He's been under watch by Bananach. Do you think *she'd* bother with him if he weren't a part of my court?"

The heat radiating from Keenan's skin made the water in the room hiss into a steam. "He's not Dark Court. He belongs among faeries who don't torment him. He's happier—"

"No. He's not. The best we can hope for, kingling, is to find ways to be at peace with what we are. You understand that, don't you? He's teetering on the edge. You've given him the keys to his own destruction." Irial watched Keenan, saw the acknowledgment he knew he'd find if he pushed hard enough.

"Don't go there." Keenan was carefully not glancing at his queen, carefully not admitting that he'd manipulated Niall and put Leslie at risk.

"Walk away from this, kingling," Irial warned. "This isn't a conversation you really want to have. Is it?"

The Summer King lashed out, a sharp wind that burned across Irial's face, drawing blood to the surface. The intensity of the fury made it all the more nourishing for Irial.

Aislinn kissed Keenan's cheeks. "Go on. I can deal with him." She waved her hand at the crowd of mortals. Too many of them were watching, curious and eager. "They don't need to see this."

Keenan made an abrupt gesture toward several of the rowan-men, and the guards—who looked like nothing more than the ominous young men in the dark alleys of most cities—moved closer. They leaned against a nearby wall, shooting menacing looks at Irial. It was a charming little show, their posturing—as if any Summer Court fey could daunt the head of the Dark Court. Without another word, Keenan vanished into the half-drenched crowd on the dance floor.

Irial smiled at the young Summer Queen. "Now that he's gone, let's you and I get to know each other."

Aislinn gave him a smile that was caught between mortal innocence and faery cunning.

I could grow fond of this one. She was a more challenging adversary than Keenan right now.

"You shouldn't try Keenan like that. I'm not sure what secrets you two were exchanging, but this is *my* court now. Needling him isn't going to help." She didn't bother to keep the heat out of her voice, but unlike her king's, Aislinn's temper wasn't a concentrated slap. Instead the blistering summer heat pushed against Irial like a sudden gust, causing him to swallow hard against the taste of sand on his tongue.

Delicious. He drank down her acrid temper with relish. "Secrets? Keenan was brought up longing for power— power I took from him under the will of the Winter Court. We have a history . . . not quite as fulfilling as my bond with Niall, mind you, but the kingling has impotence issues with me."

"I know what your court is. I know what you do. You're responsible for the evil—"

"Evil?" He laughed then, letting every bit of his court's true nature into the sound.

The Summer Queen caught her breath. Her face flamed red, and the waves of anger radiating from her brought blisters to his skin.

"Not evil, child, and I'd rather you didn't insult me so"—Irial leaned closer, watching her face as she wrestled her emotions back into place—"because as much as I like your reaction, you've too many complications to interest me that way."

"If Keenan hears—"

"Tell him. Give him the extra reason to attack me." Irial licked his lips as if sand were truly a tangible thing, not simply a flavor in the air.

She switched topics. "Why are you trying to cause him troubles with Niall?"

"It behooves me." Irial saw no reason to be other than honest. "I understand addiction: it's one of my court's coins. Niall doesn't belong with Keenan, not now, not anymore. Keenan's mistreated him more than you know."

Aislinn's placid smile didn't waver, but tiny sparks of sunlight showed in her eyes. "What difference does it make to you?"

He leaned back and stretched his legs out in the aisle, as

comfortable as he could be in the crowd of frolicking mortals. "Would you believe I care for Niall?"

"No."

"Fey don't lie."

"Not overtly," she amended.

"Well, if you won't believe that"—he shrugged—"what can I say? I enjoy provoking the kingling." He reached out for her hand. Unlike most faeries, the Summer Queen had enough speed to avoid his touch—sunlight can move as quickly as shadows—but she didn't. Keenan would've.

Queens are so much more pleasing to deal with.

Irial was assailed by the seeping heat of summer's languor, steamy breezes, and a strange-sweet taste of humid air. It was lovely. He held on to her hand, knowing that she felt his court's essence as surely as he felt hers, watching her pulse flutter like a captured thing, caught and struggling.

She flushed and pulled her hand away. "Being tempted isn't the same as being interested. I'm tempted by *my* king every moment of every day . . . but I'm not interested in sex for empty pleasure, and if I were, it wouldn't be with you."

"I'm not sure who I should envy more—the kingling or your mortal toy," Irial said.

Sparks illuminated the club as her temper finally became less stable. But even as her mood vacillated, she wasn't as temperamental as Keenan. "Seth is not a toy"—she appraised him then with a clarity Keenan didn't have—"any more than Leslie is a toy to you. Is she?"

"Keenan won't understand that. When he took mortals, he took their mortality."

"And you?"

"I like Leslie's mortality the way it is." He shook out a cigarette, tapped it on the table. "This isn't a secret you'll get from me . . . any more than I'll tell you the kingling's secrets or Niall's."

"Why not just let her go?"

He stared at her, wondering idly if she'd light his cigarette. Miach, the last Summer King, used to derive curious amusement from lighting things afire. Somehow, Irial doubted Aislinn would, so he pulled out a lighter. "I'll not answer that, not now, not without a reason. She's mine. That's all that matters."

"What if I told you our court would take her back?"

He lit his cigarette, took a long drag, and exhaled. "You'd be wrong."

Irial didn't mention that the Summer King didn't care one whit about Leslie. The Summer Queen might care for his Leslie, but Keenan? He didn't truly care for anyone other than his own fey and his queen. *And not always to their best interests.*

Irritated but still in control of her emotions, Aislinn gave Irial a look that would send most fey to their knees. Before she could speak, he caught one of her hands again. She struggled in his grip, her skin growing hot as molten steel.

"Leslie belongs to me, as surely as your Seth belongs to you, as the Summer Girls belong to Keenan."

"She's my friend."

"Then you should've done something to protect her. Do you know what's been done to her? How lost she's been? How afraid? How very, very broken?"

As much as he found it touching that Aislinn cared for his girl, it wasn't reason enough to sacrifice Leslie. They hadn't protected her, hadn't kept her safe, hadn't made her happy. He would do those things. "When she adjusts to the changes—"

"What changes? You said she was still mortal. What did you do?"

Tiny storm clouds clustered around them until the club was hazy with them. The conversation wasn't going to improve, so Irial stood and bowed. "My court deals in darker things than yours. The rest is not mine to say. Later, if she wants to, she'll tell you."

Then he left the Summer Queen and her retinue of scowling guards. Despite his court's need for dissension among the denizens of Faerie, he had no patience for politics, not now. He had something—*someone*—more important to attend to.

CHAPTER 26

Leslie and Seth were several blocks away before she finally asked, "Do you know what's going on?"

Without missing a step, Seth said, "They're not human. None of them."

"Right." She scowled. "Thanks. Joking really helps."

"I'm not joking, Leslie." He glanced past her as if someone were there and smiled at the empty street. "Ask Irial for the Sight. Tell him you deserve it."

"The Sight?" She didn't smack him, but she wanted to. She felt utterly off-kilter, and he was mocking her.

"And guards," he added. Then he stopped and motioned to the open space in front of her. "Show her."

"Show me wha—"

A girl with black leathery wings appeared. She smiled in a predatory way. "Ooh, are we going to get to play?"

Niall's voice came from behind her, "Take a walk, Cerise. She belongs to Irial now."

"Irial took a mortal? Really? I heard rumors, but . . . hmm, she's a bit plain, isn't she?" The winged girl looked astounded, amused, and curious all at once.

Leslie stared at her: she couldn't turn to look at Niall, couldn't begin to get her head around what he had just said. *Belong? What about us? What about everything he whispered to me? Belong?* A burst of anger consumed her sadness but faded immediately. *Belong? Like a trinket? I* belong *to myself.* But she didn't say any of it, didn't turn to face him with confusion written plainly on her face. Instead she stepped up to the winged girl, Cerise.

Cerise flapped her wings. "They're real." And with her backless top, it was obvious that the wings were truly sprouting from her skin. "Oh, sweetie, you're in for a good time. That one has stamina you wouldn't believe—"

Then something—unseen—grabbed Cerise from behind; she started to move backward without any obvious effort on her part. Surges of loathing for Cerise rolled through the air from that unseen thing into Leslie's skin, filling her and fleeing before they settled.

"Fine. I'm going," Cerise snapped. Then she waved as she disappeared. Her disembodied voice called, "See you around, babe."

Leslie slid to the sidewalk. She was trembling, shaking from whatever was wrong with her. It wasn't just that she could tell what others were feeling: it was more now. The feelings around her were almost tactile, and they were slithering under her skin.

"She had wings," she said.

Seth nodded.

"And vanished? She really vanished?" Leslie tried to keep her focus. Somewhere in the apartments above her, a woman was weeping with a sorrow so heavy, it made Leslie think she was swallowing copper.

Niall reached down and helped Leslie to her feet. He bent so his lips were against her face. Gently he murmured, "I've failed you yet again. But I'm not giving up. Just remember that: I won't let him keep you."

Leslie looked from him to Seth. She wanted Seth to tell her this was a joke, wanted him to tell her things hadn't become hopelessly weird. Seth had been around as long as she'd lived in Huntsdale. If he told her it was okay . . .

But Seth shook his head. "Ask Irial for the Sight and guards of your own."

"Guards? They can't protect her from what she needs protection from, from *him*," Niall snarled before looking back at her. His expression softened then, and he whispered, "Don't forget: surviving is what matters. You can do this."

Tish stepped from the shadows in front of them. "You shouldn't touch Leslie."

Leslie tried to focus on the girl. The whole world had shifted, and Leslie was starting to believe that it wouldn't be getting stable again anytime soon. The symphony of flavors wafted from the walls around her, crept toward her from nearby rooms, and battered her skin. She closed her eyes and tried to catalogue the tastes as they ran through her. There were too many.

Niall slowly stepped back, assuring that she was steady on her feet before he let go.

"Are you sick?" Tish had her tiny hands on Leslie's forehead, her cheeks. "Is it from the ink? Let me see."

"I'm fine." Leslie slapped Tish's hand away from her shirt, anxious at the thought of sharing her tattoo—*our tattoo, mine and Irial's*—right now. "What do you want? Why are you—"

"I saw you at the club but couldn't expose myself there." Tish still stared only at Leslie.

Expose herself? With the deluge of emotions distracting her so, Leslie was having trouble figuring out what to say or do. All she could ask was, "Do you know Seth?"

Tish glanced briefly at Seth, sizing him up with a look that would've done Ani proud. "Ash's toy?"

Beside Seth, Niall stiffened, but Seth put a hand out.

"I don't get it, but"—Tish shrugged—"not my business."

Then she laced her fingers through Leslie's and started talking as if there were no one else around. "You seemed like you were having fun earlier. Rabbit would kick my ass if I didn't bring you to him, though. You're pale. The first day is rough for humans."

"Humans?" Leslie almost laughed at how very surreal the night had become. "What does that make *you*?"

But Tish was still talking, ignoring the question, "Let's

get you checked out. Make sure you're all good when he comes for you."

"I'm fine," Leslie insisted although she knew she wasn't. "But yeah, let's go see Rabbit. Just to . . . He?"

"Iri," Tish said gleefully. "You want to be ready for him, don't you?"

"For Irial?" Leslie repeated, looking back over her shoulder at Niall. He had a horrible expression of pain on his face. *Chicory tangled with copper sorrow.*

"Survive," he mouthed as he touched the scar on his face.

And she paused, remembering the way her vision had shifted when Niall had walked her to Seth's. She turned her head, looking at Niall and Seth from the corner of her eye: Seth looked the same as he always had. Niall didn't. His scar glared like a fresh jagged wound; his eyes reflected the streetlight like an animal's. His bones weren't quite right, like there were extra lengths or joints where she had none. His cheekbones were too severe for a human's face, too angular, and his skin glowed as if illuminated by a light inside him, as if his skin were too sheer, like parchment over a flame. She pulled her hand out of Tish's grasp and stepped toward him.

"He couldn't tell you," Seth said.

Leslie couldn't move closer, couldn't find words, staring at Niall as he glowed.

Niall held her gaze. "I negotiated with my queen to be allowed to protect you. I'm sorry I failed, Leslie. I . . . I'm so sorry."

"Your queen?" she asked, but she suspected the answer before she heard it. She looked at Seth.

"Ash," Seth confirmed. "She didn't want you involved in this world. She wanted to keep you safe from them."

He motioned behind her, where there were now almost two dozen people who didn't look anywhere near human. Like the crowd at the Rath, they all seemed to be wearing elaborate costumes. But they weren't costumes.

"What are they?" she asked.

"Faeries."

Leslie looked at them: no one was what they'd seemed a few minutes ago. Nothing made sense. *I am angry now. I am afraid.* Yet she couldn't feel those things. She felt curiosity, surprise, and a vague sense of euphoria that she knew— objectively—should be more terrifying than the rest.

"Ash rules one of the faery courts, the Summer Court. She shares the throne with Keenan," Seth said without any inflection, but Leslie felt—*tasted*—his worries, his fears, his anger, his jealousy. It was all there under the surface.

She looked back at Niall—not from the corner of her eye, but full on. He still looked like he was glowing. She gestured at him. "What? Why can I see you like this now?"

"You already know. I don't need to wear a glamour." Niall stepped forward, walking toward her.

"She's Irial's now. *Ours.*" Tish gestured toward the shadows, and at least six of the thorn-covered men stepped in front of Leslie, blocking Niall. As they did so, the dread-locked quints from the Rath appeared beside Niall. They were growling, as was he. He bared his teeth.

More people appeared as she watched. *No, not people, creatures of some sort, stepping out of empty air.* Some were armed with strange weapons—short curved knives that looked like they were made of rock and bone, long blades of bronze and silver. Others grinned cruelly as they lined up to face one another, except for a small group that encircled her and another that encircled Seth.

Tish—who looked no different, despite claiming affiliation with whatever weird creatures these were—stepped forward slowly, like a predator stalking prey. "I speak with Irial's blessing tonight, to look after Leslie, to keep her safe for him. You don't want to try us, Niall."

Niall's tense posture—his rage humming in his bones like an elixir Leslie could drown in—said what his words did not: he very much wanted to move toward violence.

And Leslie, for all the oddity of the moment, wanted him to. She wanted the lot of them to tear into one another. She wanted their violence, their excitement, their rivalry and hatred. It was a craving deep inside her, a hunger that was not her own. She swayed on her feet as their emotions tangled into her.

Then the circle around her parted. Tish bowed her head briefly and took Leslie's hand. She raised her voice enough to be heard over the growls and mutterings of the crowd. "Would you start a war over the girl, Niall?"

"I would love to," he answered.

"Are you *allowed* to?" Tish asked.

There was silence then. Finally Niall replied, "My court has forbidden me from doing so."

"Then go home," Tish said. She motioned toward the shadows. "Dad, can you carry her?"

Leslie turned and saw Gabriel. The tattoos on his arms shifted in the low light, as if they were poised to run. *That's not possible either. But it's real. And they want me . . . for what? Why?* She couldn't panic. She felt like it was there, though, a panic just out of reach, a thought of an emotion. *What did they do to me?*

"Hey, girl." Gabriel smiled gently as he approached her. "Let's get you out of here, okay?"

And she felt herself being lifted, held aloft as Gabriel ran through the streets faster than she'd ever moved in her life. There were no sounds, no sights, only darkness and Irial's voice from somewhere far away: *"Rest now, darling. I'll see you later."*

CHAPTER 27

Niall was only halfway into the front room of the loft when he said, "Leslie's gone. I don't ask much, haven't in all these years—"

Keenan raised a hand that glowed with pulsing sunlight. "Does Irial hold sway over you, Niall?"

"What?" Niall stood motionless as he reined in his own emotions.

The Summer King scowled but didn't answer. The plants in the loft bent under the force of the desert wind that was picking up speed as Keenan's emotions fluctuated; the birds had retreated to their safe nooks in the columns. *At least the Summer Girls are out.* Keenan sent the remaining guards away with a few terse words. Then he began pacing. Eddies of steamed air swirled through the room, twisting and spiraling as if ghostly figures were hidden in them, only to be slashed apart by the hot winds already shrieking around them—all of which were then washed away by bursts of rain. Made manifest by the king's warring emotions, the climates clashed in the small space and left disaster behind.

Then Keenan paused to say, "Do you think often of Irial? Feel sympathy for his court?"

"What are you talking about?" Niall asked.

Keenan gripped the sofa cushions, clearly trying to find a way to restrain his emotions. The storm whipped through the room, shredding the leaves of the trees, sending glass-work sculptures crashing to the ground.

"I've made the choices I needed to, Niall. I won't be bound again. I won't go back to that. I won't be weakened by Irial. . . ." Sunlight shone from Keenan's eyes, from his lips. The sofa cushions caught fire.

"You aren't making any sense, Keenan. If you have a point, make it." Niall's own temper wasn't as volatile, even after all these centuries with Keenan, but it was far crueler than Keenan could ever be. "Irial took Leslie. We don't have time for—"

"Irial's still fond of you." Keenan had a pensive look as he asked a question he'd not ever asked directly before: "How do you feel about him?"

Niall froze, staring at his friend, his cause, his reason for *everything* over so many centuries. That Keenan would ask such a question stung. "Don't do this. Don't ask me questions about *before*."

Keenan didn't answer, didn't apologize for salting old

wounds. He went to stare out the window as the sandstorm in the room stilled. The Summer King was calm again.

Niall, however, fought to control his own emotions. This wasn't a conversation he wanted to have, not now when he was worried about Leslie and furious with Irial. Once, Niall had placed his trust in another king, and that had been a mistake. Back then, Irial had revealed that he'd known all along that the mortals Niall had lain with were sickened and addicted. He'd told Niall that those mortals died—but not until after the dark faeries had brought the mortals to their *bruig* for entertainment. He'd explained that Niall's addictive nature was simply part of being a Gancanagh. Niall had run then, but Gabriel had come for him. He brought Niall back into the Dark Court's *bruig*, the faery mound where Irial was waiting.

"You could rule my court someday, Gancanagh," Irial had murmured as he brought forth the mortals who'd been addicted—and were mad with wanting.

"Linger with us," he whispered. *"This is where you belong. With me. Nothing has changed."*

Around them, the addicted mortals grappled at the willing fey like they were starving for touch, too sick with withdrawal to think of the consequences of contact with thorn-covered bodies and incompatible shapes.

And Niall had been disgusted that he'd all but handed mortals over to the Dark Court, and when Irial offered him a
trade—*"You entertain the court or they can, Gancanagh. Fear
and pain is the coin for their ransom. It matters little to me
who pays it"*—Niall had thought to do the right thing,
giving his vow freely in exchange for the release of the
addicts. In the end, it hadn't mattered: the addicts still withered away, pleading for the drug that was in Niall's skin.

Keenan was speaking again. "What you are has never
been used as an asset to our court." He had a faraway look,
both pensive and calculating. "If I'm to keep our court safe,
I need to use all our assets."

Keenan uncorked a bottle that had been sitting on a
warming tray, poured the honeyed drink into two glasses,
and held one out.

Niall couldn't respond, couldn't speak. He just stared at
his king.

"Even with Irial swaying her, Leslie will want you, and
he still wants you. We can use this to learn the other secrets
Irial's court hides from us." Keenan offered Niall the glass
again. "Come now. He'll not strike out at you. Mayhap
he'll share the girl, and—"

"You knew. That Leslie was marked by him, that—"

"No. I knew there were mortals being marked and taken
in by Dark Court faeries. I hoped we'd have learned more
by now, sorting out why or how they were bonding with
mortals. Now we just need to reassess. This isn't over. She
wants you. I saw her watching you before this all began. I

can't think Irial's claiming her will erase that. This could be better than I'd hoped. If she survives, she'll be in a position to learn much. She'll tell you. She'll do what you want just to be near you." Keenan offered the glass a third time. "Drink with me, Niall. Don't let this put us asunder."

Niall took the glass and, watching Keenan as he did it, dropped it on the floor. "I've lived for you, Keenan. My life, my every decision for nine gods-damned centuries. How could you violate her like—"

"I'm not the one who violated the girl. It's not my blood under her skin. Irial—"

"*Irial* wasn't the one playing me this time, was he?" Niall bowed his head as rage vied with despair. "How could you *use me*, Keenan? How could you keep secrets from me? You manipulated me. . . ." He took a step closer to Keenan, approaching his king with anger, with the temptation to raise a hand to the faery he'd sworn to protect, to honor with his last breath. "You *still* want to use me. You knew, and—"

"I'd heard about their ink exchanges, suspected that Leslie was one of them, but finding out the secrets of the Dark Court is far from easy. She's just one mortal. I can't save them all, and if one or two fall so we can keep them all safe . . . This is no different than it's ever been." Keenan didn't back up, didn't summon guards to his side. "We can use this to have what we both want."

"You encouraged my interest in Leslie, set me up to dis-obey Aislinn, my queen, *your queen*."

"I did."

As Niall stood there, trembling in his anger, all of Keenan's statements of late came crashing in on him; the truth of what Niall hadn't seen, by trust or foolishness, was heart crushing. "And you don't feel any remorse, do you? What she's suffering—"

"Irial is a threat to our court." Keenan shrugged. "The Dark Court is too awful to be allowed to thrive. You know as well as I what they've done. You bear the scars. I won't have him strong enough to threaten our court, especially our queen. He needs to be kept in check."

"So why not tell me?" Niall watched his king, hoping for some answer that would ease the weight that threatened to break Niall's spirit as surely as the Dark Court once had.

But Keenan didn't offer such an answer. Instead he said, "And have you do what? Tell the girl? I saw you swaying to her as it was. Mine was a better plan. I needed you to have a focus, and she's as good a focus as any."

Niall heard the logic in the words, had heard his king speak thusly over the centuries when he seduced the mortals who were now Summer Girls. It didn't change anything: Niall's loyalty and partnership were rewarded by disregard and cavalier dismissal.

"I can't accept . . . won't accept this," Niall said. "I'm done."

"What do you mean?"

So Niall said the words that would undo his oath: "My fealty to the Summer Court is rescinded. You are my king no more." It was a simple thing to end what should matter so much. A few words, and he was alone in the world again.

"Niall, think about it. This isn't worth leaving." Keenan sounded nothing like the faery Niall had thought him to be. "What was I to do?"

"Not this." He stepped around Keenan. "I'd rather be solitary, courtless, without a home or king . . . than be used."

He didn't slam the door, didn't rage, didn't weep. He simply left.

Several hours later, Niall was still walking through the streets of Huntsdale. There was some sort of event, leaving the streets full and noisy, matching the din inside him. *I'm not any better than Irial. I'd have made her addicted like the junkies she fears.* And his king had known that, used that. *I failed her.*

It wasn't often that he lamented being the one who followed and never led, but as he walked through the dirty mortal streets, he wondered if he'd made the right choice so long ago when Irial'd offered to make Niall his successor. *At least then I'd have more choices.*

Niall waded through the mostly mortal crowd. The fey who mingled with them hurriedly stepped out of his path. As the crowd moved, Niall saw him: Irial lounged against a storefront.

"I heard you were out and about," the Dark King said, "but I was beginning to think my fey were wrong."

"I want to talk to you," Niall began.

"I'll always welcome you, Gancanagh. That hasn't changed." Irial gestured to the tiny park across the street. "Walk with me."

Vendors were selling sweets from their carts; drunken mortals laughed and shouted. A game of some sort or perhaps a concert must be letting out. People crowded the streets so much that traffic was unable to move. The Dark King wove through the stopped cars and angrily honking drivers, past a group of mortals singing quite poorly and doing what they seemed to think was dancing.

Once in the park, Irial motioned to a stone bench his fey had just finished clearing. "This is your sort of place, isn't it? Would you rather go—"

"It's fine." But Niall stood, leaning against a tree, not at ease with having his back to the fey roaming the street.

Irial shrugged as he folded himself gracefully onto the bench, looking perversely like an ingénue unaware of the effect he had on the gaping mortals around them. "So"—he lit a cigarette—"I expect you're here about my Leslie."

"She's not yours."

Irial took a long drag off the cigarette. "You think?"

"Yes. I do." Niall turned slightly, watching several faeries who were approaching from the left. He didn't trust Irial or the solitary faeries who were watching or—actually he didn't trust anyone right then.

Irial motioned several of his faeries closer and directed, "I want the immediate area empty." Then he turned his attention to Niall. "Sit. I'll not allow *any* harm to you while you sit with me—my vow on that."

Stunned by the generous vow Irial'd offered him—*no harm at all,* thus saying his own safety was secondary to Niall's—he sat and stared at the Dark King. It didn't change things, though: a moment of kindness didn't undo Leslie's situation or Irial's long-ago cruelty.

"Leslie's not yours," Niall said. "She's her own, bond or not. You just don't realize it yet."

"Aaah, you're still a fool, Gancanagh." Irial exhaled a cloud of smoke and leaned back. "A passionate one, but a fool nonetheless."

Niall said it then, the words he'd never thought to say to Irial, the start of a conversation that had once been his greatest nightmare. "Would you trade for her freedom?"

Something indecipherable flashed in Irial's eyes as he lowered his cigarette. "Perhaps. What are you offering?"

"What do you want?"

A weary look passed over Irial's face. "Sometimes, I'm not sure anymore. I've held this court through the wars between Beira and the last Summer King, through Beira's fits of temper, but this new order . . . I'm tired, Niall. What do I want?" Irial's usual facade—half amused and half callous—returned then. "What does any king want? I want to keep my fey safe."

"How does Leslie fit into that?"

"Are you asking for the kingling or for yourself?" Irial's tone was once more the needling one he so often used when they spoke: the Dark King had never quite forgiven Niall for running. They both knew that.

"What do you want from me in exchange? I'm here to bargain. What's your price, Irial?" Niall felt such a swirl of emotions at actually saying the words—self-disgust that he'd failed Leslie, anger that his king had failed him, dismay that he was touched by Irial's kindness. "I know how this works. Tell me what you're willing to give up and what it'll cost me."

"You never did figure it out, did you?" Irial asked incredulously. But before Niall could speak, Irial held up his hand. "Revel in the feelings you're fighting not to show me, and I'll answer you."

"Do *what*?" Niall had heard of odd bargains, but here he was exposing himself to Irial's whims, and the Dark King offered answers in exchange for "giving in to his feelings." Niall scowled. "What sort of—"

"Stop holding all those darker feelings in, and I'll give you the answers you need." Irial smiled like they were friends who'd been having a reasonable conversation. "Just let yourself feel your emotions, Niall. That's all I ask, and I'll share information commensurate in worth with what you feel and how fully you feel it."

"How will you—"

"Gancanagh . . . would you rather I ask for other favors? I'd rather not bargain with baser coins, not with you, not with anyone I have affection for." Irial leaned close enough and smiled such a wicked smile that Niall was reminded of more pleasant times with Irial long ago, before Niall knew who and what Irial was, before he knew what he himself was.

So Niall let his temper reign, released his hold on that pit of anger at Keenan's betrayal, let it bubble over. It wasn't an emotion he often let reign, but it was the one he'd been trying to quell for hours. It was almost a relief to feel the rage.

Irial's pupils dilated. His hands clenched. "That's one."

Niall thought about the mortals he'd wooed and left wasting away when he knew no better, thought of Leslie pliable and eager in his arms. He could picture her, kiss-drunk, and he wanted that—wanted *her* with a longing that was heavier for being denied.

"Two . . . Just one more emotion, Gancanagh," Irial murmured.

And Niall imagined wrapping his hands around Irial's throat, letting free the jealousy that he felt at the idea of Irial's hands on Leslie—or of her hands on Irial.

With a shaky hand Irial lit another cigarette. "You play the game well, Gancanagh. I wondered once what you'd do with the knowledge."

Niall watched, studying the Dark King with a distant calm now, feeling no true emotions at all. "What knowledge?"

"The dark fey starve without emotion, darker emotions. It's what"—Irial took a drag off his cigarette—"sustains us. Food, drink, air. Everything. There's a great secret, Niall.

There's the thing that the others would use against us if they knew."

Niall hesitated. Part of him wondered why Irial would take such a risk, why he would reveal his secrets, but another less easily embraced part knew exactly why Irial would do so: he trusted Niall. He looked away, lamenting the fact that Irial's trust wasn't misplaced. "So why doesn't Keenan notice? Or Sorcha? How did *I* not know?"

"His volatile nature? Her imperviousness to anything she doesn't like?" Irial tapped his ash onto the ground. "And you . . . I don't know. I thought you'd figured it out back then, and when I realized the kingling didn't know, I hoped that what we—"

"All of your court feeds like this?" Niall stopped him, not wanting to think about his time with Irial, the realization that Niall's blurry weeks of mad pleasures had nourished Irial—as, no doubt, had the horrific things that followed when Niall ran.

"They do, or they get weak." The Dark King's face revealed a raw pain that was almost embarrassing to see, like glimpsing someone's most private aches. "Guin died . . . from a mortal bullet. She was shot."

Irial stared at the crowd. A barefoot girl was dancing on the hood of a parked car. The driver was holding out her shoes and gesturing at the ground. Irial smiled at them before turning back and adding, "You care for Leslie. If you had known she was already mine, you would've tried even harder to keep her from me. You'd have fought for her."

I knew Irial wanted her and—Niall stopped himself, uneasy with the fact that Irial could read what he was feeling, and more important, that Niall could use this knowledge to destroy Irial. If the courts knew that they were so easily read and assessed, it would be hard to convince any of them to tolerate the Dark Court's continued existence.

"Beira knew all of this," Niall said.

"We needed her. She needed us. Else I wouldn't have helped her bind the kingling. She kept things in upheaval when my fey needed it."

"And Leslie fits in how?"

"I needed a backup plan." Irial smiled, but this time it was dark and deadly, tinged with more than a little challenge. "I need her."

"You can't have her," Niall started. But Irial gripped his arms: every lovely memory Niall had run from and every whispered horror of the Dark Court came rushing to his mind in a morass—then Niall felt like he was swallowing it, like he'd been drinking that too-sweet, forcibly forgotten wine. "Stop."

Irial let go of him. "I know Keenan has misled and deceived you. I know he was sending you to our girl, putting her in your path. Gabriel watched you struggle with your response to her. . . . I will not mislead you, not again. I would welcome you back into my home, where Leslie will be. I would still offer you my throne when you are ready."

Niall blanched. He'd been willing to endure whatever

he'd needed to in exchange for Leslie's freedom. *Kingship? Affection?* That was not at all what he'd expected. *It's a ruse, just like always. There was never anything real in what we once were.* Niall ignored all of it. "Would you let her go free in exchange for my fealty?"

"No. She stays, but if you want to be with her, you are ever welcome." Irial stood and bowed from the waist as if Niall were his equal. "I won't let my court suffer, even for you. You know what my secrets are, what I am, what I offer you still. I can promise you that she will be kept as happy as I can make her. Beyond that . . . come home with us or not. It is your choice to make. It has always been your choice."

And Niall stared at him, speechless, unsure of what answer he could offer that made any sense. He'd spent a long time not remembering the bond he'd shared with Irial, not longing for those years, and not admitting any of this each time he'd crossed paths with Irial. He realized now, though, that no matter how carefully he'd guarded his secrets, he'd been transparent to Irial. If the Dark King could read his emotions, could taste them, he'd known of Niall's weaknesses each time they'd met. *I've been exposed to him the whole time.* Irial didn't shame him for it. Instead he held out the same acceptance he'd offered centuries ago— and Niall didn't, couldn't, reply.

Irial said, "It's been a long time that you've been living for Keenan, paying back some perceived debt. We are what we are, Niall, neither as good or as evil as others paint us.

And what we are doesn't change how truly we feel, only how free we are to follow those feelings."

Then he slipped away into the crowd, dancing with mortals as he went and looking every bit like he belonged there among them.

CHAPTER 28

It was evening when Leslie woke in her own room, wearing the same clothes she'd worn the night before. She'd slept for more than twelve hours, as if her body were fighting off a flu or hangover. She still didn't feel right. The skin around her tattoo felt tight, stretched too thin. It didn't burn, or itch, or anything that would make her suspect infection. If anything, it felt too good, as if extra nerves were throbbing there.

Downstairs she could hear cartoons. Ren laughed. Someone else coughed. Others spoke in low voices and broken sentences she couldn't quite understand. She started to feel the familiar panic, terror that she was here, that she had no clue which of the others were down there.

Idly she wondered when her father had last been home. She hadn't seen him. *Someone would call if he died.* She didn't worry over him as she had done for so long. *I should.* Panic started to choke her. Then it just vanished. She knew that she had changed, and that Irial, who'd caused that change, wasn't human.

Am I?

Whatever Irial had done, whatever Rabbit had done, whatever her friends had hidden from her . . . She wanted to feel angry. Objectively, she knew she should feel betrayed, feel despair—rage, even. She tried to summon those feelings, but only the shadows of them rose. The emotions weren't hers for more than a moment before they fled.

Then Ren was calling up the stairs in a strangled voice, "Leslie?"

With a calm that should have been impossible, she rolled out of bed and went to her door. She was unafraid. It was a remembered feeling, one she liked. After turning the locks—which someone had thrown—she walked to the top of the stairs. As she looked down, she saw him, Irial, standing there beside her brother.

"What are *you* doing here?" she said. Her voice was even, but she shivered. This emotion, excitement, didn't flee. Unlike the others, this one stayed and grew.

"Seeing you." He held out a hand. "Assuring that you are well."

Ren stood beside Irial, trying to get his attention. "Umm, you need . . . anything? Anything at all?"

"Careful," Irial murmured, unmindful of everyone but her. His hands were on her hips then.

How did he get up the stairs so quickly?

"Don't. Please?" She wished she didn't feel so comforted

that he was here, wished she were sure what she was asking when she repeated, "Please?"

"I'm not here to hurt you, *a ghrá*." He stepped backward, not looking as he walked down the stairs, not removing his hands from her hips, either.

"You didn't lie, did you?"

"We don't."

Leslie stared at Irial. "Who are you? *What* are you?"

He held her gaze, and for an unreal moment she thought she saw shadows clinging to his skin like dark wings. Her body tingled all over, and she was sure that innumerable tiny mouths touched her skin all at once—soothing her, erasing everything but pleasure. She shivered against the sudden onset of cravings that made no sense. Her mouth was dry, her palms damp, her heart thundering in her head.

Without breaking her gaze, he said, "I'll take care of you, keep you from hurting or pain. You have my vow on this, Leslie. You'll never want anything again. Say the word, and it's yours. No more fear or pain. Just shadows of them, and I'll take them away. You won't have to feel them but for a moment. Look." He dropped his gaze to the air between them. A shadowy vine extended from his body to hers, coiling into her skin. She reached out as if she'd touch it; her hands brushed against the black feathers that curled from it like leaves. When she did, they both flinched.

"It's real. Whatever you did to me," she said.

"You wanted to be safe. You wanted to be without fear or pain. You have it." Irial didn't wait for her to move; he pulled her closer so she was leaning against him. He smelled like peat smoke, musty rooms full of sex and longing, sweet-strange and dizzying. She rubbed her cheek against his shirt, breathing in the scent of him.

"I'll never leave you," Irial whispered. Then he turned to the assembled crowd. "If anyone ever touches her again—"

The dealer started, "When I . . . I didn't know she was your—"

Irial made a gesture. Two very scarred guys appeared out of the empty air. They stepped forward and took hold of the dealer.

He was one of them. Leslie's knees buckled. *He . . .* Her stomach burned as she tried to let that thought finish itself. The terror of the other people in the room, of the dealer who was crying out as he was led away—she felt that too, all of it at once. The lust of the mortals—*mortals?*—in the room, the want, the desperate need. She felt a tangle of emotions assailing her. Flashes of need, of terror, of aching—they flooded her body until she swayed.

"Their feelings . . . I need . . ." She clenched Irial's hand.

"Shhh." He kissed her, and the feelings evaporated. "They just come through you. Those feeling aren't yours. Just a blink, and they're gone from you."

He had an arm around her, leading her to the sofa.

She stared at the door where the guys—*where did they come from?*—had led the dealer away.

Irial was kneeling in front of her. "It'll all be fine. No one will hurt you again. Ever. You will get used to the rest."

Mutely she nodded, watching him the way she'd never watched anyone in her life, transfixed. Irial could make everything good, right, happy. He was an answer to a question she'd forgotten to ask. Her body hummed in a pleasant blur. The feelings that had rolled through her were awful, ugly; she knew that objectively. After Irial took them, all she felt was bliss. Something heavy and floral was in her mouth, on her lips. *Lust. His. Mine.* Her veins sang with it, like fire coursing through her body, seeking her heart, flooding her nerves.

Then Niall's words echoed in her head, "Surviving is what matters. You can do this." *Do what? Survive what?* There was nothing bad here. Irial was making her safe. He was taking care of her.

"Come now. They'll pack your things." Irial motioned at three almost-androgynous guys who were headed up the stairs. "We need to get out of here. Away from so many mortals. Talk."

"Talk?" She almost laughed. Talking was pretty far from what was on her mind as he knelt there in front of her. Her eyes felt too wide. Every pore in her body was awake and zinging.

"Or whatever else would make you happy," he added with a wicked grin. "You've done me a great honor, Leslie. The world is yours."

"I don't need the world. I need—" She leaned forward until she was able to rest her face against his chest, hating the cloth that was in her way, suddenly furious at the damnable material. She snarled—then froze, realizing that her hand was already tearing at his shirt, that she'd made a sound that was so far from normal, so far from human that she should be terrified.

He pulled her to her feet, keeping her clutched tightly to his side. "It's fine. Just the initial changes. Shhh."

And as he breathed deeply, it *was* fine. He was still talking, though, asking, "What shall I do with them?"

Ren and the others were watching with looks of abject terror. But they didn't matter now; none of this mattered anymore. *Only Irial. Only this pleasure, this confidence.* That was all that mattered.

"Who cares?" she said.

Then he lifted her into his arms and carried her over the threshold into a world that was suddenly far more tempting than she'd realized it could be.

CHAPTER 29

Niall had walked out on his king; he'd failed Leslie; and he'd exposed his doubts and longings to Irial. He hadn't had such a complete feeling of loss in centuries. He'd spent part of the night and the whole of the day walking aimlessly but had come no closer to any answers or even the right questions.

He'd seen the faeries watching him: Keenan's and Irial's and those who were solitary. *Like I am again.* None of them, even those who'd tried to speak with him, had made him pause. Several times he'd had to move them bodily from his path, but he hadn't spoken a word or registered the words that they spoke.

But then Bananach was swaying toward him, moving like a shadow in the just-fallen night. The long feathers that spilled down her back fluttered and shifted in the breeze. She wore a glamour that made those feathers look like hair, playing mortal for him as she approached.

He stopped walking.

The smile she offered him was at odds with the malice in her eyes. She passed him, paused, looked back, and beckoned. She did not watch to see if he'd follow her as she walked into a narrow alley partway down the block. She did not glance back as she slipped under the metal fence or as she trailed her fingers over the razor wire that draped the top of that fence. It was only once Niall was standing behind her, like prey foolishly pursuing a predator, that she turned to face him.

Niall wondered if he was following her to his death: it was a fate he had considered and rejected after Irial allowed the Dark Court to torture him. *It wasn't the right choice then.* Bananach would gladly have taken Niall's life at the time had Irial not sent her away to indulge in her mayhem. *It's never the right choice.*

But he didn't retreat.

She leaned on the metal fence, her arm stretched over her head, her fingers curled around the loops in the fence. The barbed steel of the razor wire was just above her fingers, close enough that it looked like she was reaching for the poisonous metal. It was unhealthily attractive to him, her desire to touch pain.

He kept his distance and his silence.

She tilted her head to stare at him. The avian gesture contrasted with the mortal glamour she held on to as she waited. "Irial needs replacing," she said.

"And you're telling me this why?"

"Because *you* can give me change. He's not right for us. Not now." Her glamour shivered, flickering in and out. "Help me. Bring me my wars again."

"I don't want war. I want . . ." He glanced away, not knowing what he truly wanted. He'd followed her into a too-small space, pursuing the temptation of her violence. *And leaving Leslie to figure out the impossible on her own if I give in to the temptation of self-destruction.* He'd run away from Irial, from Keenan. He was still running. "I'm not going to help you."

"Smart answer, pretty boy." Gabriel appeared beside him. The Hound held an arm out, tattoos racing furiously over his skin, and motioned for Niall to step back. "You need to move along now."

Bananach snapped her mouth open and closed. Her glamour faded, revealing her sharp beak. "Your meddling is getting tiresome. If the Gancanagh wants to stay with me . . ."

Gabriel stepped in front of Niall just as Bananach launched herself forward. She shrieked, a sound that might have been laughter or anger or some combination of the two. Her hands were splayed open, her fingertips black talons.

"Court business, Niall. Go on now," Gabriel said without glancing back.

Gabriel lifted Bananach and hurled her into the metal fence. Her feathers snagged on the razor wire, but she yanked herself away. Shredded feathers drifted to the ground behind her and were lost on the shadowed pavement.

Niall wanted to leave, to stay, to tell Gabriel to get out of the way so Bananach could end the confusion and depression that had been weighing on him, to tell Gabriel to rip into her. Instead he stood still, watching, no more resolved than he'd been when Bananach had beckoned him to follow her.

It wasn't truly beautiful to watch Gabriel in action, but there was a brutal harmony in his movements. Like the Summer Girls' dancing, Gabriel's fighting had a rhythm to it, a song of its own. But the Hound's moves were well matched by Bananach's fury. The raven-woman was gleeful as she darted away and then returned to dive at Gabriel with abandon. From somewhere she drew a bone blade that glowed with preternatural light. Her black-taloned nails stood in relief against white bone and red blood as she slashed Gabriel from his left brow to his right cheek.

The fresh blood drew cries of pleasure from a group of Ly Ergs who filed into the enclosed lot from the street. Their red hands twitched in unison as they began circling Gabriel. They took some of their sustenance from freshly drawn blood, a habit that Niall had found disquieting when he'd learned of it. There weren't enough of them to over-come Gabriel, but with Bananach there too . . . *It's not really my business. It's Dark Court business. Which is not my court.*

Niall started to step out of their path, but leaving Gabriel to a half dozen Ly Ergs and a blood-mad Bananach wasn't something that set well with him. Gabriel's arrival had prevented Bananach from seriously wounding or killing him. He owed Gabriel for that. The Hound might not expect it, but Niall expected it of himself. That was one thing he hadn't lost, his honor.

He threw himself into the fracas—not for a court or a king, but because it was the right thing to do. Standing by while someone—even Gabriel—was outnumbered wasn't an option.

Niall didn't worry about consequences as he struck the Ly Ergs. He didn't worry about where his king was. He didn't worry about anything. He avoided some but not all of the Ly Ergs' blows. Although the red-palmed faeries were more concerned with drawing blood than with inflicting permanent injury, they had murdered their share of faeries and mortals over the years.

Bananach darted past Gabriel and caught Niall in the upper abs with the tips of her boots. Searing pain rocked him back as the boots' poisonous iron cut into his flesh. He stumbled, and she pressed her advantage with a swipe of her blood-soaked talons.

Then Gabriel grabbed her and steadfastly moved their fight away from Niall, back toward the fence, leaving Niall free to deal with the Ly Ergs. It was disturbingly good fun, salve for the gloom Niall had been trying to shake. It didn't change anything but was refreshing.

By the time Niall had most of the Ly Ergs retreating, Gabriel had bloodied Bananach severely enough that she was leaning against the one Ly Erg who'd held back from the melee. But even so, she fought until Gabriel punched her hard enough that she swayed backward and tumbled to the ground.

Gabriel told the single unwounded Ly Erg, "Take her out of here before Chela notices I've had another tussle with her." He snarled at the rest of the Ly Ergs, who'd eased closer. "I keep getting into fights with Bananach, Che's going to get all territorial. Don't none of us want that, do we?"

The Ly Erg didn't speak but merely stepped up beside the raven-woman. Bananach rested her head against his leg.

"You're inconveniencing me, puppy. If necessary, I'll see the ice queen or the kingling. Someone's"—she snapped her jaw at Niall in what was either an invitation or a warning—"going to help me get this court set right."

"Irial said how we'd handle things." Gabriel stretched out his arms to show the raven-woman the spiraling orders on his skin.

"*Iri* needs to go. He's in the way and not doing what needs done. War's what we want. Need some proper violence. It's too long." Bananach closed her eyes. "And you following me everywhere's getting old."

"So stay put and I'll stop following you." Gabriel lowered himself to the pavement with a graceless gesture and began inspecting his wounds. He grimaced, a decidedly unpleasant sight with the blood flowing down his face, as he poked at a gash on his forehead.

The Ly Erg reached an already red hand down to caress Bananach's bloody face and arms, nourishing himself on battle blood as his kind had once done on red-soaked fields. His skin shimmered as Bananach's fresh blood seeped into his palm. Another Ly Erg walked up and laid his hand on Gabriel's blood-covered face. Despite the fact that they'd all been trying diligently to skewer, maim, and otherwise incapacitate one another mere moments ago, they were almost cordial for a few bizarre moments. The Ly Ergs took the pain and blood into their skin, unmindful of past conflict in the moment of postfight pleasure and sustenance.

Then Gabriel swung at the Ly Erg who stood patting his still-bleeding wounds and said, "Enough. Get her out of here. Maybe you could try being obedient tomorrow?"

"Maybe you should try staying out of my way tomorrow." Bananach stood and flicked her long hairlike feathers over her shoulder with a look of disdain. She might be bruised and unsteady on her feet, but she wasn't cowed by anyone. Then, with a solemnity that was as eerie as her violence, she shifted her attention to Niall. "Think about what you want, Gancanagh—what's *right*. Forgiving the Dark King? Forgiving the Summer King? Or letting me bring you justice, pain, and war, and *everything* you desire. We'd both be happy."

Once she was out of sight, Gabriel asked, "You might have walked away from Irial, Gancanagh, but do you really want this lot influencing our court? Do you want to *help* her?"

"I'm not getting involved. It's not my court." Niall sat beside the Hound. He wasn't sure, but it felt like one of his ribs had been cracked.

Gabriel snorted. "It's yours as much as mine. You're just too much of an ass to admit it."

"I'm not like you. I'm not out looking for fights or—"

"You don't back down from them, though. 'Sides, Irial's not all about fighting either. That's why he keeps *me* around." The Hound grinned and gestured at the shattered windows and cracked bricks. "There's more to the Dark Court than violence. You bring out another sort of darkness. We both belong in the shadows."

Niall ignored the implications of Gabriel's words. "I left the Summer Court. That's why Bananach was here— because I am solitary, fair game, *prey*."

Gabriel clasped Niall's shoulder approvingly. "I knew you'd get it figured out eventually: you don't belong with them. You get a few more things figured out, you'll be all right."

Then he lifted a broken brick and tossed it at a still-lit streetlight. As the glass shattered and clattered to the ground, Gabriel stood and started to walk away.

"Gabe?"

Gabriel's steps didn't slow or waver, but Niall knew the Hound was listening.

"I'm not letting him keep Leslie. She deserves a life. Irial can't take hers like this."

"You're still a slow learner, boy." Gabriel turned back.

"She's part of the court now. Just like you. Been part of it since that first touch of ink went in her mortal flesh. Why do you think we're all called to be nearer her? I watched you try to resist it. Like draws to like. You're both Irial's, and with her being a mortal . . ."

Niall froze.

Gabriel gave him a pitying smile. "Don't beat yourself up over things that are out of your control . . . or worry so much after the girl. You of all faeries ought to know Iri's not going to give up on the ones he claims as his own. He's just as stubborn as you."

Then the Hound was in his Mustang and vanishing into the darkened street, and for the third time in less than two days Niall was left with answers that did more to confuse him than ease his worries.

CHAPTER 30

Leslie rolled over, out of Irial's reach. Despite the vastness of the bed, she still felt too close to him. She'd meant to move several times already, to get up and leave. She didn't. She couldn't.

"It'll get easier," he said gently. "It's just new. You'll be fine. I'll—"

"I can't step away. I can't. I keep telling myself I'm going to go. But I don't." She wasn't angry even now, when her body ached. She should be, though. She knew that. "I feel like I'll throw up, like if I move too far from you . . ."

He rolled her back over so she was being held in his arms again. "It. Will. Fade."

She whispered, "I don't believe you."

"We were starved. It's—"

"Starved? We?" she asked.

He told her what he was, what Niall was, what Aislinn

and Keenan were. He told her they weren't human, not any of them.

Seth was telling the truth. She'd known somehow, somewhere, but hearing it said again, hearing it confirmed was horrible. *I am angry. I am afraid. I am . . .* She *wasn't*, though, not any of those things.

Irial kept talking. He told her that there were courts and that his—the Dark Court—lived on emotions. He told her that through her he would nourish them, that she was their salvation, that she was his salvation. He told her things that should terrify her, and every time she felt close to afraid or angry he drank it away.

"So you're what in this faery court?"

"In charge. Just as Aislinn and Keenan are for the Summer Court." There was no arrogance in his statement. In fact, he sounded weary.

"Am I"—she felt foolish, but she wanted to know, had to ask—"human still?"

He nodded.

"So, what does this mean? What am I then?"

"Mine." He kissed her to emphasize his point and then repeated, "Mine. You are mine."

"Which means what?"

He looked perplexed by that one. "That whatever you want is yours?"

"What if I want to leave? To see Niall?"

"I doubt that he'll be coming to see us, but you can go to him if you want." Irial rolled on top of her again as he said it. "As soon as you're able, you can walk out the door anytime you please. We'll look after you, keep you protected, but you can always leave when you want to and are able to."

But she didn't. She didn't want to, and she wasn't able. He wasn't lying: she believed that, tasted it, felt it in his words, but she also knew that whatever he'd done to her made her not want to be anywhere other than with him. For a brief moment, she felt terror at that realization, but it fled, replaced by a craving that made her sink her fingernails into Irial's skin and pull him closer—again and again, and still she was nearly shaking with need.

When Gabriel walked in, Leslie was dressed. She wasn't sure how the clothes had ended up on her, but it didn't matter. She was sitting up and covered. There was an apple in her hand.

"Remember to eat now." Irial stroked her hair back from her face, gentle like his voice.

She nodded. There were words she was to say, but they were gone before she could remember what they were.

"Troubles?" Irial asked Gabriel. Somehow Irial was at a desk far away from her.

She searched for the apple she'd been holding. It was gone. She looked down: her clothes were different. She had on a robe; red flowers and swirling blue lines covered it. She tried to follow them with her finger, tracing the pattern.

"The car's here." Gabriel had her hand and was helping her to her feet.

Her skirt became tangled around her ankles.

She stumbled forward and was folded into Irial's arms as they went into the club. The glare of lights made her hide her face against his shirt.

"You're doing fine," he told her as he combed out her hair, stroking his fingers through it, untangling it.

"It's been a long day," she murmured as she swayed under his caresses. She closed her eyes and asked, "The second day will be better, right?"

"It's been a week, love." He pulled the covers up over her. "You're doing much better already."

She listened to them laugh, the strange people—*faeries*—with Gabriel. They told her stories, amused her while Irial talked to a faery with raven feathers for hair. She was lovely, the raven-woman, Bananach. They all were. Leslie stopped staring at Bananach, trying to focus instead on the Vilas that danced with whichever of the Hounds beckoned, swaying through the shadows in the rooms like they felt the touch of shadows as Leslie did—like teasing hands, promising bliss that was too intense to allow for speech.

"Dance with me, Iri." Leslie stood and, ignoring the Hounds, went over to where Bananach was talking to Irial. It occurred to Leslie that this was a repetition of a tableau she could remember from other days: Bananach was around too often, taking Irial's time and attention. Leslie didn't like it.

"Move," she told the raven-woman.

Irial laughed as Bananach tried to raise a hand, only to

have it forced down by Gabriel and another Hound who both grabbed at her.

Irial said, "Bananach was just explaining why you aren't of any use to us."

Leslie felt the shivering in the tendrils that tied her to Irial, and she knew with perfect clarity in that moment that he had tamped down on their connection so she could have a few extra moments of lucidity. He did that.

"And what use am I, Irial? Did you tell her?" she asked.

"I did." Irial was standing now, hand outstretched, palm up.

Leslie put her hand in his and stepped closer.

Beside Irial, Bananach had gone still. She tilted her head at an angle that made her look far less human than the other faeries. Her eyes—which were similar enough to Irial's that Leslie paused—narrowed, but she did not speak. *She does not speak to me.* Leslie remembered that from other nights: Bananach refusing to address "the pet."

Leslie glanced at Gabriel, who stood waiting, and then around the club. They were all waiting. *For me. For food.* She thought she should feel frightened, maybe angry, but all she felt was bored. "Can you keep a leash on her while I relax?"

Gabriel didn't look to Irial for the Dark King's accord. He smiled. "It would be my pleasure."

Leslie knew that almost everyone in the club was watching her, but she suspected they'd seen her in far more mortifying circumstances. She slid her hands up Irial's chest, over his collarbone, and down his arms—feeling the tension in him that was utterly absent from his posture and expression. She tilted her head up and waited until he looked down. Then she whispered, "Am I just for using up, then?"

She knew it, knew that the ink under her skin was intended to let him—let *them*—do just that. She knew that the bone-melting bliss she felt each time he funneled the storms of emotion through her, forcing a tidal wave through a straw, was a trick to keep her insensible to the clarity that she had grasped *again* in that moment—and she realized that she'd had similar moments of clarity other nights and forgotten each time when the rush hit.

"Am I?" she repeated.

He leaned closer still, until she could feel his lips on her neck. There was no sound, only movement, when he said it. "No."

But she was willing to be: they both knew that as well. She thought about the life she'd had before—druggies in her home, drunken or missing father, bills to pay, hours waitressing, lying friends. *What's to miss?* She didn't want to return to pain, to worry, to fear, to any of that. She wanted euphoria. She wanted to feel her body go liquid in his arms. She wanted to feel the mad crescendo of pleasure that hit her with enough force to make her black out.

He pulled away to look at her.

She twined her arms around his neck and walked forward, forcing him to walk backward as she did so. "Later I'm going to be too blissed out to keep my hands off you. . . ." She shivered against him at the thought, at the admission here in public of what she was going to be like, not sure if admitting the desire was worse or better than telling herself some pretty lie to allay the blame. "This is fun, though. Being here. Being with you. I'd like to start remembering more of the fun stuff. Can we do that? Let me remember more of the good times with you? Let me have more of *this*?"

The tension fled then. He looked beyond her and gestured. Music filled the room; bass rumbled so heavily, it felt like it was inside her. And they danced and laughed, and for a few hours the world felt right. The disdainful and adoring looks on the faces of the mortals and faeries didn't matter. There was only Irial, only pleasure. But the longer she was clearheaded, the more she also remembered things that were awful. She didn't feel the emotions, but the memories came into sharper focus. There, in Irial's arms, she realized that she had the power to destroy every person who'd given her nightmares. Irial would do that: he'd find out who they were, and he'd bring them to her. It was a cold, clear understanding.

But she didn't want it, didn't want to truly destroy anyone. She just wanted to forget them again—even knowing she should feel pain was more than she wanted. "Irial? Feed them. Now."

She stopped moving and waited for it, the flash of emotions ripping through her body.

"Gabe," was all he said. And it was enough to start a melee. Bananach shrieked; Gabriel growled. Mortals screamed and moaned in pleasures and horrors. Cacophony rose around them like a familiar lullaby.

Irial didn't let her turn around. He didn't let her see anything or anyone.

Stars flashed to life in some too-close distance. They burned her up for a few brief heartbeats, but in their wake they pulled a wave of ecstasy that made her eyes close. Every particle of her body cried out, and she remembered nothing—knew nothing—but felt only the pleasure of Irial's skin against hers.

CHAPTER 31

Snatches of time were nothing but blurs and blank spaces, but the lucid periods were becoming more frequent. *How long has it been?* Her tattoo had been healed for a while. Her hair was longer. Often she could feel Irial close the connection, stopping the pull of emotions that slithered along the black vine that hovered between them. On those days almost everything was in order, sequential. So much of the time was a long blur, though. *Weeks?*

She hadn't left his side yet. *How long? How long have I . . .* Today she would. Today she would prove she could. She knew she'd tried—*and failed*—to do this more times than she could guess. There were bits of memories jumbled together. Life was like that now: just montages of images and sensations, and through it all there was Irial. He was constant. Even as she moved, she heard him in the other room. *Always at my reach.* That was dangerous too. The raven-woman wanted to change that, take Irial away.

Leslie slipped into one of the countless outfits he'd ordered for her, a long dress that clung and swirled when she moved. Like everything he bought, it was of material that felt almost too sensuous as she slipped into it. Without a word, she opened the door to the second room.

He didn't speak; he just watched her.

She opened the door to the hallway. Faeries followed her—invisible to any other human in the hotel, but she saw them. He'd given her the Sight with some strange oil he'd rubbed on her eyelids. Lanky creatures with tiny thorns all over their skin were silent, respectful even, as they followed her. Had she been able to, she'd have been terrified, but she was nothing but a conduit for emotions. The walls didn't keep her safe from them. Every fear, every longing, every dark thing those passing mortals and faeries felt flowed through her body until she couldn't focus. Only Irial's touch kept her from madness, calmed her.

The elevator door slid shut, closing the watching faeries out, taking her to the lobby of the hotel. Others would be there, waiting for her.

A glaistig nodded as she stepped out of the elevator. The glaistig's hooves clattered as she strode across the expanse of the room. Leslie's own footsteps weren't much quieter; Irial had bought her only ridiculously expensive shoes and boots with heels.

". . . the car brought around?" The doorman was speaking, but Leslie hadn't noticed. "Miss? Do you need your driver?"

She stared at him, feeling the flood of fear in him, feeling Irial several floors above her tasting that fear through her. It was like that, endless blurs of nothing but feeling emotions slither through her body to Irial. He said he was stronger. He said they were doing well. He said the court was healing.

The doorman stared at her; he spilled his fears and disdain onto her.

What does he see?

Irial had the appearance of someone far from responsible. He had the money and the constant flow of criminal-looking guests: the faeries' human masks did little to hide the aura of menace that clung to them. And she—when she left the suite—moved through the halls like a zombie, clinging to Irial, and on several occasions coming close to putting on a public show.

"Will you be going out today?" the doorman asked.

Her stomach cramped. Being away from Irial made her sick.

Gabriel swooped in behind her. "Do you need help?"

The doorman glanced away: he mightn't have heard the inhuman timbre of Gabriel's voice, but he'd felt the fear the Hound's presence elicited. All mortals did. It was what Gabriel was, and as he became agitated, he became more frightening.

The doorman's fear spiked.

"You made it to the door, Leslie. That's good." Irial's voice slipped into her mind. It was no longer surprising, but she still winced.

"Not his driver. Grab me a taxi?" she asked the doorman. She clenched her hands: she wasn't failing, not this time. She didn't faint or crumble. *Little victories.* She forced the words from her lips, "Taxi to take me to warehouse . . ."

She swayed.

The doorman asked, "Are you sure you're well enough to—"

"Yes." Her mouth was dry. Her hands were fisted tightly enough that it hurt. "Please, Gabriel, carry me to the taxi. Going by the river . . ." Then she toppled, hoping that he'd listen.

When Leslie woke in a patch of grass by the river, she was relieved. She could feel relief. Irial didn't drink her good feelings away. That should make her happy, knowing she wasn't numb. If not for the other thing—that maddening craving for Irial's touch, the awful sickening longing when darker emotions filled her to choking but didn't touch *her* emotions—she might be okay.

A bit away from her, several of Gabriel's Hounds waited and watched. They didn't frighten her. They seemed pleased that she liked them. A few times, she'd seen Ani and Tish— and in that shock-free way she lived now, she'd accepted their mixed heritage without pause. She'd come to terms with the realization that Ani—and Tish and Rabbit—had known that the ink exchange would change her.

"But you're strong enough, Les, really," Ani had insisted.

"And if I'm not?"

"You will be. It's for Iri. We need him to be strong." Ani had hugged her. *"You're his savior. The court's so much stronger. He's so much stronger."*

Ignoring the Hounds, Leslie walked along the river until she came to a warehouse where she and Rianne used to go to smoke. She slid open the window they'd climbed in together so often and made her way to the second floor— just high enough to see the river. Out here, away from everyone, she felt the closest to normal she had since the morning she'd left her house with Irial.

She sat watching the river race away. Her feet dangled out the window. There were no mortals, no faeries, no Irial. Away from all of them, she felt less consumed. The world was back in order, more stable somehow now that she was on her own. *Is it the distance?*

It didn't matter, though: she felt his approach. Then Irial was in the street, looking up at her. "Are you going to come down from there?"

"Maybe."

"Leslie—"

She stood up, balancing on the balls of her feet, hands above her head like she was preparing to dive into a pool. "I should be afraid, Irial. I'm not, though."

"I am." His voice sounded jagged, not tender this time, not reassuring. "I'm terrified."

She swayed back and forth as the wind batted against her.

In that implacable way he always seemed to have, Irial began, "We'll get better at this and—"

"Will it hurt you if I step forward?" Her voice was dispassionate, but she felt excitement at the idea. *Not fear, though.* There still wasn't any fear, and that's what she wanted—not to hurt, but to feel normal. She hadn't been sure before, but in that moment she knew that's what she needed: the whole of herself, all the parts, all the feelings. *And they're as far gone as normal is.*

"Would you feel it? Would *I* feel it if I fell? Would it hurt?" She looked down at him: he was beautiful, and despite the fact that he'd stolen her choices, she looked at him with a strange tenderness. He kept her safe. The mess she was in might be his fault, but he didn't abandon her to the madness it caused. He took her into his arms no matter how often she sought him, no matter that he'd had to move his court, that he looked positively exhausted. Tender feelings surged as she thought about it, about him.

When he spoke, it wasn't to say anything gentle. He pointed at the ground. "So jump."

Anger, fear, doubt, rolled over her—not pleasant, but real. For a brief moment, they were hers and *real* this time. "I could."

"You could," he repeated. "I won't stop you. I don't want to steal your will, Leslie."

"You have, though." She watched Gabriel walk up and whisper to Irial. "You did this. I'm not happy. I want to be."

"So jump." He didn't take his gaze away from her as he told Gabriel, "Keep everyone back. No mortals. No fey in this street."

Leslie sat down again. "You'd catch me."

"I would, but if the fall would please you"—he shrugged—"I'd rather you were happy."

"Me too." She rubbed her eyes, as if tears would come. *They won't.* Crying wasn't something she did anymore— neither was worrying, raging, or any other of the unpleasant emotions. Parts of her were gone, taken away as surely as the rest of her life. There were no classes, no melodramatic Rianne; there'd be no laughing in the kitchen at Verlaine's, no dancing at the Crow's Nest. And there was no way to undo any of the things that had changed. *Going backward is never an option.* But staying where she was wasn't true happiness either. She was living in a hazy dream—or nightmare. She didn't know if she could tell the difference just now.

"I'm *not* happy," she whispered. "I don't know what I am, but this isn't happiness."

Irial began climbing the building, grabbing hold of crumbling brick and broken metal, piercing his hands on the sharp edges, leaving a trail of bloody handprints as he made his way up the wall to her.

"Grab hold," he said as he paused in the window frame.

And she did. She clung to him, holding on to him like he was the only solid thing left in the world as he finished scaling the building. When he reached the barren rooftop, he stopped and lowered her feet to the ground.

"I don't want you to be unhappy."

"I am."

"You're not." He cupped her face in his hands. "I know everything you feel, love. You feel no sorrow, no anger, no worries. How is this a bad thing?"

"It's not real. . . . I can't live like this. I won't."

She must have sounded serious enough because he nodded. "Give me a few more days, and I'll have a solution."

"Will you tell—"

"No." He watched her face with something almost vulnerable in his eyes. "It's best for everyone if we don't talk of this. Just trust me."

CHAPTER 32

Irial had spent several days watching Leslie struggle with the urge to feel something of the emotions she'd lost now that he drank them through her. It was an unexpected dilemma. She'd stepped into traffic, provoked the increasingly aggressive Bananach, and interfered in an altercation with two armed mortals: the moment he relaxed his guard she was out endangering herself. She didn't make sense to him, but mortals rarely did.

Today she was exhausted—as was he.

He pulled the door to the bedroom closed, tearing his attention away from his sleeping girl. She required so much careful handling, so much hiding of his true feelings. He'd not expected a mortal to change him; that wasn't part of the plan.

Gabriel looked up as Irial sat at the other end of the sofa and resumed the conversation they'd been having every time Leslie napped. "We haven't had a good party with mortals in a while." He held out an already open long-neck bottle.

"That's because they break too easily." Irial took the bottle, sniffed it, and asked, "Is this actually *real* beer? Just beer?"

"Far as you know." Gabriel leaned back on the sofa, legs stretched out, boot-clad feet tapping in tune to some song that only he heard. "So, party with the mortals?"

"Can you get some that'll survive for a few nights?" Irial glanced at the closed door, behind which his own too-fragile mortal slept fitfully. "It'll be better if we don't need to replace them each week. Just gather the same ones up every few days until we see how it goes."

He didn't add that he wasn't sure how well Leslie would cope with channeling too many mortals' deaths, fear, and pain. If there were enough of them and they were terrified and angry and lustful enough, she'd be so intoxicated that he doubted that she'd notice a few deaths, but if too many of them died at once, it could upset her.

"A bit of war might be good too. Bananach is testing every boundary you set. Give her a small skirmish?" The fact that Gabriel had mentioned it at all was reason enough to worry.

"She doesn't have the support yet to get very far." Irial hated that she was always there at his heels, looking for weaknesses, stirring her small mutinies. In time, she would wear him down. If he didn't keep the court strong enough, she would rally them to true rebellion. It wouldn't be the first time. He needed to lull her back to moderate rumblings of war, not give her reason to get more bold. *First get Leslie situated.*

"Bananach tried for Niall again." Gabriel flashed his teeth in his glee. "Boy still holds his own in a fight."

Irial would've enjoyed seeing that. Niall tended to go for logic before violence, but when he did indulge in a fight, he did it like he did everything: with singular focus. "He's . . . well still?"

Gabriel shrugged, but his gleeful expression wasn't dimming. "He'll come back sooner or later, Iri. You need to think long term, that's all."

Irial didn't—*couldn't*—ponder what Niall would do just now. He had hopes, but hope wasn't a solution. Gabriel was right: Irial did need to think long term. He'd been too focused on his initial ideas. It had been too long since he'd needed to truly plan. During the nine centuries Beira ruled unopposed, Irial had allowed himself to grow weak, to assume that their nourishment would always be so easy. The past few months of having a true Summer King and a new Winter Queen had shown him how quickly change could come—and he hadn't been ready.

"Tell Bananach to gather whoever wants to go and start a little chaos with Sorcha. I can't nourish everyone long term. If the seasonal courts are determined to be uncooperative for now, let's see what we can do with her royal tediousness. If anyone can provoke Sorcha, Bananach is our best choice."

Gabriel's forearms grew dark with the details he'd carry

to Bananach—and hopefully satisfy her enough that she wouldn't be underfoot for a while.

"And Ani"—Irial paused to measure his words carefully—"bring Tish and Rabbit to stay with her. Have them move into the house where we took Guin. With Sorcha's penchant for stealing half-fey, they'll be too much at risk once Bananach starts her assault. Now that peace is here, Sorcha won't keep the High Court in seclusion."

For a moment, Gabriel hesitated. Then he said, "You'll be careful with my pups. Ani's being able to feed off mortals doesn't make her any less mine. Experimenting on—"

"We won't do anything she doesn't consent to." Irial lit a cigarette. He'd taken to smoking more frequently since Leslie had come to them. *Worry, for her.* He took a few drags before he spoke again. "Let Ani loose with the mortals, too. I want to see what she can drink off them. Maybe she's what we need to sort this all out."

"That'll mean two . . . parties . . . because I'm not going in there if my pup is." Gabriel's menace had vanished under his disgust at the idea of his pup loose in a crowd. "She's a good girl."

"She is, Gabe. Pick a few Hounds you'd trust to mind her. Two rooms, the ones across the hall. We'll see what it'll take to fulfill me—and the court, before Leslie slips into a coma. We'll watch her, keep track of her reactions, and stop when we get close to her limits." Irial cringed at the idea. A few of the mortals seemed to suffer neural damage if they were pushed too far.

"Gather up a few of Keenan's Summer Girls too. They work well as enticement for good behavior. Prizes for those with the most surviving mortals come dawn." Irial lowered his voice at the sound of movement in the bedroom. Leslie shouldn't wake just yet, but she was too stubborn to sleep as she should.

Irial held a hand out to Leslie as she walked into the room. She took his hand and curled into his arms.

"You'll take care of the party plans then?" Irial asked, absently petting Leslie's hair as she nestled closer.

Gabriel nodded. "Need at least two days, though."

"That works." Irial turned his attention back to his girl then, pleased to hear the soft click of the door closing behind Gabriel. "If you can be patient for two more days, we can work on your feeling a little less trapped by this." He motioned to the feathered vine that bound them together.

"What are—"

"No questions, Leslie. That's the condition." He kissed her forehead. "You want more freedom, room to roam?"

She nodded mutely.

"I just need you to stop putting yourself at risk. If you keep doing that, I won't be able to give you your space." He watched her face as he spoke, wondering yet again what she'd be like if she could keep some of her emotions, not all of them, but a few.

"Will what you're doing hurt?" She looked excited at the idea for a moment, interested in the idea of feeling the very thing from which she'd been seeking oblivion.

"Did the first couple weeks with me hurt?"

"I don't remember." She licked her lips as if she could taste his worries. She couldn't because of their tie, but sometimes he felt the tug as she tried to reverse the flow, as if she'd steal *his* emotions. "I don't have many clear memories of *that.*"

"Exactly."

"You're cruel, Irial." She wasn't angry, accusing, none of those things. She couldn't be.

And for a moment, he realized that they both wished she could be. *My Shadow Girl.* He kissed her before he made the mistake of saying what he was thinking.

"I can be, Leslie. And if you keep trying to do damage to yourself, I will be." He had a brief hope that—even without feeling fear—her basic intellect would be enough to make her realize that this wasn't something either of them wanted. But she sighed, as if it weren't a threat but a reward, so he asked, "You remember Niall's scars?"

"I do." She watched him carefully, staying motionless.

"You won't like me if I'm cruel." He lifted her to her feet.

She stood motionless, hand outstretched. "I don't like you now."

"We don't lie," he reminded her as he took her hand and pulled her into his arms yet again.

"I'm mortal, Irial. I can lie all I want to," she whispered.

He let go of her, hating that it was hard to do. "Get changed, love."

They had a riot to attend. He hadn't walked her through

hospitals, sanitariums, or the like—*yet*—but tonight he'd take her to the feasts of anger. If he filled her up with all the darkness she could stand and channeled it out to his court, then he could let her breathe for a little while. It was either that or lose her, and right now, that didn't feel like an option. He'd been trying to build her tolerance slowly, but her stubborn streak—and his desire not to destroy her—had made his timeline no longer workable. Not for the first time since the damnable peace had begun, Irial wanted nothing more than to walk away from his court, from his responsibilities—except now he wanted to take Leslie with him.

CHAPTER 33

Over the next week, he pushed her until she was so shadow drunk that she retched, but they didn't discuss it.

They fell into a routine she thought she could accept. Irial didn't tell her what happened during the nights, and she didn't ask. It wasn't a solution—not really—but she felt better. She told herself it was progress of a sort. Sometimes, she felt brief tendrils of lost emotions when Irial kept the connection between them tightly closed, when the shad-owed vine stretched like a sleeping serpent between them. In those moments she could lie to herself and say she was happy, that there were benefits to being cosseted so—then the weight of what she had become rolled over her until the cramps of need made her insensible.

No different than any other addict.

Her drug might have a pulse and a voice, but he was a drug all the same. And she'd sunk to depths that would make her dissolve in shame if such feelings were still in her reach. They weren't, though: Irial drank them down like some exotic elixir. And when the awfulness reached its pinnacle, Irial's touch was all that would assuage the maw that yawned open inside of her.

What is it doing to me? Will the darkness consume me?

Irial didn't have that answer; he couldn't tell her what it would do to her body, her health, her longevity—anything. All he could tell her was that he was there, that he'd protect her, that he'd keep her safe and well.

Now that she was able to go out walking regularly—away from Irial—she knew it was only a matter of time until she saw Niall. Of all the people from her life before the ink exchange, he was the one she was loath to encounter. He'd been beside Irial once: he knew what the Dark Court was like, what the world she lived in was like, and that lack of secrecy was something she didn't know how to deal with.

She'd looked for him, and today he was there. He stood across the street, outside the Music Exchange, the shop where Rianne was most often found. Beside him was a man—a human—playing music that was foreign and familiar on a bodhran. Her pulse picked up the rhythm, the pace of the music settling in her stomach as if each touch of the beater were on her skin, in her veins.

Then Niall turned and found her watching him.

"Leslie." His lips formed the word, but the sound was too slight to hear.

Traffic on the street moved faster than seemed safe to

enter, but Niall wasn't human, hadn't ever been human. He slid through gaps that weren't quite there, and then he was beside her, lifting her hands to his lips, crying tears she wasn't able to shed.

"He wouldn't let me see you," he said.

"I told him not to. I wasn't in a place where I'd have wanted anyone to see me." She looked away, watching the faeries watching them.

"I'd kill him if I could," he said, sounding crueler than Irial ever did.

"I don't want that. Not—"

"You *would* if he hadn't done this to you."

"He's not awful."

"Don't. Please." Niall held her, silent but for the sound of his tears. He acted like it was her he wanted, like all that she thought he'd felt was real, but she wondered. That urge she'd felt *before*, that compulsion to touch Niall, to press closer—it was gone. *Had it been an illusion? Was it there but swallowed down by Irial?* She looked at Niall's beautiful scarred face and felt a flash of tenderness, but there was no temptation.

Along the street, the faeries watched with expressions gleeful and heinous. Chattering and murmurs rose as they speculated on what Irial's fey would do, what Irial himself would do when he heard.

Kill the boy. He will.

Give him grounds to start a melee.

Nothing. She's not reason enough to—

Is. Irial never took a mortal till this one. She must be—

Irial hasn't allowed us to strike his lovely Gancanagh *in almost* always.

Torture him then? Make her *do it?*

They chortled and carried on until Leslie turned her eyes to the shadows and shot a pleading look at one of Gabriel's Hounds. In less time than it would've taken to speak, the Hound cleared the crowd, sent them scurrying by threat or force, hefting a few of them like misshapen balls and launching them down the street. Horrid splattering noises and shrieks resounded until even the man with the bodhran paused for a moment, looking about as if he heard some slight echo of the horrors he couldn't quite sense.

"They listen to you?" Niall asked.

"They do. They are good to me. No one has hurt me." She touched his chest where she knew his scars were hidden. Those scars told the answers to so many questions about him, about Irial, about the world she now called her home. She added, "No one has done anything but what I've asked of them. . . ."

"Including Irial?" Niall's face was as unreadable as his voice. His emotions, though, she felt those—hope and longing and fear and anger. He was a tangled mess.

Leslie wished she could lie, but she didn't want to, not to him, not knowing that he *couldn't* lie to her by word or emotion. "Mostly. He doesn't touch me without asking, if that's what you mean . . . but he made me this without asking, and I'm not sure anymore what's my choice and what's his. When I . . . I *need* him or I'm . . . it kills me, Niall. It's like starving, like something eating me alive from deep inside. It doesn't hurt. *I* don't hurt, but I know it should. The pain isn't there, but it doesn't stop me from screaming under it. Only Iri makes it . . . better. He makes everything better."

Niall leaned close to her ear and whispered, "I can stop it. I think I can undo it. I can get what I need to break his tie to you." And he told her that Aislinn would give him sunlight and the Winter Queen would give him frost, and he would burn and freeze the ink from her skin. "It should work. You'd be free of him. All of them."

Leslie didn't answer, didn't tell him yes or no. She couldn't.

"It's your choice." Niall cradled her face in his hands, looking at her the same way he had before, when she was not this. "You have a choice. I can give you that."

"What if it makes it worse?"

"Try to think what you'd choose if you weren't under his sway. Is this"—he paused—"what you would have chosen?"

"No. But I can't unchoose it either. I can't pretend I haven't become this. I won't be who I was before . . . and if the feelings come back, if I *can* leave, how do I live with what I've—"

"You just do. The things you do when you're desperate aren't who you are." Niall's expression had grown fierce, angry.

"Really?" She remembered the feeling, that moment when she looked at the ground and knew that even if Irial caught her the first time she jumped, there would be other times when she felt that desperation. The emotions she could just barely touch in that moment were a part of her as well. She was the person who chose this route. She thought back over the signs and warnings that something was amiss. She thought of the shadows she'd seen in Rabbit's office. She thought of the questions she hadn't asked Aislinn or Seth or Rabbit or herself. She thought of the shame she'd bottled up instead of seeking help. That was who she was; those were parts of her. They were all choices. To not act is a choice too.

"I don't think so, Niall," she heard herself say. Her voice wasn't soft or afraid. "Even under the addiction, it's me. I might not have had as many choices, but I'm still choosing."

She thought again of standing in the window of the warehouse. She could have chosen to jump. She hadn't. *It would be giving up, giving in if I actually jumped. Isn't it better to endure?* The person she was under the weight of her addiction was stronger than she'd realized she could be.

"I want a choice that doesn't hurt Irial or me," she said, and then she left him. Her choice would come—maybe not now, maybe not the choice Niall held out, and she wasn't going to let Irial or Niall or anyone else make it for her.

Not again.

CHAPTER 34

The moon was well overhead when Irial crept across the room. It wouldn't do for mortals to see doors opening and closing on their own, so he stepped into the hall wearing his mortal-friendly facade. Several of the Hounds were standing guard outside the room, invisible to any mortals that might pass. There weren't any in the hall, though, so Irial let go of his glamour and shut the suite door behind him.

"Keep her inside if she wakes," he told the Hounds. "No wandering tonight."

"She doesn't cooperate so well. We could just follow, keep her safe and—"

"No."

Another Hound objected, "We don't want to hurt her . . . and she's so unhappy if we stop her from going out."

"So block the doors." Irial grimaced. He wasn't the only one swayed too much by his bond with Leslie. His weakness for her flowed into his whole court: they all had an unreasonably hard time doing anything Leslie disliked.

I weaken them. My affection for her cripples them.

The only way to work around it seemed to be keeping her from asking his faeries to do anything asinine. The alternative, breaking her irreparably, wasn't a path he wanted to consider.

Could I? He suppressed the answer before he let himself go further in that thought. Handing Niall over to his court had been horrific enough that he still dreamed of it. For centuries, he'd dreamed of how Niall had rejected him afterward. Weak kings didn't thrive. Irial knew that, but knowing didn't undo the ache when Niall chose to go to another court. That was a long-dead pain.

Being tied to Leslie, indulging in parties with the mortals as he and Niall once had, these things had brought long-silenced memories back to the surface. It was yet another proof that her mortal influence had tainted him, changed him. It wasn't a change he liked. The vine that stretched like a shadow between him and his mortal grew suddenly visible in the air before him as his agitation increased.

He told the Hounds, "Don't speak to her other than to tell her that I forbade you to let her leave the room. Tell her you'll bleed for it if she goes anywhere. If that doesn't work, tell her *Ani* will."

They snarled at him, but they'd tell Leslie. Hopefully, it

would inspire her to obey his wishes for a few hours while he cleaned up the latest mess.

Inside the first room the floor was strewn with the weeping mortals who'd survived the most recent round of festivities. They'd endured longer than the last batch, but so many broke in mind or body too easily. They were wailing as the madness of what they'd seen and done settled on them. Give them a few drugs, a little glamour, and some simple enticements, and mortals willingly dived into the depths of hidden depravity. Afterward, in the light, when the bodies of those who'd died were entwined with the still living, there were those who didn't know how to hold on to their sanity.

"Chela's found a few sturdy ones to replace them. They're enjoying the amenities over in the other room." Gabriel tossed a girl's handbag into one of the bins and then motioned at a corpse.

"Dibs." Two of the Ly Ergs lifted her. A third opened the door. They'd take her somewhere else in the city to leave her for the mortals to find. "She's ours."

"No posing this one," Gabriel snarled as the Ly Ergs left. The faery who opened the door lifted his hand in a dismissive gesture, flashing his bright red palm.

Irial stepped over a couple who stared blindly past him.

"She kept encouraging them to fight over her. Whatever's spliced with that new X made her violent." Gabriel emptied pockets and stripped away some of the shredded clothes, directing grinning thistle-fey as he went about the grisly task. "They've been posing the ones they like. They set tea for several yesterday."

"Tea?"

One of the Ly Ergs grinned cheekily. "We got them proper things, too. They'd have been naked but for the hats and gloves we nicked."

A leannan-sidhe added, "We painted their faces, as well. They were lovely."

Irial wanted to chastise them, but it wasn't any worse than most of the things they'd done for sport over the centuries. *The Dark King doesn't require kindness for mortals.* He tamped down his unease and said, "Maybe we should set up a stage over in the park by the kingling's loft. . . . A scene from *Midsummer Night's Dream* . . . or—"

"No. The other mortal that was scrawling plays then. What's the one with the parade of sins?" A Ly Erg rubbed his blood-red hands over his face. "The fun one."

"I like sins," a leannan-sidhe murmured.

One of Jenny's kin picked up a corpse. "We've got our gluttony right here. This one serviced every willing faery in the room."

They were laughing.

"That's *lust*, sister. Gluttons have the extra meat on their middles. Like this one."

The surly Ly Erg repeated, "What's the play?"

"Faustus. The Tragical History of Doctor Faustus," Leslie said. Her voice was soft, but they all turned to the doorway where she stood. Her lacy pajamas were mostly covered by

the robe she'd slipped on. "Marlowe wrote it. Unless you believe the theory that Marlowe and Shakespeare were the same person."

None of the faeries answered. Had it been anyone else, they'd have snarled at her or invited her to join the fun. With Leslie, though, they did neither.

She pulled a pack of Irial's cigarettes out of her robe pocket and lit one, silently watching as they gathered the newly mad mortals. When they approached her, she opened the door for them.

They crossed the threshold and extended their own glamour to mask what they carried. She saw it, though. She got a close-up view of wide-eyed madmen, a fresh corpse, and bare flesh. Her horror and disgust peaked. She didn't feel it, of course, but the rush of emotions she should feel swarmed to Irial.

Once the faeries were all gone, she walked toward him, flicking ash on the red-stained floor. Her bare feet were stark white against those stains. "Why?"

"Don't ask me that." Irial saw the fine trembling in her hands, watched her resist the backlash from the feelings he'd sought out.

"Tell me why." She dropped the cigarette and ground it out under her bare foot. The trembling became worse as waves of mortal terror surged through her.

"You don't want this answer, love." He reached out for her, knowing that despite her best intentions, the backlash would soon pull her under.

She backed away. "Don't. I want to"—she stopped—"it's my fault, isn't it? That's why you're—"

"No."

"I thought faeries didn't lie." Her knees gave, and she dropped to the floor. She knelt on a wide red stain.

"I'm not lying. It's not your fault." His attempts to be the King of Nightmares, the Dark King, all faded because she looked lost. It was him who faltered, not her.

She gripped the carpet, bloodying her fingertips as she tried to hold on to the floor so as not to reach out to him. "Why were they here? Why are they . . ."

She obviously wasn't going to stop asking questions, so he stopped avoiding them. "If I'm sated, I feed the court enough that you can have some freedom. The court starves a little, but not enough to cripple them . . . and as long as you stayed in the suite you didn't need to know."

"So we tormented them so—"

"No. *You* didn't torment anyone." He watched her grasp at the horror she wanted to feel, felt it slither into his skin. He sighed. "Don't overreact."

She laughed, a sound as far from humorous as a scream would be.

He sank to the floor beside her.

"There are worse things." He didn't tell her that those worse things were inevitable if the peace between the seasonal courts grew much stronger, that this was just one step in their path. She stared at him for several heartbeats, and then she leaned forward and laid her head against his chest.

"Can you pick criminals or something?"

Somewhere inside he was saddened by her acceptance of these mortals' deaths, but that was her mortal essence tainting his judgment. He pushed the sorrow away. "I can try. . . . I can't change what I need you for, but I would spare you details of it."

She tensed in his arms. "And if I can't take it? What then? What if my mind . . ."

He said it then, admitted his weakness, "I hadn't planned this part, Leslie. I just needed your body to stay alive. Most of the mortals from the earlier exchanges . . . they didn't fare as well, but I'd like you not to be comatose. If that means a few other mortals die or slip into their own minds while you black out for a few hours or days—"

"Then that's what you'll do," she whispered.

CHAPTER 35

Niall had stopped by the loft to gather a few belongings when Aislinn walked in. "I don't want to discuss it again," he started, but then Aislinn stepped to the side. Leslie stood behind her. She was wan, with dark circles under her eyes. Bluish veins were so clear through her skin that, to his vision, she had a slight blue tint to her.

Aislinn said, "She wants to talk to you . . . not to me." Then his queen-no-more left, closing the door behind her, leaving Niall alone with Leslie.

"Has something happened?" he asked.

"Irial sends his regards." Her movements were as stilted as her words. She wandered away to stare out the window. Shadows danced in the air around her; he'd seen those same shadows dance in Irial's eyes, formless figures that leaped and spun on the edge of the abyss. Now they hovered around Leslie, a retinue of nightmare's handmaidens.

Niall didn't know what to do or say or think. So he waited.

"Can we leave?" She looked over her shoulder. "I can't do this here."

"Do what?"

She watched him, dispassionately it seemed. "What we talked about *before*."

And he knew that whatever she wasn't saying was horrific enough that she'd decided to leave Irial.

"Will you help me, Niall?" she asked. "I need to set things right."

For a moment, Niall wasn't sure if it was Leslie or Irial asking: her voice sounded wrong, her words not matching the intonations he'd heard from her before. But it didn't matter. The shadows danced around her, and he gave the only answer he could offer either of them: "Yes."

Leslie felt the strange whisper of Irial's nature rustling through her, even now. And it was a comfort, even though she was hoping to end it. What he gave her, what he cost her, it wasn't right for either of them. She would find it easier if she could call him evil, but none of this was about values or ethics. Those answers were too simple. Irial did what he deemed necessary to save his fey, what he thought best for his court—including her. It wasn't what was best for her or for the people who'd been brought to terror in the hands of the Dark Court. It wasn't best for the thousands of mortals who'd inevitably get drawn into Irial's plans once she grew less important to him or he grew more desperate.

She smiled at Niall. They stood in her old room. She hadn't been back there since she'd left with Irial. When she'd walked in, the house was empty, as if no one else had been there in weeks. If she could feel it, she might worry about her father, but as it was she merely noted that she wanted to worry.

Deal with that later. After.

Niall pulled her into his arms, holding her as securely as if she'd been falling only to be snatched back from the edge. His hand cradled the back of her head. "Will you look poorly on me if I admit that I wish I weren't the one to do this?"

"No." Later, though, when Irial's influence wore off, she suspected she might.

"Come on." She took his hand in hers and led him to the bed, her bed, inside her house. It was safe. *Because of Irial.*

Niall stood motionless as she sat down on the edge of the faded rose covers. She could feel rare brushes with her feelings—thanks to what Irial had done, thanks to the mortals who'd fallen into the arms of the Dark Court—not all of her feelings, but a few of the stronger ones. She felt disgust at the way the faeries treated the dead bodies, horror at the fact that people had suffered because of her. She cringed at the sin-sick weight of it . . . and at her yearning to return to numbness so she didn't have to feel it. That's what she'd pursued—numbness—and it wasn't worth the cost to her or anyone else.

She pulled Niall toward her; he looked at her with sad eyes.

Her stomach clenched at the fear that threatened to smother her—not in the way it once had, but in hunger.

Irial's hunger.

Then her fear fled, swallowed down by Irial as he sat in one of his clubs, surrounded by the fey who'd been slowly flocking to his side. Hopefully Irial's hungers would take the edge off the pain she knew was coming.

She rolled over, removing her shirt as she did, and tried not to think of what was about to happen. Eyes closed, she said, "Please?"

Niall lowered his hands onto her skin, onto her ink, onto that mark where Irial's presence was anchored into her skin. His touch burned from the small ball of sunlight that Aislinn had given him at the loft, that he'd carried inside him, that he'd brought.

At my request.

The frost that the other queen—the Winter Queen—had given him followed the sunlight: Leslie thought she felt icicles piercing her skin. And she screamed, though she tore at her lip to keep that sound inside. She screamed as she'd done only once before.

This isn't Niall's fault. MY choice. Mine.

"Forgive me," he begged as he forced the sunlight and

frost into her skin, freezing the tears in the ink, searing away the tinge of Irial's blood that was blended into that ink, killing the roots of the black vine that Irial's ink had anchored in her body.

"Leslie?" Irial whispered.

She could see him clearly enough that he looked like a hologram in the room. If her eyes hadn't been closed, she would have believed he really was there. Startled, he stood, unsettling the faery who'd been curled on his lap. *"What are you doing?"*

"Choosing." She bit the coverlet to keep from screaming again. Her hands were fisted so tight that she felt the cover rip. Her spine bowed. Niall's knee was on her back, holding her down.

Tears were soaking the blanket under Leslie's face.

"I'm mine. *Not anyone else's."*

"I'm still yours, though. That won't ever change, Shadow Girl." And then he was gone, and her emotions crashed over her.

Niall pulled his hands away, and she turned her head to look at him. He sat beside her, staring down at his hands. "I'm sorry. Gods, I'm sorry."

"I'm not." She wasn't sure of much else, but she knew that. Then the agony in her skin, the memories, the surge of horror, it was too much: she rolled over and threw up in the wastebasket. Her entire body clenched as pain coursed through her. Tears joined the perspiration on her face as hot and cold flashes switched in and out of control. Muscles she hadn't known she had were knotting up in response to the pain inside her.

She smiled despite it all; for just a moment, she smiled. She was free. It hurt like hell, but she was free.

CHAPTER 36

Leslie drifted in and out of consciousness for several days while the world moved around her. Niall stayed beside her. Aislinn and Seth visited. Ani and Tish and Rabbit visited. Gabriel visited, carrying more flowers than could be considered reasonable. He set the flowers down, clasped Niall's shoulder and nodded, kissed Leslie's brow, and left. The others all talked—words of support and apology from Aislinn, praise from Seth and Rabbit, forgiveness for leaving the court from Tish and Ani. Irial did not come to her.

She lay on her stomach wearing jeans and a bra. She hadn't spoken more than a few words yet. There had been too many things in her mind for her to try to formulate sentences. Neither her father nor her brother ever showed up at the house. She didn't know where they were, if they were coming back, or if they were being *prevented* from coming back. She was in her home—healing and safe. That was what mattered right then.

Niall was putting some sort of soothing cream on the sun- and frost-burned skin of her back. She turned her head to look at him. She saw them, stretched across the room: burned tendrils of the shadowy vine flowing from her skin—a connection still, but not a conduit. "It's never going to go away, is it?"

Niall stared at the blackened vine. "I don't know. I couldn't see it before. I can now."

"It's closed off. That's what matters. And it's not going to open again." She sat up and had to bite her lip to keep from crying out.

"Are you . . . how do you feel?" He was tentative, still not pushing her to words or actions. He was near enough that she could take his arm if she needed support, but he didn't get in her space.

"Awful, but real," she said.

"The aloe should help. It's the best I can do. The mortal things won't work since it was faery. . . . I called Aislinn and—"

"It's good, Niall. Really. I don't mind that it hurts." She watched him look at her with such sorrow that it broke her heart to see it, to realize how difficult the past days had been for him too.

"Help me up?" She held out a hand so he could steady her until she saw how she was going to handle moving. Sometimes standing was painful enough that she'd fallen back down. This time she wavered a bit as Niall helped her to the bathroom, but it wasn't as awful as it had been. She was recovering, physically and mentally. *It's time.* She leaned on the doorframe and motioned toward the cupboard under the sink. "There's a hand mirror under there."

Without comment he got it out, and she turned in front of the large mirror and held the hand mirror up so she could see her back. The ink in her skin had faded to white and gray. It was as beautiful as before, but it'd been bleached, lightened by the sunlight and frost Niall had pressed into her skin.

My *art now. My body.* She lowered the mirror and smiled. It wasn't the tattoo that had changed her, had given her repossession of her body. It was her actions, her choices. It was finding the path when it looked like there weren't any paths to be found.

"Leslie?" Niall stepped behind her and looked at her in the mirror, holding the reflection of her gaze. "Are you going to be all right?"

She turned so they were face-to-face and gave him back the words he'd offered her their first night together: "I survived. Isn't that what matters?"

"It is." He pulled her closer and held her carefully.

They stood there, quiet and together, until she started to sway. Blushing, she said, "I'm still weak, I guess."

"You're not weak at all. Wounded, but that's nothing to be ashamed of." He helped her to the bed. Hesitantly he said, "Aislinn would come care for you if you'd allow it. I've left them, left Keenan, but they'll look after you. We can sort it out, and then—"

"Niall?" She tried to keep her tone gentle as she said, "I . . . I can't deal with your faery courts right now. I just want my life. This"—she gestured around her room—"isn't good, but it's better than your world. I don't want to be a part of the faery world."

"I can't change what I am. I'm not a part of the court, but I can't *not* interact at all with my world. . . . I . . ." He let his words fade.

This wasn't a conversation she wanted to have, not now, but it was there. "I still feel . . . something, whatever it was, for you, but right now . . . I need to start over, somewhere else . . . on my own."

"I tried to keep you safe." He told her that he'd kept guard over her for months, that he—and other of Aislinn's faeries—had walked beside her in the streets of Huntsdale. He told her that he'd tried to not speak to her before because Aislinn had ordered him not to, that she didn't want Leslie drawn into their world—and that he'd thought his queen wise to decide thus.

"I want to be with you. I'm not with the court now. I'm . . . solitary. I could come with you . . . take care of—"

"I'm sorry," she said.

"Right. You need time, but when you're ready . . . or if you need anything *at all,* ever . . ."

"I know." She leaned back on the pillows. "Can you call Ash to come over? I need to talk to her before I see Irial."

"Irial? Why would you—"

"I'm not the only mortal. There's plenty of people he

could replace me with"—she kept the pain out of her voice, but she still had to pause—"if he hasn't already. I'm not going to walk away and leave someone else in my place." She thought about the weeping mortals on the floor, the bloody fights she'd seen the starts of before she blacked out, the knowledge that this was all Irial's being *careful*, gentle with her. What he'd be like without that caution was too much to consider. "I need to talk to Ash before I see him. I can't wait too long."

Niall sighed, but he went. She heard the front door open and close as he went to seek whoever waited outside. And she let herself drift to sleep, knowing that she was safe, free, and going to find a way to make sure that her freedom wasn't at the cost of another girl's life.

When Leslie walked into the suite that night, there was no one there but Irial. He didn't comment, didn't ask questions. He poured her a drink and held it out.

Silently she took it and walked over to the sofa. He followed but didn't sit near her. He pulled a desk chair over. It was uncomfortable to see him sit where she couldn't touch him.

"Are you okay?"

She laughed. "Niall thought it was unsafe to come here, and the first thing you ask is if I'm okay. Whatever you did to him must have been hellish."

"Our boy's not as quick to forgive as you are." Irial smiled, a sad smile that made her want to ask questions.

She didn't. She moved, trying to find a comfortable position that made the pain on her back less awful. She was glad it was there, but it still brought tears to her eyes when she moved. "I couldn't watch people die for me. Or whatever else you weren't telling me."

"It would've been worse in time," he admitted. It wasn't an apology, but she hadn't really expected one.

"Do I want to know?"

He lit one of his seemingly constant cigarettes, watching her in a way that was almost comforting in its familiarity. Then he made a dismissive gesture with his hand, the cherry of the cigarette waving in the air as he did so. "War, more effort on the drug front, an increase in the number of dark fey kept nearer to me. Maybe a bit of negotiation with Far Dorcha's fey in the sex and death markets."

"Would I have survived it?"

"It's possible." He shrugged. "You were doing pretty well. Most of the mortals don't stay conscious as long as you did. And since it was me that you were bound to . . . you really might have. I wanted you to survive."

"I've talked to Ash, and if you take another mortal—"

"Are you threatening me, love?" He grinned at her.

"No. I'm telling you that I don't want you to replace me."

His smile faded. "Well, then . . . and if I do?"

"Then Ash will work with the other one, the Winter Queen, and *they*'ll threaten you, hurt our—your—court." She watched him, not sure that her approach was the right one, but certain that she couldn't let someone else suffer like she had. "But here's the thing they *don't* get: I don't want you to be hurt. It would hurt me. If you let some other mortal channel that awfulness for you, that would hurt me. What they'll do to you when they find out, that will hurt me."

"And?"

"And you promised me that you wouldn't let anyone hurt me." She waited as he sat staring at her, smoking silently. Leslie's friendship with Aislinn might not be anywhere near repaired, but if the advice she'd given Leslie worked, it would go a long way toward setting things right. For now, that was Leslie's goal: getting things put to rights—her life, her future, and if she could, things with those who mattered to her. Irial was still on that list.

"The Dark Court is what it is. I won't tell them to change their natures to appease—"

"You're playing word games, Irial." She gestured for him to come closer.

His surprise was enough to offset her twinge of fear. He ground out his cigarette and moved over to sit on the sofa, near enough to touch—but not actually touching her.

She turned so they were facing each other. "You gave me your vow, Irial. I get that now. I'm telling you what will happen if you let them wound you: you will be hurting me, and if you know that and still take another mortal . . . What you are, what you do isn't my business, but doing another ink exchange, starting wars in my world, killing mortals, that *is* my business, and if my caring for you means that you can't do it . . . I'll admit that I still care."

He reached for her and she didn't flinch. She closed her eyes and gave herself over to his kisses. It was Irial who stopped.

"You aren't lying." He gave her the strangest look, a bit like awe and a bit like fear.

Having her autonomy back was a beautiful thing. And she realized that how she felt about Irial hadn't changed all that much.

"Tell me what you feel for me?" she asked.

He backed up just a little, no longer holding her. "Why?"

"Because I asked."

"I'm glad you won't end up comatose or dead," he said, his tone revealing nothing.

"And?" She watched him wrestle with his temptation to tell her. If he didn't want to, she couldn't make him.

"If you wanted to stay . . ."

"I can't." She squeezed his hand. "That's not an emotion, by the way; it's an offer. *You* of all people know the difference. What I'm asking—and you're avoiding—is whether you still care for me now that we're not connected. Was it just the ink exchange?"

"The only thing that's changed is that you're free of me and I'm left trying to figure out how to feed my court properly." He lit another cigarette and gave her his answer. "It was the exchange at first, but . . . that wasn't all. I do care for you. Enough to let you leave."

"So . . ." she prompted, needing the words.

"So, my vow's going to stay intact: no mortal ink exchange."

She stood awkwardly for a few moments. Leaving wasn't easy, no matter how right it was. There were so many things she wanted to say, to ask. They wouldn't change anything. They wouldn't make a difference, and really, they were all things that she suspected Irial already knew. So she said, "In the morning, I get the key for my apartment. Ash took care of it for me . . . not the money, but finding one and the paperwork and everything."

"You'll tell me if you need anything?" He sounded as tentative as she felt.

She shook her head. "No. I'm pretty sure seeing you— or Niall—is a bad idea. I told him, too . . . I don't want this world. Ash was right about that part. I want to go live my life, be normal, and sort out what happened—before you."

"You'll do well, better than if you stayed." He took another drag off his cigarette and exhaled.

She watched the smoke twist into strands in the air, not shadows, not anything mystical or ethereal, just the air that he'd exhaled—normalcy. And it made her smile. "I will."

EPILOGUE

As he often had over the past few weeks, Niall watched Leslie step out into the street. The mortal boy waiting there shrugged off whatever she said to him with a smile. He watched her with a protectiveness Niall approved of—putting his body streetside, keeping alert to the passing mortals. She needed friends like him. She needed the way the mortals made her laugh. *Not me. Not now.* The shadows under her eyes were fading; her stride was steadier, more confident.

"Looks good, doesn't she?" said an unwelcome voice behind him.

"Go away." Niall pulled his gaze away from Leslie, turning to face the king of the Dark Court.

Irial lounged against the newsstand, hat tipped low on his brow.

How did I not notice him?

"Healthier too, without that wretch of a brother causing her trouble," Irial added. With a friendliness that seemed at odds with the situation, he stepped forward and draped an arm over Niall's shoulder. They were of equal height, so it was an almost embracing gesture.

Niall shrugged off Irial's arm and asked, "What do you want?"

"To check on our girl—and you." Irial watched Leslie with a strange look that Niall would call protective if it were anyone else.

He's not capable of that, though. He's the heart of the Dark Court. But Niall knew he was trying to lie to himself, knew he'd been lying to himself for centuries: Irial wasn't what Niall had let himself believe. He was neither as awful as Niall believed nor as kind as he'd first seemed. *He still doesn't deserve to be near her.*

Leslie had been joined by several other mortals. One of them said something that made her laugh out loud.

Niall stepped in front of the Dark King. "She's free of you. If you—"

"Relax, boy." He laughed softly. "Do you really believe I'd hurt *her*?"

"You *did* hurt her."

"I took away her choices when I didn't warn her about the ink exchange. I used her. I did what we have both done with mortals forever."

Niall started, "It's—"

"*Exactly* what your last king did with his lovely queen and the rest of his formerly mortal playthings"—Irial paused, a strange solemn look on his face—"but you'll figure it out soon enough." Then, staring past Niall toward Leslie and her mortal friends, Irial said, "Once I gave you the choice between giving me the mortals you'd addicted or giving me yourself. You gave me yourself. That's what a good king does, Gancanagh—makes hard choices. You know what we are, yet you kept our secrets. You're setting aside your love for Leslie for her best interests. You're going to make an excellent king."

And before Niall could react, Irial pressed his mouth to the long scar that he'd once allowed Gabriel to carve on Niall's face. Niall felt his knees give out under him, felt a disquieting new energy flood his body, felt the awareness of countless dark fey like threads in a great tapestry weaving his life to theirs.

"Take good care of the Dark Court. They deserve that. They deserve *you*." Irial bowed his head. "My king."

"No," Niall stumbled back, tottering on the sidewalk, nearly falling into the traffic. "I don't want this. I've told you—"

"The court needs new energy, Gancanagh. I got us through Beira's reign, found ways to strengthen us. I'm tired—more changed by Leslie than I'll admit, even to you. You may have broken our tie, seared me from her skin, but that doesn't undo my changes. I am no longer fit to lead my court." Irial smiled sadly. "My court—*your court now*—needs a new king. You're the right choice. You have always been the next Dark King."

"Take it back." Niall felt the foolishness of his words, but he couldn't think of anything more articulate.

"If you don't want it—"

"I don't."

"Pick someone worthy to pass it on to, then." Irial's eyes were lightening ever so slightly. The eerily tempting energy that had always clung to him like a haze was less overwhelming now. "In the meantime, I offer you what I've never offered another—my fealty, Gancanagh, my king."

He knelt then, head bowed, there on the busy sidewalk. Mortals craned their necks to stare.

And Niall gaped at him, the last Dark King, as the reality settled on him. He'd just grab the first dark fey he saw and . . . *turn over this kind of power to some random faery? A dark faery?* He thought of Bananach and the Ly Ergs circling, seeking war and violence. Irial was moderate in comparison to Bananach's violence. Niall couldn't turn the court over to just anyone, not in good conscience, and Irial knew it.

"The head of the Dark Court has always been chosen from the solitary fey. I waited a long time to find another after you said no. But then I realized I was waiting for you to leave Keenan. You didn't choose me over him, but you chose the harder path." Irial stood then and took Niall's face in his hands, gently but firmly, and kissed his forehead. "You'll do well. And when you are ready to talk, I'll still be here."

Then he disappeared into the throng of mortals winding down the sidewalk, leaving Niall speechless and bewildered.

Irial didn't look back, didn't turn toward Leslie or Niall. He kept moving until he was lost in the crowd of mortals whose feelings he could read but not drink.

Not without her.

He could feel her out there, confident in her world, seeing the things that watched her from the shadows and not flinching. Sometimes he felt teasing tastes of her longing—for him and for Niall—but he'd not go to her, not now, not with her happy in her new world. She was making up the courses she'd missed during her time with him, proud of herself, rebuilding herself. She'd start college in the fall.

Not mine, not his, but Her Own. It pleased him, knowing that, and having those brief bursts of connection with her. He'd had a fear that relinquishing his throne would also end his tie with Leslie. He'd let that fear delay his stepping down. *Fear of losing my last link to my Shadow Girl.* Her actions had burned away the tendrils of vine where they'd burrowed into her flesh. He'd felt it, like losing feeling in a limb, setting him off-kilter so badly that he'd been despondent at the loss. But he could still taste the echo of her—not always, not even often, but there were moments when he felt her—like phantom pains in a missing limb. It was his craving for those moments that proved his inadequacy to lead his court. He might be out of her skin, but she'd left him as something other than what he'd been before—not mortal, but not strong enough to deserve the title of Dark King.

What does it mean when nightmares dream of peace? When shadows wish for light?

She might not be bound to him, but she was still his Shadow Girl. He'd given her his vow: to take care of her, to keep her from hurt or pain, from wanting for anything. Her leaving didn't negate his promises; they weren't conditional. And if Niall wasn't bound to a court, kept tied to some cause or purpose, he'd eventually go to Leslie. Their Gancanagh might mean well, but his nature—like Irial's—was to be addictive to mortals. He was still a thing of shadows despite how long he'd run from who he was. *Not now.* Now that Niall was bound to the Dark Court, his addictive nature was nullified. *And mine is returned.* Like Irial had once been, Niall was strengthened by his court, just as the court would be strengthened by Niall.

To look after the Dark Court, Irial had found them a better king. To care for Niall, Irial had given him the court. And to love Leslie, Irial would stay away from her. *Sometimes love means letting go when you want to hold on tighter.* It was the only way he knew to protect the court, the faery, and the only mortal who'd ever mattered to him.

AUTHOR'S NOTE

I wanted the representation of all things tattoo-related to be as accurate and respectful as possible, so every tattoo reference in this book was handed to my tattoo artist, Paul Roe, to examine. Along the way, I've learned a great deal about the history of the art, the assembly of the machines, and minutia ranging from the metals one could use (what with faeries being sensitive to steel/iron) to why tattoo artists position the canvas in various ways. If there are errors, I hope you'll forgive me. If there aren't, the credit goes to Paul.

Leslie's tattoo is at the center of *Ink Exchange*. I knew that early on; I just didn't know exactly what the tattoo looked like. It needed to be a representation of Irial's nature, and while I had the words that made Iri come to life for me, I didn't have a visual that captured his essence. The universe gives us what we need, though; I believe that. What I needed was Paul's art and wisdom. To say that he was essential to the creation of this novel would be an understatement.

As with the tattoos I wear on my skin, I gave Paul my words; he answered with his images. The final result was the art that's hung in my direct line of sight for the past year. Thanks to Paul, Irial's eyes look back at me every day while I work.

It's an amazing thing when two people's muses can dance together.

35674050229500